Eric Wilder

Big Easy

Gondwana Press
Edmond, Oklahoma

Other books by Eric Wilder

Ghost of a Chance
Murder Etouffee
Name of the Game
A Gathering of Diamonds
Over the Rainbow
Just East of Eden
Lily's Little Cajun Cookbook
Bones of Skeleton Creek
Of Love and Magic
City of Spirits
Primal Creatures
Black Magic Woman

Gondwana Press LLC
1800 Canyon Park Cir., Ste 401
Edmond, OK 73013
gondwanapress@gmail.com

Front Cover by Higgins & Ross Photography/Design

Anniversary Edition
ISBN: 978-0-9791165-8-2

Acknowledgments

Big Easy was completed ten years ago, just before Hurricane Katrina devastated New Orleans and the Gulf Coast. Homes and lives were destroyed and thousands of people displaced, many of them permanently. At the time, I didn't know if the city would survive, and *Big Easy* languished on a shelf for two long years. New Orleans not only survived, it has prospered. This novel would have never become reality except for the people of the region. This edition of *Big Easy* commemorates these wonderful folks for their pride, stamina, and resilience, and for coming back from one of the most destructive hurricanes in Louisiana history.

For Anne

Big Easy

A novel by
Eric Wilder

Prolog

Gaylon LeBlanc was a collector. Not stamps or coins, but shriveled objects, much like the one he carried in his pocket for luck. He fingered it as drums echoed from the cultural center in Louis Armstrong Memorial Park. Intent on the arrival of someone he knew and his upcoming task, He paid no attention. The drummers had no idea their hectic tempo would backdrop an actual Vodoun ceremony. One that would culminate in someone's death.

Gaylon waited in a part of the park named Beauregard Square. Also known as Place du Cirque, or Place des Negres at different times, most locals still called it Congo Square. Dressed as voodoo deity Baron Samedi, in tuxedo, top hat, and flowing cape, Gaylon had arrived at Congo Square long before dark. Near the fountain centering the cobblestone pavement, he awaited a woman's arrival.

His cigar remained unlit, and his purple sunglasses served no purpose except to save his blue eyes from the glare of a full moon. He removed them as a taxi halted at the entrance to the square. When the passenger, a nun dressed in a black habit, offered the driver a ten, he motioned it off with a wave of his head. After crossing himself, he pulled away in a screech of burning rubber.

The nun stuffed the note in her clothes and turned to the man awaiting her, no words exchanged when she reached him. Strapping her arms around him, she probed his mouth with her tongue and groped his privates. Undisturbed by her blatant, sexual advances, Gaylon reciprocated, returning her ardor with his own. Wild drumming continued as he tore open her robe, ripped off her starched head cover, and tossed them to the ground.

She stood before him in only a knee-length mantle of beaded seashells that did little to hide her athletic body. Blonde hair tumbled to her waist. The fake sister had something else hidden beneath her robe.

Backing away from him, she grasped a black rooster by its neck in one hand, an opened bottle of Jamaican rum in the other. The rooster, sedated by strong rum poured down its throat, was alive, though not for long. Gaylon watched as she twisted the head off the bird, tossing its lifeless body to the ground.

The headless rooster ran in circles until it finally dropped, blood gushing from its neck. When it did, she grabbed its pulsating body and held it, along with the bottle, over her head. Warm blood and strong alcohol poured down her face, mixing with beads of sweat on her bare neck and breasts.

Drawing ever closer to Gaylon, she began dancing the wild bamboula, her sultry moves daring him to join her. The percussive melody pervading the park had become more frantic as if feeding on the strength of the two dancers. Her beaded wrap glistened with sweat and blood as the drumming reached a crescendo. When it did, she stopped dancing.

When she smacked his forehead with her bloody palm, he dropped to his knees, grabbing his temples as if they were about to explode. He was no longer Gaylon LeBlanc when he arose from the ground. He was now Baron Samedi as the voodoo deity had taken possession of his body.

The woman began dancing again, her gestures sexual and overt. Baron Samedi finally reclined her on the cold stone and began humping her in a ritual manner. At the climax of the wild, yet simulated performance, a man burst from the shadows.

He was huge, his crooked smile imparting a fierce look in light reflecting from the full moon. Moving away from Baron Samedi, she danced toward the man with unkempt hair, and then blew something up his nose. The inhaled powder caused an instant change to his persona. A smile replaced his scowl as she tore open the front of his shirt and clawed deep scratch marks down his chest with her long fingernails. Voodoo drums continued as she stood on her tiptoes, accosting him with her lips.

"This is the night you've waited for, my handsome lover. The great Ghede himself has sent Baron Samedi to assist you. Tonight, he will help you revenge yourself on the person that has wronged you."

She turned when Baron Samedi spoke. "You are not yet done. You have one more thing to do before satisfying my needs."

Prostrating herself, she crawled toward Baron Samedi and licked his shoes with her tongue.

"I pray you will return him to my bed," she said.

Baron Samedi dusted his tuxedo, reached into his pocket and removed a frightful object, showing it to her.

"He will have his revenge, and I will have another nipple for my collection."

As Baron Samedi left Congo Square, a bus passed on the street, saturating humid air with the momentary odor of burning diesel. Before following him, the other man bent the woman over a park bench. This time, the sex wasn't simulated.

"Go now, and return triumphant to my bed before the sun rises," she finally said.

The drums had gone silent as the man followed Baron Samedi out of the square and vanished into the night.

Nearby, a dog howled at the moon, its mournful sound melding with the screech of brakes on N. Rampart. As a tugboat sounded its whistle, dark clouds shrouded the moon. They masked the man as he left the nun alone in Congo Square and followed Baron Samedi down Rue St. Peter.

Chapter 1

Torrential rains had moved in from the North, cooling afternoon heat twelve degrees in less than fifteen minutes. As I sat in Bertram Picou's bar, on Chartres Street in the French Quarter, shucking oysters from a pile of seafood laid out on paper spread across a table in back, I could still see the headline through the oily stains: *Strangler claims victim near Lee Circle.*

The headline didn't surprise me. The Big Easy is a violent city, a fact usually hidden from tourists, again visiting after Hurricanes Katrina and Rita. This murder had touched me personally because the victim was my high school English teacher.

Something, maybe the bottle or perhaps hundreds of unmotivated students, had driven Sally to madness. She had disappeared for a while, finally surfacing on St. Charles Avenue, pushing a grocery cart she'd stolen from a nearby grocery store. No one seemed to care. Rain gusted through the door, freeing my thoughts from the disturbing murder of Miss Sally Gerant.

The drop in temperature provided a welcome respite to Bertram's overworked air conditioning—a bonus for the few lucky customers enjoying the fragrant mix of rain and spicy seafood. Junior Picou, Bertram's brother, had taken his flat-bottomed skiff out at dawn, into the splay channels beyond Yscloskey.

Junior had returned before noon with a wealth of shrimp, oysters, and redfish. What Bertram hadn't used in his pot of gumbo, simmering in the kitchen, he'd boiled up and put on the table as complimentary appetizers for his customers to enjoy. Who said there was no such thing as a free lunch?

Despite the enticement, the bar remained virtually empty, except for a few mostly out-of-work regulars. Everyone, especially Bertram's female customers, gawked when the front door opened, and a handsome, middle-aged man entered. After spotting me by the table, he smiled and walked toward me. An expensive raincoat draped his elbow. Despite afternoon humidity through the roof, he was still wearing his tweed sports coat, and had not bothered to loosen his tie.

"That you, Wyatt Thomas?" he said. "Remember me, Beau Kaplan?"

How could I have forgotten? Captain of the L.S.U. football team and student voted most likely to succeed. How could anyone forget handsome Beau Kaplan, big man on campus, and the one voted by everyone most likely to succeed? He needn't have worried about his popularity as Bertram's women regulars, and a table of local legal secretaries stared goggle-eyed at him from across the room. He palmed my hand with the secret fraternity handshake I'd almost forgotten.

"How are you doing, Beau? Help yourself to some of Bertram's grub."

Beau's grin vanished. "Ate already. Can we talk?"

"Sure. There's a booth in back."

"No, I mean somewhere else, like over in Jackson Square."

"You bet," I said, taking one more bite of the shrimp po'boy.

Not knowing why Beau had bothered looking me up after all these years, or for all the secrecy, I wiped hot sauce off my mouth with a bar rag and followed him out the door. We found the sidewalk almost deserted. Rain had moved south toward the Gulf. Dark clouds hung directly overhead, weighing heavily on already thick, humid air. Too hot for most tourists, the square was almost deserted. They were probably visiting the endless miles of air-conditioned shops that began where Canal Street intersects the Mississippi

River. Most any place that had air conditioning. Only a white-faced mime and a few persistent portrait artists occupied the Square when we reached it.

I followed him through a wrought iron gate to a secluded park bench. His physical appearance had hardly changed since I'd seen him last. Just a touch of gray rimmed his full head of dark, wavy hair. He and his wife Kammi owned a mansion near Pontchartrain and many expensive toys. One of New Orleans' leading neurosurgeons, he'd only added to his family's impressive wealth. His trademark grin soon returned.

"Seeing you again has really brought back memories."

I knew what he meant. My sudden recollection of Kammi had sent a wave of melancholy nostalgia cresting across my bow.

"Those days at L.S.U. were the best of my life," he said. "Remember the frat parties down by the river with the bonfires, barbecue, and kegs of ice cold beer? Those hot young things all loved you, Wyatt."

"You kidding me, Beau? When it came to women, you were the pro. I'm just an amateur."

"Kammi didn't think so. She never gave me the time of day till you had that fight at the Old South Party. When you broke up, she gravitated to me. On the rebound, I guess."

Kammi and I were a number for a while. Now I couldn't remember why we'd argued, but I hadn't forgotten her large green eyes. Not long after breaking up with Kammi, I took a real job and moved out of the frat house. Sometime after that, I'd married Mimsy, my ex and had lost touch with the frat crowd.

As we talked, a half-grown yellow tabby with a stump for a tail appeared from under the park bench. After rubbing against my leg, he bounded into my lap.

"Didn't know you like cats," Beau said.

"Never had one."

"I think you do now. That one looks like he hasn't had a meal since the last time he sucked his mama's tit."

When I stroked the cat, he promptly closed his eyes and fell asleep in my lap. "What's bothering you? You didn't look me up to talk about cats or old times."

Beau stared at the sky as a gull, winging toward

Pontchartrain, disappeared into the clouds. Rolling thunder rumbled in the distance.

"It's Kammi. She's trying to kill me."

I waited for the punch line. Beau's puckered brow and bowed head soon informed me there wasn't one.

"You're kidding me?"

"It's true. You handle this kind of work. I'll pay you to help me."

Beau's insinuation that I'd only assist an old friend for money stung me, even though I'd experienced a prolonged dry spell with few clients and fewer payments. Still, I could see he was serious, and I was in no position not to hear him out.

"If what you say is true, you should go to the police."

"They'd never believe me."

"I'm finding it hard myself. Why would Kammi want to kill you?"

Beau sank back against the bench and squeezed the raincoat still draped over his arm. "Cause I got a girlfriend," he said, averting his eyes. "Well, more than a girlfriend, a mistress, really. Kammi must have found out about Sheila, and now she's trying to even the score."

His admission failed to surprise me. Beautiful women had flocked around Beau, always ready to comfort the moody young man. I couldn't believe Kammi wasn't aware of her husband's wandering ways, or that she was capable of sustaining any negative emotion other than mild anger.

"What did she do? Threaten you with a gun or knife?"

"Worse than that. She went to some witch doctor one of her girlfriends told her about. I know because Sandi, another of her girl friends, confided as much to me at the country club barbecue last Saturday."

I could only imagine the confiding scene at the country club with Sandi and Beau.

"Witch doctor? What the hell are you talking about?"

"Voodoo, Wyatt. It is real around here, and you know it. Kammi found some voodoo witch doctor to cast a spell on me. Pretty soon I'll be dead, and no one'll be the wiser."

"I don't believe that for a minute and neither should you. How is this spell affecting you?"

"It's bad, Wyatt. I wake up in a cold lather, my head

pounding, and bones aching. I'm so nervous I can hardly do my business down at the hospital."

Beau grew silent as heat lightning pulsed across the horizon behind St. Louis Cathedral. Another clap of thunder quickly followed, frightening the pigeons on Andy Jackson's statue. The white-faced mime had gone, the few remaining artists busy packing their brushes and easels and hurrying off toward Pirate's Alley. I waited for Beau to resume his wild tale.

"One thing though. All this malarkey with Kammi has made me realize the one I love is Sheila. You know, Wyatt, what's so strange? I never felt this way about Sheila before and never thought of her as anything except a mistress. Don't mean a thing, though. When I get this situation behind me, I'm going to divorce Kammi and marry her."

"Why wait?"

"Cause I got to break the spell first. That's why I need you."

"I'm no voodoo expert," I said, half in jest.

"I bet you know someone that is because you know everybody. Always did. Can you help me?"

Warm rain began falling in the vacant Jackson Square. A clap of thunder almost masked my answer.

Chapter 2

Another hot day in New Orleans and Detective Tony Nicosia ran chubby fingers through thinning hair, trying to ignore the Chief's angry words that had greeted him when he arrived at work. Although barely July yet, the city had already experienced more than three hundred homicides. Tony seriously considered packing up and moving to a safer place. New York City, maybe.

The daydream was fleeting when his partner, Tommy Blackburn, entered the office unannounced.

"Don't you ever knock?"

"Sorry, Fat Tony," Tommy said as he pulled up a chair.

Detective Nicosia had lost seventy-five pounds in the last two years and had so far, managed to keep the weight off. At five-eight and two-twenty-five, he was still not exactly svelte. He continued working at it, walking two miles before work, lowering his cholesterol and blood pressure as he cinched his belt tighter by the month. He detested the precinct nickname he had lived with for twenty years. Despite constant appeals to his fellow officers, he couldn't get them to stop calling him Fat Tony. Not even Tommy Blackburn, his young partner.

Tony had grown up in a rough, New Orleans area known as the Irish Channel, a neighborhood once populated by Irish workers. His accent was clearly recognizable by locals from other parts of the city. Many ethnic and racial groups lived there now, and the low-income neighborhood still maintained its tough appearance.

Tommy Blackburn, ten years younger and forty pounds lighter than his partner, had also grown up in the Channel. A raw-boned six-footer, Tommy's ruddy complexion matched his unruly growth of flame red hair. Tony often accused the bachelor of sleeping in his clothes. His rumpled sports jacket provided no evidence contrary to that accusation. Tommy was like the little brother he'd never had, so he didn't bother reminding him not to call him Fat Tony. He poured two cups of coffee from the percolator on the corner table instead.

"What's up?" Tommy asked.

"My blood pressure," Tony said, testing the coffee with a careful sip. "Chief Wexler chewed my ass this morning. Second time this week, and it's just Tuesday."

"Can't be that bad. Chief Wexler's not much of an ass chewer."

When Tony failed to answer, Tommy sipped his own coffee, knowing better than to ask what was caught in Wexler's throat.

"I'm starved. Let's grab a po'boy at Nicoletta's."

"We'll get something on the way," Tony said. "The chief didn't like our report from last night's murder scene. We're going back down and look again. See if we missed something."

Tony grabbed his own coat from the rack and started out the door. After a final swig of his coffee, Tommy followed.

Sergeant Blackburn and Lieutenant Nicosia worked out of the 8th District Station on Royal Street, in the French Quarter. The 8th District includes the Central Business District—what the locals call the C.B.D.—the prime downtown and business district, and of course the French Quarter.

The vaunted 8th District was well known for providing outstanding police service for significant events that included Mardi Gras and the Super Bowl. For a while after the hurricane, Detectives Blackburn and Nicosia had wondered if there ever would be another Mardi Gras or Super Bowl in New Orleans.

Tony was the chief detective, a job he considered one of the city's most essential. He was also one of the few older officers in the District that had survived the firings to clean up what some had deemed the most corrupt police department in the country. Many close friends and associates had lost their jobs, and not all had been dishonest. Tony still smarted from the experience, and his early morning meeting with the Chief brought unwelcome memories.

The district firings were only a blink of the eye compared with the loss caused by Katrina. One of Tony's oldest and dearest friends had committed suicide during the immediate aftermath of the devastation. Many officers fled New Orleans with their families. A few particularly heinous individuals had even joined in the looting. Most of the decent cops had stuck it out, performing like champions through the ordeal. Now it was summer, and many things had changed.

July in New Orleans is tolerable, although only barely, even for the locals. Prickly heat and intense humidity drape the city like a damp washcloth. Tourists planning their visits usually wait until spring or fall. Driven by the need for tourism, city leaders promote such minor events as the Festival of the Tomato and Crawfish Week.

Usually, only sweaty tourists tempted by off-season hotel bargains frequented these events. It was usually so hot in July that many of the locals took their vacations, traveling to cooler climes. After driving down St. Charles Avenue in a police car with inadequate air conditioning, Tony wished he'd gone with them.

"Roll down your window," he said as they passed a clanging streetcar. "It can't be any hotter than the air coming out of the vents."

"That's the truth," Tommy said. "What's the matter with our report?"

Tony remained silent as he parked on the street, just before reaching Lee Circle. The Garden District, one of the oldest and classiest neighborhoods in the city, lay further down St. Charles. Businesses and warehouses populated the C.B.D., between Lee Circle and downtown New Orleans. Interspersed between them were a few tiny eateries, visited during the day by hordes of workers. They usually closed around five.

Lunch hour, aromas of gumbo and frying shrimp wafted from the many cafes and bistros. Tony's stomach growled as he and Tommy threaded their way down the sidewalks filled with people dressed in industrial uniforms, and white shirts and ties. There were also the invisible, homeless people living on the streets, some asleep on the sidewalk while others extended hands to the passing herd of office workers. Many were already sipping from bottles of Tokay and Mad Dog 20-20. All they had in common was they didn't care what people thought about them.

The latest murder had occurred in the early morning hours of the previous day, Tony and Tommy called at two in the morning. Now they were returning to the crime scene, an alleyway leading to a large dumpster surrounded by crime scene tape. Tony stepped over the yellow plastic barrier, walked behind the dumpster and stared at the bloody patch of concrete. After several minutes of silence, Tommy finally tapped his shoulder.

"What do you think?"

"There's blood all over the dumpster. And over there," Tony said, pointing at a spot on the brick wall he had overlooked in the dark. "The old lady was probably going through the trash, trying to find something to eat. That door is the back of a café that closes around five. Her killer probably dragged her behind this dumpster. Must be a big one, him, considering the way he manhandled her."

"Or maybe two murderers," Tommy said. "The victim looked at least one-seventy five. Living on the street and all I doubt she was a shrinking violet."

Tony thought about his comment. "The killer cut her clothes off with a razor and then used it on her. Bruising and loss of blood means she was alive while all this was happening."

Tommy shook his head. "The coroner's report will be interesting, especially if she put up a fight."

"He'll have something for us, always does."

Tommy mopped his brow with a handkerchief. "No wonder the Captain is pissed. This one could be bad for the recovery, being so close to the Quarter and all."

Tony crossed over the tape and started for the car. "We'll nose around the streets and see if anyone saw something that didn't get reported."

Lunch hour was near an end, and it didn't take long to find two of the many homeless people who lived in the C.B.D. The men were sleeping on the walkway covered by remnants of a day-old Times Picayune. An empty bottle of Tokay lay between them. Tommy prodded one man's ribs with the toe of his shoe.

"You boys seen anything unusual lately?"

Both men blinked and rubbed their eyes. "Like what?" one man said.

"Like a large man, maybe a stranger to the area? Maybe you saw him drive up in a car."

The man shook his head and pulled the paper back over his head. The other man refused to answer at all. When further questioning provided only a consumptive cough, Tony motioned Tommy to give it up and move on. They continued questioning panhandlers, bag ladies, and winos, again with no success.

"These zombies aren't alive just yet. Make a note to have the uniforms come back after dark. Maybe they'll be more receptive."

As they returned to the car, someone caught their attention. The big man walking toward them was tall and sallow, his face scarred by acne and exposure to the sun. He also had the muscled physique of a smack-down wrestler. A red ski cap topped his dark and greasy, shoulder-length hair. His thousand-yard stare glared at them as he passed on the sidewalk. Despite his disheveled appearance, the man appeared sober.

"You looking at me?" he said.

"N.O.P.D.," Tony said. We need to ask you a few questions."

"I didn't say anything to you," the man said with an angry edge to his voice as he continued walking.

Tommy started to grab him, but Tony shook his head. "Call for backup to take this guy downtown for questioning. He's not a wino, but he's large enough to be our killer, and clearly not normal."

Tommy quickly used his cell phone. Until help arrived, they followed the large man who was apparently indifferent to their presence. Shortly, two uniformed police officers arrived in a cruiser and went after the suspect as soon as Tony had pointed him out.

"Sir, you need to come downtown for questioning," one of the officers said.

The man ignored the request, brushing past them. The two officers grabbed his arm.

"Hey Mac, didn't you hear me?"

The suspect wheeled around, his face red and wild eyes accentuating his tortured complexion. Without warning, he swiped at the cop with a small knife he had hastily pulled from his pants pocket.

"Don't kill him!" Tony yelled, sensing what was about to happen.

Without waiting, Tommy knocked the knife-wielder to the ground with a flying body roll from behind.

"You sons-of-bitches," the man screamed as three cops descended on him, cuffing and dragging him to the awaiting squad car.

Tony and Tommy watched as the two uniformed police officers screeched off downtown, the suspect in handcuffs in the backseat.

"Now that's one crazy dude. You think we're lucky enough for him to be our killer?" Tommy asked.

"Never know. One thing I do know. We got about all the information we're gonna get today from this damaged mass of humanity. Let's head uptown and visit the morgue."

A tanker coming up the river blew its whistle, the mournful sound melding with blaring car horns involved in traffic congestion on Canal. As they drove down Camp Street, the air conditioning worked no better than before. Despite their impending confrontation with death, both men welcomed cooler air as they entered the building housing the morgue. Dr. Bernard's office was at the end of a long hallway and they entered without knocking.

"Got anything for us, Doc?" Tony asked.

Dr. Bernard nodded and began reading from the report on his desk. "As you already know, her name was Sally Gerant, white female, sixty five years old, hundred and eighty pounds, raped and sodomized. We have a sufficient sample of semen. The murderer bruised and cut her with a straight razor. He also took some trophies, pieces of her skin and snippets of hair. Some of the cuts in her chest look like symbols."

"Of what?" Tommy asked.

"Can't tell because of the swelling, but they look like patterns. He kept her alive while he was torturing her although there's no evidence of a struggle from the woman. I found no hair or skin under her fingernails and no bits of anything human I can identify. She was a practicing alcoholic. No other diseases and was in reasonable health, except for her scarred liver. No physical abnormalities and excellent muscle tone for a woman her age and weight. Cause of death was strangulation."

"Ligature," Tony said. "He kept her alive by applying the right amount of pressure to whatever he used to strangle her with."

"Probably a thin wire," Dr. Bernard said. "There's swelling around the ligature mark which means he worked her over for ten minutes or more. He gloved her so she couldn't scratch him, but he didn't bother tying her hands."

"Find any prints?" Tony asked.

Dr. Bernard shook his head. "The killer probably wore gloves. Not that it matters. Besides his semen, we got samples of his saliva where he drooled on the old woman, and some long hairs from someone other than her. When you catch the man, we'll have all the evidence we need."

"Crazy," Tony said. "He wore gloves but not a rubber. What's the point?"

"What color are the hairs?" Tommy asked, ignoring his partner's question.

"Dark, almost black, but definitely Caucasian," Dr. Bernard said

"What's the victim's history?" Tommy asked.

He cast a questioning glance at his partner when Dr. Bernard said, "From New Orleans. She used to teach English over in Metairie. So far, no relative has come forward to claim the body."

The footsteps of Tony and Tommy echoed down the empty hallway as they departed the coroner's office. Though Tony was moving ahead with authority, Tommy had no trouble keeping up with his short-legged, older partner. They went straight to the snack shop on the ground floor and poured coffee from the urn. Tony's stomach growled again, louder this time as he glanced at the doughnuts lined up in the cabinet by the cash register. Tommy joined him at a table in the back corner.

"What's your take on all this, Fat Tony?"

"Your ass if you don't quit calling me Fat Tony."

"Sorry," he said, sipping his hot coffee.

"These street people are tough. They had to be to survive Katrina. Sally was a bag lady, living alone on the street. Reason for murder is random selection. At least that's my first take, though we need to check her family and acquaintances to verify that. Our killer is big and unusually strong."

Tommy frowned and folded his arms. "What else?"

"The killer seems to know something about police procedure, or he wouldn't have gloved her. Even that fails to make a lot of sense because he didn't bother using a rubber. Sounds like something a crazy asshole might do."

"Something else puzzles me," Tommy said. "Even with a crazy asshole, he could have found a better candidate to satisfy his sexual needs."

"It had nothing to do with sex," Tony said. "That old woman was physically unattractive, bordering on the grotesque. Probably hadn't bathed in years and smelled like a distillery. Our man had another motive in mind."

"Such as?" Tommy asked.

"Humiliation," was Tony's terse reply.

Chapter 3

Beau Kaplan was right. I did know a voodoo practitioner. So did almost every other resident of the Big Easy. Beau picked me up in front of Picou's bar in his maroon Lexus coupe for a little trip to see the one I knew. Mama Mulate lived in a two-storied Victorian house not far from the river. Age and decay typified most of the homes in the old neighborhood, crumbling brick walls only partially concealing junk cars littering many of the yards.

Mama's house resided at the end of the block. A horn sounded from a nearby tugboat plying its business as we parked in her drive. I kept my fingers crossed the fancy chrome hubs of Beau's Lexus would still be there when we returned.

A jungle of garden plants covered Mama's front porch, banana palms, and other semi-tropical plants that melded with fragrant bougainvilleas draping from the ceiling in wicker baskets. Hibiscus and morning glories crammed well-tended beds surrounding the porch, and a small truck garden teemed with peas and carrots on the side of the house.

Mama answered the door, Beau instantly smitten by the handsome woman. When I introduced them, he became all charm and Pepsodent. Ignoring his blatant flirtation, she led us down a narrow hallway to a room where she donned a black lace shawl retrieved from the closet. Only flickering light from several well-placed candles lit the room, and it took a moment for my eyes to adjust to the dimness.

Mama was sensually stunning, slender and nearly six feet tall, in her thin caftan. Coffee-colored flesh accentuated finely chiseled features and flowing black hair that draped to her shoulder blades. When she finally spoke, she did so with no discernible accent. Mama's understanding of the black arts wasn't all she possessed. She also had a doctorate in English, and she taught classical literature at Tulane University.

She took a seat at a table near an elaborate shrine decorated with glowing candles, various bones, feathers, and crucifixes. The room reeked with the cloying odor of melted wax and burning incense. She motioned us to join her at the table and quickly locked Beau's eyes in her intense stare. Her eyes soon mesmerized Beau, reducing him to swaying passivity. When Mama finally spoke her Oxford-flavored accent had disappeared, replaced by the rhythmic singsong of a Haitian field hand.

"Why you come see Mama?"

"A spell," Beau's voice droned. "Someone put a spell on me."

Mama tossed her head, causing a strobe-like passage of light to permeate her thick black hair. She closed her eyes and slowly raised her chin, stretching her arms toward the ceiling. Soon, she began to shake. It started with a barely noticeable palpitation in the hollow of her long neck and then quickly shimmied down the length of her body.

Absorbed in a trance of his own, Beau didn't seem to notice Mama's fit. I did, reaching a hand across the table to help her. I didn't get far—a force, like repelling magnets, stopped my hand, locking it in midair. All the candles flared at once as if pure oxygen had suddenly surged through the room. Mama's head slammed against the table with such force I thought she must have knocked herself out. Again, the force kept me from touching her.

For the better part of a minute, I watched as Mama's upper torso writhed on the table top; her dark eyes rolled back in her head and a thin strand of saliva drooled from the side of her open mouth. When her convulsions finally ceased she lay on the table for a long moment before a piercing sound emanated from her unmoving lips—a moan that seemed to come from another world rattled the walls

18

and whipped the softly glowing candles into orange and crimson flame.

"Who dares awaken me from my sleep?" a deep voice said.

Beau's eyes were open, his body rigid; almost as if he were in an advanced stage of rigor Mortis. The voice, pealing from Mama's lips, repeated the question.

"Mama, is it you?" I asked.

"Mambo asleep. I am Bon Dieu. What is it you want?"

Mama was a close friend, and from my many discussions over the years with her, I knew Bon Dieu was the High God of Voodoo. The voice coming from her body had to be a hoax, but I didn't believe it. Mama had too much integrity to stoop to such theatrics. Maybe I was wrong. Still, feeling quite the fool, I answered the question.

"My friend thinks someone has cast a spell on him."

The spirit's laughter echoed inside the smoky room. When the laughter died away, the voice said, "A powerful spell, an unbreakable spell cast by a mighty houngan."

"If you're the Bon Dieu, you can surely help us."

"Such a powerful spell cast cannot be undone," the indignant voice replied. "Finality is the only solution."

"What finality?"

A cold wind chilled the room before I'd gotten my answer. It rattled the walls, sending files and feathers flying and flaring candle flames. When the wind ceased, Mama moaned, raised her head, and stared around the room. Beau shook the cobwebs from his head, opening and closing his mouth, trying to pop his ears as his eyes began to refocus.

"What was that?" he asked.

"The Bon Dieu," I said.

"Hardly," Mama said, making the sign of the cross. "It was only a loa, a simple spirit of the dead, but he told you what you came to hear. A voodoo priest we call a houngan has cast a powerful spell that you cannot break."

Beau's Lexus had survived the stay in Mama's driveway. He returned me in silence to my apartment over Bertram Picou's bar. Two days later, I discussed the incident with Bertram as he polished glasses behind the bar, his collie asleep on the floor beside him.

Cajun slang peppered Bertram's colorful vocabulary. His bar on Chartres, hidden two blocks from Bourbon Street, was a favorite of the locals as well as the occasional tourist that stumbled in to escape the heat or rampant humidity. Bertram's bar never closed its doors during Hurricanes Katrina and Rita. Bertram, like many of his regulars, refused to evacuate.

Much of New Orleans became flooded when several levees failed. Most notably, the Lower 9th Ward remained underwater for several weeks, first by Katrina and then by Rita. The French Quarter was different. The original inhabitants of New Orleans constructed the city on the area's highest ground. The forethought of the founding fathers helped spare the Quarter and the C.B.D. from the storm's destruction.

Bertram never stopped serving whiskey and beer—cold as long as the ice lasted and warm after that. He soon found a generator, solving even the problem of warm beer. The main drawback was the smell of garbage, dead fish, and mildew that lingered long after the clearing of the carnage of the two monster hurricanes.

Bertram always wore a trapper's hat that framed his square face, emphasizing his gapped teeth, and graying ponytail. He always smiled, even when tossing the inevitable unruly drunk out the front door. Bertram was French Acadian—an authentic Cajun. That meant he was friendly though distant with people he didn't know. Like most Cajuns, he would do anything in the world for a friend.

"What's up, my man? You look like you seen a ghost."

"Maybe I did," I answered, relating as briefly as possible my experience at Mama's séance.

"Your doctor buddy sounds beaucoup screwy," Bertram said, tossing Lady a treat from a canister kept beneath the bar.

"He is just a little eccentric from growing up the only child of one of the city's wealthiest families."

At that moment, Beau Kaplan entered the bar, dressed like a Calvin Klein runway model. "You wouldn't be talking about me, now would you old buddy?" he said, pulling up a bar stool beside me.

"One and the same," I said. "Beau Kaplan, this is

Bertram Picou, proprietor of this fine establishment."

The usually moody Beau pumped Bertram's hand across the bar, his smile celebrating every perfect tooth in his mouth.

"Proud to meet you."

"Sorry about what happened at Mama's house," I said.

"You kidding me? That was the most awesome experience of my life, and the spirit told me exactly what I need to do."

"Oh? And what's that?"

"I had Kammi served with divorce papers. I'm moving in with Sheila. Best thing I ever did and I owe it all to you."

I had a feeling Kammi would be less than thrilled with me if she knew of my involvement in her impending divorce. Without asking, Bertram poured himself and Beau shots of Jack Daniel's, and a cold glass of lemonade for me.

"Here's to you!" Bertram said as he and Beau drained their shots.

"Wyatt, I got a business proposition for you. All my friends at the club are just as curious as I am about my voodoo experience. They all want to learn more about this city's best kept secret, and you're just the one to teach them."

I glanced at Bertram and noticed his usual smile had changed into a wry grin. "I really don't know that much about voodoo."

"That's bullshit, and you know it. Here's the money I owe you for solving my problem," he said, peeling off ten crisp Benjamin Franklins from the roll he pulled out of his sport coat. "I know you can use the money, and you can easily make this much and more. All you gotta do is introduce some of my friends into the voodoo inner circle. You know what I mean?"

I had no idea what he meant, and I wanted to return the thousand dollars to Beau. I knew that I couldn't because I owed Bertram two months' rent. After Katrina, he needed the money and so did I. With his 100-watt smile still intact, Beau patted my shoulder and headed for the door.

"I'll be back in touch," he said. "Thanks a bunch, Wyatt."

I watched him go then turned to find Bertram waiting

with an outstretched palm. Counting out half the bills, I pocketed the rest. Was Beau was the answer to my prayers, or a nightmare waiting to happen? I didn't have an answer.

"You haven't had a paying customer since February," Bertram finally said, sensing my hesitation. "You need some work, and to tell you the truth I'm tired of seeing you sit in that booth back there sulking all day."

"I'm not a tour guide," I said.

"Now you listen to me," he said, thumping his chest. "If someone wants to give you a job plucking chickens, you better take the plucking job. You ain't got nothing else going right now."

Bertram was right. Still, I knew little more about voodoo in New Orleans than Beau. It didn't matter because Mama did. I called later and left a message on her answering machine.

❧

Although my room upstairs was small, it was all I needed. Just a bedroom, closet, and bath, but it did have a wrought iron balcony overlooking Rue Chartres. I had a potted palm growing on it, and hanging plants draping the colorful awning that shielded it from the heat of the day. Oh, and now there was Bob, the cat I'd rescued in Jackson Square during my meeting with Beau.

Despite my better judgment, I'd grown fond of the yellow tabby. He looked as if his name should be Bob because all he had for a tail was a stump. Once I'd named him, like the saying goes, he was my cat. More likely, I was his human.

Bertram had frowned on me keeping him. It didn't matter because Bob had taken to the balcony. He wasn't about to leave, and I wasn't about to make him. He spent his days sunning, stretching and watching the action on Chartres from a perch in my potted palm. At night, he'd go tomcatting. I always knew when he'd returned because he would scratch on the patio door until I let him in. He'd also taken to sleeping at the foot of my bed, and I'd finally given up trying to put him out. Soon, I didn't know if he were my pet or the other way around.

❧

Toward the end of the week, Mama returned my call. "I

22

feel terrible taking the poor man's money when there's nothing I can do for him."

"There's nothing poor about him Mama, and he thinks you hung the moon. Anyway, I called you about another matter Are you interested in a potential business deal?"

"What kind of business deal?"

"Let's talk about it in person."

Mama hesitated, and then said, "I'm working late tonight, grading a few papers. Will you stop by? When I'm finished, we'll get some oysters and barbecue shrimp at Pascal Manale's."

Later that night I took Mama up on her offer.

When the streetcar rattled to a stop at Tulane, I stepped off into a world of towering oaks and academia. The old university was stately and rather imposing. I entered the large building housing the English Department and took the stairs to Mama's office. It was the weekend, the building near deserted. I found her alone at her desk, dressed quite differently from our previous meeting. Instead of the revealing caftan she'd worn at the ceremony her pinstriped dress imparted a stately and intellectual persona. Steadfastly refusing to discuss my business proposal while grading papers, she made me wait in silence. When she finally finished, we drove down the street in her fully restored Bugeye Sprite to Pascal Manale's.

While waiting for a table in the crowded restaurant, we enjoyed two-dozen freshly shucked oysters at the bar in the front. After making it to a table in back, we barely talked while eating the succulent shrimp and didn't discuss business at all until we had finished our bread pudding. Finally, I told her about my meeting with Beau Kaplan.

"You know I'm a practitioner of Vodoun because it is very real to me," she said. "What you saw and heard the other day was not a sideshow attraction."

"That's exactly why I called you. Beau wants an expert. I'm not, but you are. His friends have money, Mama, and they will gladly pay. I propose a fifty-fifty partnership. I bring you the clientele, and you take it from there. I'll help all I can, of course. I think we can make some real money."

"Well," she finally said. "I would love an extended trip

to Europe this time next year. When do we start?"

"When Beau calls. He is setting us up with someone as we speak. Are you in?"

Mama smiled, shook my hand, and motioned our server for more coffee.

Chapter 4

Detectives Nicosia and Blackburn waited a day before stopping at Sergeant Tim Conahan. He knew something about the person they were about to question, and they wanted to know what it was. Conahan was a balding, twenty-year veteran. Once a beat cop, he'd grown pudgy working behind the booking desk the last five years. Bags beneath his eyes were just one of the telltale signs that the job had perhaps aged him prematurely.

"You got anything for us, Sergeant?" Blackburn asked.

"You guys really picked a doozy this time," Conahan said. "He kicked out one of Martinez's front teeth and gave Jon a black eye. Believe me when I tell you that those two are not happy campers."

"I'll bet," Tony said. "How's he doing now?"

"Still pissed. Had to lock him in the padded cell to keep him from beating his brains out against the wall. Didn't stop him from screaming bloody murder until two this morning. Bet he's staring at the wall right now. If I didn't know any better, I'd say he's about two bricks shy of a load."

"You got an I.D. for him?" Tony asked.

Conahan consulted his notepad and said, "Jason Stampler, thirty two, from Gonzales. Has a long history of mental illness."

"What's he do for a living?" Tommy asked.

"Professional street person, but he comes from a wealthy family. They haven't disowned him, but it seems like they gave up getting him out of scrapes years ago. He has a box at the Lafayette branch Post Office. His family keeps him supplied with enough money for him to leave them alone."

"Any priors?" Tony asked.

"No, but he has a history of unprovoked violence. Nothing serious, but he was permanently expelled from high school for attacking a teacher."

"A female teacher, I bet," Tommy said.

Conahan tapped his notepad and nodded as Tony and Tommy exchanged glances.

"What did he have on him when they brought him in?"

"Not much," Conahan said. "No wallet or I.D., pictures or letters from home. Just fifty bucks stuffed in his shirt pocket. A derelict at the soup kitchen on Camp gave us his name after we described him. Seems he's well known and not particularly liked."

"I hear that," Tommy said. "What else you got?"

"Doc Warner got some snippets of hair and samples to check his DNA."

"Must have had a tough time doing that," Tommy said.

Conahan chuckled. "How do you think Ernie got his tooth kicked out?"

"We want to question him," Tony said.

"Waste of time. You won't get nothing out of that one," Conahan said.

"What do you suggest?" Tommy asked.

"Confine him for seventy-two hours. Pump him full of drugs and maybe you'll get something coherent out of him."

"That'll pollute our case if he's our man," Tommy said.

"We'll worry about the consequences later," Tony said. "Meantime, let's check forensics and see if they have anything."

Carnahan folded his report. "I'll have the psych boys take care of Stampler. And Tony, I think you owe Jon, Martinez, and me a few Dixies after work."

"You got it," Tony said, pointing his finger at Carnahan as he and Tommy walked out the door. "Meet you at Carlucci's around six."

Tony and Tommy went down the hall to forensics, several distinct odors assaulting their senses as they entered. It sent Tommy into a sneezing fit. The technicians at work in the lab barely looked up from what they were doing. The spasm did bring a wry grin to Doctor Warner, the chief of Technical Services and Support, or T.S.S. as the cops called it.

Warner was a small man with tiny hands and feet, and an elfin face. Though he spoke sparingly, his facial expressions always seemed to indicate he knew more than what he was telling. Tony suspected that Warner considered the give and take of questions and answers an entertaining game. Tony didn't like games even though he knew it was the fastest way to get answers from the little man. This time he was in a hurry and decided to take the direct approach.

"Doc, you figured out who murdered our victim yet?"

Doc Warner didn't take the bait. "Maybe," he said.

"I need more than a maybe. I want to know who and why?"

"I can't tell you who. I can give you a clue as to why."

"I'm all ears," Tony said.

"Information doesn't come for free," the little man said, grinning. "You owe me a dart game."

"I've beaten you ten games in a row. Don't you know when to say uncle?"

"I've been practicing, and you owe me the chance to even the score."

"Okay; we're having drinks at Carlucci's after work."

"You buying?"

"Don't I always?" Tony said, throwing up his hands. "Yesterday was payday. You may as well bring Paul and Donna along."

Forensic technicians Paul Portie and Donna Fonteneau worked for Doc Warner. Paul was a pleasant young man with Cajun roots and Donna a cute, blonde-haired woman with blue eyes. Tommy had a crush on Donna, and Tony thought it might be worth buying a few beers to get the young woman and his shy partner together. Let chemistry do its work. Outside the T.S.S. lab, if such a possibility existed.

"Thanks, Fat Tony," Paul and Donna echoed from the back of the lab.

Tony winced at their unintended insult. He wanted to say something, but decided to lose those last few pounds first.

"Okay, Doc. You got your darts and free beer; now what you got for me?"

"Lots of physical evidence. Blood, semen, and fingerprints. If Stampler is our man, we'll know soon. We gave the area a thorough scouring but found no footprints because the ground around the murder site is mostly covered with concrete and brick."

"You said you had something for me right now," Tony said.

"Those strangely shaped plugs of skin cut from the victim. We made drawings for you," Doctor Warner said, handing Tony a piece of paper with various patterns drawn on it.

"What are they?" Tommy asked, staring over Tony's shoulder.

"Symbols of some sort," Warner said.

"Like what?" Tommy asked.

The doctor shook his head. "Your guess is as good as mine."

Tony and Tommy waited for more. "What else?" Tony finally asked.

"That's it, boys. You now know as much as we do."

"See you tonight, Tommy," Donna Fonteneau said with a pretty smile as he and Tony started out the door.

Tommy ducked his head so that Tony wouldn't see the glow of red moving up his already flushed neck. It didn't matter. Knowing Tommy too well, Tony already realized without looking that Donna's open flirtation had caused his nervous partner to blush.

✥⊂✈⊃✥

Carlucci's, a neighborhood bar frequented by police personnel, was nothing special except for its proximity to the precinct and distance from the typical tourist paths. The dark bar had two pool tables, three dartboards, cold Dixie and Abita on tap. Mike, an ex beat cop, tended bar. As always, Mike, gesturing wildly as he related some cop story, was holding sway when Tony and Tommy entered. Carnahan and the others were waiting at a big table near the dartboards. Doc Warner, a look of determination on his face, had a handful of darts.

28

"We thought you two had stood us up," Jon Do said as Tony and Tommy approached the table.

"Two pitchers of Dixie, Mike," Tony said. "And keep them coming. We might be here a while."

Mike was already pouring beer from the tap. "That would be a change," he said. "How you doing, Cuz?" he said to Tommy, his real-life first cousin. The family resemblance was unmistakable.

Tommy acknowledged the greeting of his cousin with a wave of the hand. He noticed the chair beside Donna Fonteneau was empty, though he was too nervous to take it. Quickly assessing the situation, Tony plopped down in the only other empty seat.

Seeing Tommy's discomfort, Donna grabbed a chilled glass and poured him a beer. "How are you doing, Tommy?"

"Oh, I'm okay. You?"

"Super. Hey, they told me you were the shy type. I like that. Most of the cops in the precinct are so into themselves they drive me crazy."

"Yeah, well just don't get him drunk," Ernie Martinez said.

Ernie was a short cop with a fast mouth and full head of straight, black hair that had begun turning gray around the edges. He had a perpetual smile. Today, it highlighted his recently missing front tooth.

Having slugged his first glass of Dixie and already working on his second, Tommy was feeling slightly more confident. "Say Ernie, how'd you lose that tooth?" he said.

"Doing your job," Ernie shot back.

"Ernie blinked when he should have ducked," Jon Do said. "How could anyone miss those teeth?"

Like Ernie Martinez, Jon was short and sturdy and had closely cropped black hair. Ten years younger, his hair had yet to start turning gray. The two men were practically inseparable, either on or off the job. They could have been brothers except that Ernie was of Mexican descent, Jon Vietnamese. Jon's name evoked endless jokes. Being a police officer only compounded the problem.

Tony and Doc Warner had begun their dart game, Warner already losing badly. Despite his tendency to put on weight, Tony was a terrific athlete with a good eye. During his younger days, he'd played pro baseball, albeit in the minors, for two years. Now he had a wife and five kids. His athletic endeavors consisted of bowling and coaching little league baseball, and an occasional game of darts that he rarely lost.

Tony's wife Lillian was a police officer's dream. She understood his erratic schedule and had always forgiven him for his occasional over-indulgence. Most of his drunken escapades were in the past. Now, he made sure to check his Timex, and his sobriety, often.

"Give it up, Doc," he said after pasting Warner for the second time. "I'll let you have another shot later. Let's have some Dixie before those pups drink it all."

"Good idea," Doc Warner said.

Tim Carnahan poured Tony a glass of Dixie as he joined the throng at the table and motioned Mike for two more fresh pitchers.

"The boys from psych picked up Stampler. Took four of them, along with Jon and Ernie, to restrain and sedate him."

"He's one crazy dude, all right," Jon said. "And strong as an ox. You think he's the killer, Fat Tony?"

Brushing off his irritation, Tony said, "All I know is he's big, strong, and mean, and he don't like teachers for some reason. I still got a few problems, though."

"Like what?"

"He doesn't strike me as the type that would use a wire garrote instead of his bare hands to strangle someone."

"What else you got on him?" Martinez asked.

"Not much. He doesn't have an apartment to check out. Tommy and I are going over to the rescue mission on Camp Street tomorrow and interview the people who run it. Maybe they have some of his possessions, or know something about him. Right now I'm more interested in finding out what these things are."

Tony pulled out a copy of the symbols Doc Warner had sketched for him and handed it across the table to Jon Do. Anyone that has visited New Orleans has heard of Marie Laveau and the practice of voodoo. There are at least six shops in the French Quarter alone specializing in selling potions, amulets, and literature. Every citizen knows something about voodoo. Most have little more than a passing knowledge of the complex religion. This was true, even for the beat cops working the streets. Tony, a devout Catholic, didn't even know that Vodoun, the real name for voodoo, is a religion.

"Does anybody recognize anything on this sheet?" he asked.

Jon Do glanced at the symbols and passed it around the table. No one seemed to know what they meant until Paul Portie returned to the big table to replenish his beer. Portie, shooting pool since Tommy and Tony had arrived, was young, tall, and wiry. He also spoke with a distinct Cajun accent, pronouncing sink as zinc.

"They's hex signs," he said. "My grandma knew a lot about voodoo, and she showed me some when I was a little kid. Voodoo priests and priestesses use them to cast spells."

"Oh?" Tony said. "What else you know about voodoo?"

"A few stories I heard while growing up. My grandma's gone and Mama thinks it is evil."

With everyone's attention immediately rapt, Tony glanced around the table. "Anyone else got anything for me?"

Donna, by now, was holding Tommy's hand. Despite his anxious expression, he wasn't trying to loosen it from her grasp. His question caught her attention.

"Paul is being coy," she said. "He's even been to a voodoo ceremony."

"Now don't be telling all my secrets, Miz Donna."

"Quit talking like a field hand," Donna said. "Everyone knows how smart you are."

Paul Portie was a smart man with a bachelor's degree from Southeastern Louisiana University in Hammond. Mulatto or quadroon, just two of the many local nouns indicating the percentage of white blood a person of color could have, might have described him during antebellum times. Most such inhabitants were freeborn and held respected positions in local society. Such was the anomaly and mystery of life in New Orleans, both then and now.

Because of the diverse influx of many nationalities for many years, ethnic groups that included French, Germans, Irish, English, Chinese and Native Americans coexisted in relative harmony. This diversity continues in modern New

Orleans, the Vietnamese perhaps the latest addition to the melting pot. Paul Portie and Jon Do were both excellent examples of New Orleans racial, national, and cultural diversity.

Tony finished his beer, glanced at his watch, and stood to go. "Do some more thinking on the subject and I'll catch you a little later, Paul. See you all tomorrow. Lillian's got meatloaf waiting."

Tommy reluctantly freed himself from Donna's grasp and hurried after him. Stopping him at the front door, he cupped his hand to say something in private.

"Can you beg off for me tonight, Fat T? I'm not ready to leave yet."

"Must be love for you to pass up Lillian's meatloaf," Tony said. "I'm sure Lil won't forget you next time she makes gumbo. Have fun and I'll see you tomorrow."

Chapter 5

Thanks to Beau Kaplan, word of my reported voodoo knowledge spread quickly, and I began fielding calls, inquiries, and jobs. Along with the notoriety came newly found wealth, at least by my humble standard. Being a glorified tour director was not the career path I would have chosen, but it quickly allowed me to remove most of my debt. Too broke to turn business away, and lacking more than a basic knowledge on the subject of voodoo, I happily allowed Mama to help bail my leaky boat.

Bertram's cousin Buddy DeJan had passed away. He and I would have gone to the wake in any event. Because of my current popularity in the subject of black arts, Beau Kaplan had recommended me to a client who had paid handsomely to attend the event with us. I felt guilty after feeding Bob and giving him a few quick, good-bye strokes down his back. His eyes and twitching tail signaled my neglect, and I tried to ignore his indignation as I walked out the door.

Mama joined us on our trip in Bertram's old truck. Two of Beau Kaplan's out-of-town friends followed us in a rented Lincoln. City lights disappeared in our rear-view mirror as sub-tropical vegetation and endless splay channels gradually became the norm. Soon, there was no sense of urban proximity at all on either side of the road as scrub oak and cypress knobs replaced riverfront hotels.

Distraught over his cousin's death, Bertram drank Cuervo and sniveled all the way from the city. Having my own memories of Buddy, and little patience for Bertram's stories I'd heard before, I stared out the window, trying to block out his mindless chatter. Respectful of the somber situation, Mama also remained silent. When we reached the wake, Bertram's bottle was already empty. No problem for him because he always kept spares in his truck.

Foxy and Buddy lived in a fishing camp beside a murky channel that snaked into the Gulf of Mexico. Wooden stilts raised their home above a soggy yard marked by muskrat hides in frames, catfish bones, and flat-bottomed fishing skiffs. The high stilts had saved the house from Katrina as they had for many previous hurricanes. By midnight, the affair had become almost festive. Bertram was leading the charge.

The color black swathed all two-hundred pounds of Foxy DeJan, although she had long since discarded her shawl of mourning. Like many of the mourners crowding the room, she clasped a half-empty glass of bourbon in her hand. Black crepe paper draped the front door, all the clocks stopped to coincide with the exact moment of Buddy's death, and mirrors turned to face the wall. Lying in his mahogany coffin, Buddy seemed more resplendent than in life.

Our guests were Maurice Duples and his daughter Celeste. Mama knew more about Cajun burial customs than I could have ever hoped, and she provided a streaming fount of information. As she had Beau Kaplan, striking Mama immediately smote Maurice Duples, and he stayed close by her side as the wake progressed. Duples' daughter Celeste was a stunner, and her dark eyes sparkled in the flickering, candle light. She was only five-three or four, her raven hair and flawless complexion leaving little doubt of her own Acadian genealogy.

Both Duples and Celeste seemed engrossed in the wake, and Mama's running commentary. I was happy because Foxy and Buddy were longtime friends. Buddy's passing, even though I was reluctant to admit it, had affected me deeply. Amid the wake, I slipped out of the house, seeking solitude in the darkness below. When someone tapped my shoulder, my trance shattered abruptly.

"I didn't mean to startle you," Celeste Duples said when I jumped.

"It's okay. Guess I was thinking about Buddy."

"I see that. I'm so glad you brought Dad and me. He has some unresolved questions about his family and his Acadian heritage. I think this event will help him immensely."

"Glad to be of service."

Although I didn't recognize Duples as a Cajun name, I kept my opinion from the attractive young woman.

"Thank you."

"Where are you and your dad from?"

"I grew up in Philadelphia with my mother. Now I live in Starkville and teach psychology at Mississippi State. Dad owns a real estate company. How did you learn so much about voodoo, Mr. Thomas?"

"Wyatt," I said. "Picked it up here and there."

"Fascinating," she said.

Even though the night air was humid, she crossed her arms and shivered. Too dark to see, I could only imagine the goose bumps rising on her slender arms.

"You can have my sports coat if you're cold."

"I'm okay. Dad has lots more questions for you."

"Maybe, between Mama and me, we can give him some answers."

I'd stepped out of the shadows, into the beam of the floodlight suspended from the roof, when I heard someone calling my name. It was Mama.

"Down here," I said, waving.

Mama joined us, along with an attentive Maurice Duples. A catfish jumped in the water, disturbing the night's silence, and temporarily distracting us from the ruckus coming from Buddy DeJan's wake.

"All of this ceremony seems so strange to me," Duples said.

Unlike Celeste, he was quite tall with the erect posture of a military officer. His full head of hair was stately gray. Along with his Rolex and expensive cut of his sports coat, it imparted the striking appearance of a wealthy man. Mama responded to his remark.

"A ritual mixture of Protestant, Catholicism, and even Judaism, with a smidgen of black magic from Africa and Vodoun from Haiti tossed in for good measure."

Dueling strains of mandolin and accordion, saturating moist air with a Cajun melody, quieted the chorus of frogs in a nearby pond. A shooting star streaked across the sky, disappearing over the horizon.

"Buddy's wake will be a party before morning," I said.

Celeste yawned. "I won't last that long. Have you seen enough, Dad? Let's go back to the hotel."

Maurice Duples nodded. "Your friend seems engrossed in the wake. Would you like a ride back to the city with us?"

"Thanks," I said. "Bertram was one of Buddy's closest cousins. He won't stop grieving till he runs out of Cuervo. Judging from the extra bottles he keeps in his truck that might be a long time."

My description of Bertram's alcoholic proclivities amused Celeste. Leaning closer, she said, "Do you need to tell your friend?"

"He'd never miss us," I said. "But I'll run up and tell him anyway. Be right back."

Bone tired, I needed little encouragement to leave the wake and return to the city. After paying my last respects to Foxy, I joined Mama, Celeste and her father in the driveway. Maurice Duples continued asking questions during the trip back to New Orleans, and I was glad that Mama, sitting in the front seat beside him, remained alert and responsive.

Celeste and I rode in back. I didn't mind when she fell asleep on my shoulder shortly after leaving the wake. When we reached New Orleans, we dropped off Mama at her house. Celeste and her father left me in front of Bertram's bar, and I didn't expect to see them again. I was wrong.

The next morning I opened the bar for Bertram, even managing to turn a small profit. Lady, Bertram's collie licked my hand, alleviating any guilt derived from missing Buddy's funeral. Bertram, hung over and his head pounding, showed up at noon. Seeing that I was holding down the fort, he went straight to his apartment in back.

I continued working until five when Maurice Duples strutted through the front door. Back-dropped by bright sunlight, he seemed quite different from the person I'd sat behind all the way to the city. He wore a different, though just as expensive jacket than the night before. Now he sported combed gray hair, a clean shave, and seemed if possible, even more dapper than before. He greeted me with a vice-like handshake.

"I was hoping I'd find you here," he said.

"Bertram's a little under the weather. I try to help out when I can."

"That's amiable of you. Celeste said you were a decent man."

Celeste's approval secretly pleased me, although I had little time to ponder it. The thought crossed my mind that he had come for a refund of his money, and I'd already given Mama her split. "I hope you weren't disappointed in the wake last night," I said.

"What I saw and experienced was wonderful," he said, gazing around Bertram's bar. "Now I'm convinced you can help me."

"How so?" I asked.

"I have the distinct impression you make it your goal to see things others don't. Our trip last night gave me no reason to believe otherwise. I need your help in visiting a place."

"Such as?"

"A grave that I have no earthly idea where to find."

"The city has dozens of cemeteries and thousands of graves. Do you know which cemetery?"

"No, and that's exactly why I need your help. I'll pay you whatever it takes to achieve it, and to answer my questions."

I motioned him to join me at the bar, and he sprawled his elbows against the zinc counter top. He exhaled deeply before resting his head in the palms of his hands, and then nodded an affirmative when I asked if he needed a drink.

Maurice Duples was much older than was his daughter Celeste. I guessed his age as seventy something, even though he carried himself like a much younger man. He swept hair off his forehead with the back of his hand and blinked twice, letting his eyes adjust to the dimly lit room.

"Jack Daniel's, neat," he said.

I poured him a glass of straight Black Jack. When I pushed it toward him, he seemed almost asleep, his left hand dangling off the counter. Lady's warm tongue revived him, and he patted her head affectionately before tasting the whiskey. It made me realize he was a gentle man. At least that is what I thought at the time.

"Interesting place," he said, noting the severed ties, bras, panties and other personal undergarments draped from the ceiling and mirror behind the bar.

"New Orleans is an easy place to lose your inhibitions."

Duples smiled for the first time since I'd met him. "Don't I know it? During a particularly eventful Mardi Gras, Celeste was conceived here."

"She said you live in Mississippi."

"Yes but I was born in New Orleans. My mother worked for a man named Duplesses, and we lived with his family until she died. An aunt from Starkville took me in. I never knew my father, or my real mother's burial place. I'm desperate to find her grave. Will you help me?"

Removing the bottle of Jack Daniel's from the rows of liquor behind us, I topped up his glass and said, "Anything else you remember about New Orleans?"

"Is that a yes?"

"Look, Mr. Duples, you don't need me. If you know your mother's name and her estimated date of death, you can go over to the Notarial Archives and find where her grave is. No place on earth has kept better records than New Orleans, and they weren't disturbed by the latest hurricanes."

"Tried that already. The two investigators I hired found nothing. If you can't help me, I don't know where to turn."

I could feel his desperation, even deeper than Celeste had implied. "Tell me what you remember, and I'll do my best."

The look of utter despair melted for a moment from his face, replaced by a grateful smile. "Thank you, Mr. Thomas, thank you."

Tourists were beginning to reach the Quarter. We could hear them talking as they passed on the banquette in front of the bar. A couple from New York wandered in, sat at an empty table, and ordered mugs of cold Dixie. After serving them, I returned to Maurice, waiting at the bar.

I topped up my lemonade and his whiskey, and said, "Let's go over to the booth. We'll find it more comfortable. You can fill me in on everything you know about your mother."

He followed me to a booth in one of the dark recesses of the bar. Most of Bertram's regulars never appeared before nine or ten at night. Except for Maurice and me, and the couple from New York, the place was empty. The young couple held hands, kissing and otherwise oblivious to anyone else, so I decided not to disturb them for a while.

Turning my full attention to him, I said, "Now tell me what you remember."

"I was only five when they buried her. Seems I've blocked most of the details from my memory."

"No hurry," I said. He closed his eyes. "You must be tired from last night. Just keep your eyes closed. Pretend you're five again, at your mother's funeral. Don't try too hard. Just let the memories waft over you like a gentle breeze."

"You have a soothing voice," he said.

"Then just listen to it. Breathe deeply. In," I said softly. "Out."

His head was sagging, chin touching his chest, his breathing becoming ever slower.

"Now tell me what you see," I said.

He began reciting in low tones—the voice of a five-year old as spoken by someone much older.

"Rows of rectangular structures topped with crosses and Greek statues. Beautiful flowers with colors, and smells you can almost feel wide streets separating the structures. I see an impatient horse, snorting and kicking up grass with his hoof. He's pulling a black carriage. It's almost like a city. Everyone is dressed in black."

"Is there any particular statuary, or perhaps a convenient name you can see? Anything specific you remember?"

"Yes," he said. "Lots of Xs on one of the ornate graves."

Chapter 6

Tony, suffering from a case of indigestion, arrived at the station earlier than usual the next morning. Lil, his wife of thirty years, was a fabulous cook although lately her enthusiastic use of spices and seasonings had begun affecting his digestion. Despite his discomfort, he would never recommend to her to use less garlic in her meatloaf.

He swallowed four antacids before brewing a pot of Community coffee. Today, he cut the number of scoops in half, long suspecting the strong, local coffee he preferred might be part of his problem. He had completed thirty minutes of paperwork, his stomach feeling better, when Tommy arrived.

"How's your head?" Tony asked when his younger partner entered without knocking.

Tommy didn't answer until he'd poured a cup from the pot on Tony's file cabinet. "I feel fine," he said after the first sip. "But your coffee tastes like hell."

"Then you make it next time. I don't remember asking you to drink it."

Tommy ignored the scolding comment. "Why so touchy, Fat T? Lil give you a ration of shit about something this morning?"

"She didn't, and I'm going to kick your Irish Channel ass if you don't stop calling me names and complaining about my coffee." Tony poured another cup. The Tums had kicked in, and the coffee did taste a little weak. "You and Donna looked like a real couple last night. You didn't blow it after I left, did you?"

"She was riding with Portie, and they left right after you did," Tommy said. "But not before I asked her out Saturday night."

"Who did the asking, you, or her?"

Tommy ignored his partner's apparent suggestion. "We're going to Lafourche's, for gumbo and dancing."

"Good for you," Tony said. "She's a lovely lady. Hope you hit it off and have a terrific time. I need a few God children"

"It's just a date. We're not getting married, or nothing."

"Not yet, anyway."

Ignoring his partner's wry comment, Tommy said, "What's on the agenda today?"

"Check out the Rescue Mission on Camp. Ask around about our suspect. They should be more helpful than the street people we talked with. At least I hope so."

"What about the hex signs?" Tommy asked.

"We'll talk to Paul about them when we get back from the Rescue Mission. Then we'll question Jason Stampler and hope he's in more control than the last time we saw him."

They left the office and drove down St. Charles Avenue, past Gallier Hall, the fancy Greek revival building that had once served as the New Orleans City Hall. Tony remembered a story his grandmother had told him of a particular mayor of New Orleans, forcibly removed from the building after losing the election. Politicians are a strange lot, and New Orleans' politicians rank right up there with the strangest of them all.

The sidewalks bustled with tourists, dressed in shorts and tennis shoes, taking pictures of the historic surroundings. They mingled with office workers, many wearing suits, on the way back to their offices. Although it all seemed bright and worldly, Tony knew the area had a seamier side.

The business district during the day grew deserted at night, except for muggers, thieves and the walking wounded of the city—its skid row derelicts. Someone had killed one of these derelicts, cut her up, and raped her before strangling her to death. Tony intended to find out whom. A ship, its horn blaring as it plied its steady progression up the nearby Mississippi River, snapped him out of his daydream, reminding him to cut across to Camp Street before reaching Lee Circle.

Both men were sweating and loosening their ties when they found a parking spot a block away from the Camp Street Rescue Mission. They reached their destination on foot. An attractive older woman wearing a simple though timeworn polka dot dress, her hair covered with a bright, paisley scarf, met them at the door. Both immediately noticed her eyes—a deep, blue color neither had ever seen.

"I'm Sister Agnes," the woman said. "Are you the reporters from the Picayune?"

"No, ma'am," Tony said, showing her his badge. "I'm Detective Nicosia, and this is my partner, Detective Blackburn. Can we ask you some questions?" Sister Agnes seemed noticeably disturbed, "Did I say something wrong?"

"I'm sorry. I was just expecting the reporters. They were going to do a story on the mission. Our money tends to dry up in the summer. It's hard keeping our doors open. A sympathetic story does a lot to raise donations."

"I'm sure they'll be here soon," Tony said, glancing at his watch, and then around the large open space.

They weren't alone. Rows of cots lined one wall, a temporary food line another. Several men wearing tattered clothes served soup from large, metal containers. Bewhiskered bums ate at picnic tables beside young families with babies and older children. Several cats roamed freely between people's legs, and more than one little boy held a puppy in his lap. A teenager with an old hound at his feet strummed a guitar in the corner. No one seemed to notice, or to care.

The place had the musty smell of an old, wood-framed building whose foundation had spent years under a few feet of water. After Hurricane Katrina, Tony had grown used to the smell. A streetcar on nearby St. Charles Avenue rang its bell as it approached Lee Circle. The sound comforted him. At least some things never change.

"Oh," Sister Agnes said. "You must be here to ask about the murdered woman."

"Yes ma'am," Tommy said.

"The police visited us earlier. We've already told you everything we know."

"We're just following up. What can you tell me about the victim?"

"She was a loner and rarely took advantage of our soup kitchen and never spent the night here, no matter how cold or wet it got outside."

"Sounds eccentric."

As Tommy's comment brought a smile to Sister Agnes, Tony noticed that beneath her pale cheeks was the stunning, bone structure of a truly, handsome woman.

"She was more than eccentric. The regulars called the old woman Crazy Sally. I don't want to make light of her nickname," Sister Agnes said, her smile disappearing. "Mental illness is rampant on this part of Camp Street."

"The people we serve are all cripples," a woman's voice said from behind. "And we are their crutch."

They turned to see another woman dressed as garrulously as Sister Agnes was, and she stood as tall as Tommy. Unlike Sister Agnes, this woman had long red hair.

"This is Sister Rose," Sister Agnes said. "She founded this mission and has watched over the people of Camp Street for almost two decades."

Sister Rose was as thin as she was tall, and she mimicked a gypsy peasant woman in her red plaid skirt. Though the room was not air-conditioned and the ceiling fans did little to curb the humid air, a tattered shawl draped her shoulders. She gripped it as if there were some strange chill in the air.

Bums, homeless families, and alcoholics milling around reacted to every inflection in her voice and each ever-so-slight wave of her arms. A man dressed in tattered shirt and pants smiled and bowed his head as he walked past. His deference to the tall woman seemed inevitable. Tony noticed that everyone's attention to Sister Rose was as reverent as an Irishman was to St. Pat.

"The city knows the fine job you're doing for the people here, Sister Rose," Tony said. "Our job is to find out who murdered one of your people, and keep something like this from happening again. Can you help us?"

"Like Sister Agnes said, we told the other policemen everything we know. What else can we tell you?"

"Please just search your mind for that last minute detail

that didn't seem significant enough to report the first time. We're grasping for straws here, Sister, and desperate for a clue. There isn't much dirt left on the floor, but we need to sweep it again, just in case. Maybe there is something under the rug we missed the first time, you might say. Think hard. Maybe you saw someone out of the ordinary about the time Sally was murdered." Sisters Agnes and Rose exchanged an amused glance. "Did I say something funny?"

"Everyone you see here is out of the ordinary," Sister Rose said. "Some are hopeless alcoholics or drug addicts. Many are mentally ill, like the Vietnam War veterans who can't resolve their pasts. There are the homeless, with children, that have no work, or food and little hope. We let them keep their dogs and pets, or they wouldn't stay here."

"Are they capable of murder?" Tommy asked.

Sister Rose's mouth opened wide, her lips petrified by Tommy's question.

"Sorry about my partner's bluntness," Tony said.

"We're all a little weird sometimes, although not everyone is capable of murder. You noticed anyone lately you think might be?"

Sisters Rose and Agnes remained silent until Tommy showed them a picture of Jason Stampler. "You know this man?"

"We know him!" Sister Agnes said. "He's one of the few lost souls that Sister Rose ever banned from the Mission."

Neither Sister Rose nor Tony missed Sister Agnes' almost accusatory tone.

"He is a violent man suffering from severe mental illness," Sister Rose said. "He tried to strangle someone. It took every healthy person in the mission to stop him."

"That someone wouldn't have been Sally Gerant, would it?"

"It was another woman."

"Whose name is?' Tony asked.

"Sandra Tillson," Sister Agnes said.

Tony made a note to interview the woman. "Did you call the police after the incident?" he asked.

"That's not our way," Sister Rose said.

"You didn't even report it?" Tommy said.

"He's not at fault," Sister Agnes said. "It's our job to

heal the spirit, not condemn the soul."

"Commendable," Tony said, wondering about the strange comment. Tommy's blank expression told him the observation had flown over his head. "Is Sandra Tillson around? We'd like to talk to her. Maybe she knows why Stampler attacked her."

"We never know when she will come around," Sister Agnes said. "She's out there, on the street somewhere."

"We'll put the word out that you want to talk to her," Sister Rose said. "She'll show up in a day or so."

Tommy and Tony completed their tour of the shabby facility. Before leaving, Tony cleaned out his wallet of forty-two dollars and gave it to Sister Rose.

"You're buying lunch, cheapskate," he told Tommy as they hiked back to the car.

"What's the story of those two?" Tommy asked, ignoring his partner's rant.

"The story I heard is that Sister Rose showed up twenty years ago. Some say she was a street person herself. She moved into an old two story off Tchoupitoulas Street and started taking in homeless people, sometimes thirty, forty people a night. She got some publicity and the public started donating money to the cause. They moved into that big building on Camp about ten years ago. Sister Agnes appeared three years later—a drunk when Sister Rose took her in. She gave up the bottle overnight, they say, and has helped Sister Rose ever since."

Tommy thought a moment and said, "You think Stampler would have killed the woman he attacked at the Mission?"

"Don't know," Tony said. "We'll ask her when she shows up. I just hope he's our man since he's already in custody."

Tommy and Tony continued to the city-run psychiatric hospital. They pulled into the large parking garage, finding an empty spot out of the sun. From there, they took a back corridor to the hospital and a service elevator to the third floor. The hospital's air conditioning was cranked up, frosty air heavy with the smell of antiseptics, illness and death. Refrigerated air quickly chilled their sweaty backs, arms, and something unspoken deep in their souls. An overweight nurse behind the reception desk greeted them with a frown when they arrived at their destination.

"You here to see Dr. Goldman?"

"You got it, Tootsie," Tony said.

He wasn't being rude. The nurse's name was Tootsie. Both detectives had known the woman for years. Their long acquaintance apparently meant little to Tootsie. Her frown intact, she picked up the phone and called Dr. Goldman.

"I wondered when I'd see you two," Goldman said when he arrived.

He held the self-locking door for them to enter. Young Dr. Goldman's silver bifocals balanced on top of his thick swath of dark hair like a tiara. Although as tall as Tommy, he was as lithe as a racehorse, and both detectives had trouble keeping up with him as he power-walked down the empty hallway. When they stopped at a door guarded by a uniformed police officer, he signaled him to open the door and let them in.

"We've had him under heavy sedation since he came in, and have him in a jacket, just in case," Dr. Goldman said. "Call if you need me."

"Thanks Doc," Tommy said.

As Tony glanced around the room, he got a decent look at Jason Stampler for the first time. The large man, wrapped in a straight jacket secured by straps attached to the wall, sat on a metal cot. Despite the drugs in Stampler's system, he stared at the two detectives with a gaze that made them feel like garden spiders about to be stomped.

"Where you from, Mr. Stampler?" Tony said.

"How long you been in New Orleans?" Tommy asked.

Stampler remained silent. Instead, he yanked the straps securing him to the wall with such force the resultant pop sounded like the crack of a well-used leather strap. Tommy and Tony stepped backwards in unison.

"You think you're bad?" Tommy said, regaining his composure.

Tony grabbed Tommy's arm and eased in front of him. "Did you kill Crazy Sally, Jason?"

"I killed lots of people," Stampler said.

"I only need to know about the old bag lady off Camp. Did you kill Sally Gerant?"

46

Stampler didn't bother responding to Tommy's question.

"You know anything about voodoo?" By this time, he'd had lost interest in both Tommy and Tony. Ignoring them, he stared at the windowless area's fluorescent lighting. Tony had yet to see him blink. "Let's go, Tommy," he said. "I've heard enough."

"You think he's our murderer, Doc," Tony asked as the young doctor hurried them back down the hallway.

"He's paranoid, delusional, and capable. So are dozens of others out there on the streets. Mental health isn't a key priority these days. Still, a little birdie told me a fascinating tidbit of info."

Tony stopped in the hall. "Such as?"

"Doc Warner got a positive match on Stampler's hair sample."

"Is that enough to pin him as the killer?" Tommy asked.

"Probably," Dr. Goldman said. "If he's the murderer, his DNA will match the semen samples from the crime scene."

Tony thought about Dr. Goldman's terse comment as they left the hospital and returned to downtown. "We need to book him for suspicion of murder."

"You want me to call in a report?" Tommy asked.

"We'll have plenty of time to do it when we get back to the precinct. Right now, he's fine just where he's at."

The day was slipping away as they hurried to speak with Paul Portie. It was rush hour, and Big Easy drivers are some of the worst in the United States, and maybe even Mexico. Tommy counted three crashes before they'd gone a mile. Par for the course, he thought. Donna Fonteneau and Paul Portie were preparing to leave for the day when they reached the lab.

"Can we talk at Carlucci's?" Paul Portie said. "I'm ready to get out of this place, and I have a powerful thirst."

Feeling exhausted, Tony wanted to go home. Tommy didn't. "One beer, Tony. It won't hurt you."

Tony nodded when Donna grasped Tommy's elbow and gave him a friendly nudge with her elbow. Who was he to stand in the way of his partner's budding romance?

"Okay. One beer and no darts," he said.

As a group, they headed for Carlucci's Bar. Doc Warner was out of town so Tony could focus on questions about voodoo and not darts. Carlucci's was empty as they took their usual seats at the table in the back. Tommy ordered a pitcher of Dixie before settling in next to Donna. Her unwavering attention had succeeded in dissipating Tommy's shyness. Tony could see he wasn't going to be of much help quizzing Portie. It didn't matter. He knew what he wanted to ask. When their beer arrived, he posed the voodoo question to Paul.

"You thought any more about what those voodoo signs may mean?"

"Like I said, Lieutenant, I know a few stories my grandmother told me when I was a boy. Other than that, I don't know any more than you do."

"You know anyone that does?" Tony asked.

"Wish I could help you," Paul said. "My grandmother passed away years ago, and my mom would never let us mention the subject in the house."

Donna was ignoring Tommy's advances and listening to Paul and Tony's conversation.

"There was an article in the Picayune last week," she said. "A guy downtown is an expert on voodoo. He's become quite the media darling."

"You remember his name?"

"Yeah, it's Wyatt Thomas."

Chapter 7

It quickly became apparent that Maurice Duples had an almost manic personality, one minute moody, and the next upbeat. When he awakened from his trance in the booth, his mood was nothing less than exuberant.

"Amazing," he said. "I feel better than I have in years. And I remember things now."

"You never actually forgot. You just had them blocked."

By now, Bertram had arisen from his drunken stupor, seemingly unaffected by the excess alcohol he'd consumed. As he cleaned up with a wet rag behind the bar, a few afternoon patrons began straggling in, along with some curious sightseers. A street band fired up a hot jazz number outside, hoping to elicit some hefty donations from the throng of tourists filing into the French Quarter. Maurice was grinning madly, the back of his head resting in his hands.

"I haven't visited the cemetery since my mother's funeral. I'm truly amazed that now I remember it vividly. It was almost like a little town, with rows of houses and narrow streets."

"That's why they're called Cities of the Dead. Since much of New Orleans is below sea level, the water table is close to the surface. The only choice citizens had before the city set up a drainage system was to bury their dead in a puddle of water, or above ground."

There were other reasons, most of which involved customs of different religions brought to the city by its multinational immigrants. Maurice wasn't interested in the city's history, his thoughts focused on only one thing.

"You said you knew where to find my mother's grave."

I did know. Voodoo was not my forte, but I did possess a thorough understanding of New Orleans and its rich history. I'd earned a decent living for many years with little more than my knowledge of New Orleans. His problem was no mind bender. After hearing his account of his mother's funeral, any New Orleans schoolchild could have told him where to find her grave. Still, he listened to my explanation with the doubt of a non-resident.

"Close enough, anyway. We should find it somewhere in the St. Louis Cemetery No. 1, over on Basin Street."

"Pardon my skepticism, Mr. Thomas, but how can you be so sure?"

"St. Louis Cemetery No. 1 is the oldest cemetery in the city. Many famous people lie buried there. Etienne Bore, father of the sugar industry, and Homer Plessy to name two. You may remember the pivotal cemetery scene from *Easy Rider*. It was filmed there."

Maurice didn't seem to know about *Easy Rider* or the two names I'd mentioned and said, "Homer Plessy?"

"Plessy v. Ferguson was an 1892 Supreme Court decision establishing separate-but-equal Jim Crow laws for blacks and whites in the South."

"Sorry," he said. "I'm in real estate and not a first-year law student."

Biting my tongue, I refrained from asking him if real estate people could read. Instead, I continued my explanation.

"Many of the rich and famous had expensive and often ornate tombs built for themselves and their families, and it's not uncommon to see forty-foot tall Greek statuary or tons of carved and polished stone. I was hoping you would remember a landmark grave we could zero in on."

"But I didn't."

"Yes you did. You remembered seeing the most famous tomb in New Orleans—that of Marie Laveau, queen of voodoo."

"Of course, you're a voodoo expert."

"I would have known it at any rate because it's a huge tourist attraction. Visitors mark **X**s on the grave with chalk for good luck. Supposedly, if you make a wish after chalking Marie Laveau's grave, your wish will come true."

Marie Laveau's powers are strong, long after her death, and her believers still have ceremonies at the gravesite. I'd heard this all my life but had never had an opportunity to ask Mama about it. Maurice didn't care. His mood had changed from animated to unusually quiet. Light from the jukebox reflected off the deep, green of his eyes.

"Take me there."

"Sure. Is tomorrow soon enough?"

He folded his arms, crossed his feet, and shook his head. "We must go now. I won't wait another day."

Maurice didn't realize that there are places in New Orleans you never visit at night, only during the day when accompanied by a large group of people. The city's cemeteries are such places. For years, they had fallen into decay from age, thieves, and lack of maintenance. A group called the New Orleans Cemetery Society had finally formed to rectify the problem, and tourist groups now visited the cemeteries regularly. They did so only during daylight hours because many of the cemeteries were located near public housing developments where even the tenants were often in danger of mugging.

"It's too late to arrange a visit today. The St. Louis No. 1 is near an area known as the Iberville Project, and crime is rampant there. Maybe the worst in the city and that is saying something. You may remember the looting after Hurricane Katrina. Even tomorrow we'll need to go with a group."

"I'm not going with a group, and I won't wait until tomorrow. There's a full moon tonight, and that's when I want to see my mother's grave. I have a thousand dollars. It's yours if you show me. If not, I'll find someone who will."

I had no idea what mysterious reason Maurice had for visiting the St. Louis Cemetery No. 1 by the light of a full moon. I only knew that doing so would be like smearing blood on your body before jumping into a shark tank. The offer of a thousand dollars, however, caught my attention. Though no longer in debt, I clearly remembered how it felt and didn't relish returning to that past situation. Before I could give him an answer, the finishing school voice of

Celeste spoke from behind us.

"My, my," she said. "You have such wild expressions on your faces. You both look almost ready to fight."

Bob rubbed against my legs as I combed my hair in front of the bathroom mirror. Although cats are usually solitary creatures, they have all the insecurities of a dog or child sensing neglect. Feeling badly about the problem, I picked him up and stroked him until he purred. It was then I noticed he had lost weight. I suspected he might have worms, probably picked up from one of the garbage cans out back in the alley he liked to frequent. I made a note to get him to the vet as soon as I had the time.

When I put him down, he retrieved a cat toy from beneath the bed and dropped it at my feet. With all the extra business lately, I'd begun ignoring our daily playtime ritual. Obviously, Bob had not forgotten. Picking him up again for a few more strokes failed to relieve the guilt I felt when I shut the door behind me and left him alone in the apartment.

Much later that night, I left the irresistible thousand dollars with Bertram for safekeeping and accompanied Maurice and his daughter Celeste up Basin Street, past the housing project to the St. Louis Cemetery No. 1. Although the cemetery had closed to the public for the night, I knew a place where we could enter at any hour. Likely every grave robber in New Orleans also did. He had armed me with two vital bits of information—the probable location of his mother's grave, and the name of a shadowy figure from his past. Arthur Duplesses was still alive, living on St. Ann.

Last glimmers of red and orange disappeared over the treetops as we opened a heavy, wrought-iron gate and entered the City of the Dead. Dormant pigeons roosted in eaves around the tombs, barely budging as we trod past. Bats, chasing insects mesmerized by soft, streetlight, strafed our heads with wildly beating wings. Up the way, a tomcat's screech abruptly silenced the cooing of pigeons. Celeste was mesmerized. Apparently unaware of the prevalence of impending danger, she sported a blissful smile on her pretty face.

"If Marie Laveau's grave is unmarked," she said. "How did you know Daddy saw it?"

"I knew it was her grave because freshly chalked Xs generally cover it. The superstitious believe if you make a wish, and then mark the grave with the letter X, the wish will come true."

Celeste squeezed my hand. "What do you believe, Wyatt?"

"I believe we should find your grandmother's grave and then get the hell out of here."

"You really think we're in danger?"

Her question went without an answer. By now, it was dark, with only the dim fluorescence of a few streetlights and the bright glow of my Mag-Lite illuminating our path. Because of darkness, we hardly noticed two figures as they stepped from the shadows directly in front of us.

"Well, what do we have here? Grave robbers or midnight mourners?" one of the men said.

Several missing front teeth made the man's heavy accent all but incomprehensible. It didn't stop his partner from laughing at the joke. His laughter quickly died away when we tried to walk around them. Despite the darkness, I could see they were big, mean, and ugly. To make matters worse, both men brandished switchblade knives.

"Where you think you're going?" the leader said, digging his knuckle into my breastbone.

To my surprise, Celeste answered with an angry retort, knocking the man's hand away with the palm of her hand.

"Leave us alone. This is a public place."

Celeste's anger brought an even greater burst of laughter from the two men.

"Lookie here, Biggs. We got ourselves a sassy one."

"Jackson, we surely do."

"You heard the lady," I said. "I'm an off-duty cop. Make trouble with us at your own risk."

I forced as much authority into my voice as I could muster, and it had some success. Biggs and Jackson both took half steps backward. The N.O.P.D. is notorious—that's spelled B.A.D. The force had once turned around a group of Hell's Angels, preventing them from attending and disrupting Mardi Gras. I hoped my bluff would get us safely out of the cemetery. Something else happened instead.

Two pistol shots, fired right behind my head, almost

caused me to lose my lemonade. Diving to the turf, I wrestled Celeste down with me.

"You'd better run. I'll blow your heads off, you lice-infested ghouls."

It was Maurice, screaming like a banshee and firing an old German Luger into the air. Biggs and Jackson didn't wait around, racing away into the shadows. They took Celeste's smile with them, and she trembled like a frightened puppy as I helped her to her feet. In the distance, sirens wailed. They weren't coming our way.

"Are they gone?" she asked.

"Yes," I said. "Let's get out of here."

"Not until I see Mother's grave."

Celeste and I stared into her father's eyes, now wildly green amid dim light from the street. Celeste continued to shake, as if suddenly the victim of an uncontrollable chill. When I put my arm around her shoulder, she nuzzled against my chest. My own racing heart did little to diminish her chill.

"This is frightening your daughter. I'll bring you back tomorrow. What are you doing with that gun, anyway?"

"It saved our lives, didn't it? If you're so frightened, then go. Take Celeste with you. I'll find the grave myself."

When I nudged Celeste toward the street, she looked at me and shook her head. "I'm all right now. I have to go with Daddy. I can't leave him here by himself."

"He has the gun," I said.

Celeste ignored my advice.

Maurice had already struck out alone, trudging blindly along the path lined with stone and broken shells. I thought about leaving them both. When Celeste tugged on my arm, I quickly changed my mind. Retrieving my flashlight from the ground, I followed them. We were close to Marie Laveau's grave when his manic yell pealed through the cemetery.

"Here it is!"

We found him squatting beside a large tomb bedecked with faded marble and statues of Greek gods. He was sobbing. Celeste knelt beside him, putting her hands on his shoulders.

"What is it, Daddy?"

"The name," he said. "It's not our name. Someone

removed my mother's body. Please tell me why anyone would want to do that to her?"

For once, he was right. During the plague years of the 1800s, when cemetery space was at a premium, residents often sold or bartered grave rights to those more prosperous. This practice continued to some extent until recent times with bones often moved hither and yon, and to who-knows-where. Although still alive, Arthur and Megan Duplesses had their names already engraved in stone on the tomb. The two people Maurice and his mother had lived with had apparently taken her grave.

"Probably a mistake," I said. "We'll check the public records in a day or two."

After helping Maurice and Celeste to their feet, I pointed the light until it reflected off Marie Laveau's grave. Celeste stopped beside it. Maurice and I watched as she took a bit of chalk from the sidewalk, closed her eyes, and marked three large Xs on the side of the tomb.

Chapter 8

New Orleans has two exclusive men's clubs—the Pickwick and the Boston Club, both formed before the Civil War, and both associated with Mardi Gras krewes. The Pickwick Club is associated with the Krewe of Comus, and the Boston Club the Krewe of Rex. Membership in either organization is almost impossible to achieve, and only the strongest and most influential of the city's richest families are members. Membership carries with it a position that the wealthiest outsider cannot buy—not for any amount as many Texas oil barons have learned.

There is a third club in New Orleans, more powerful and more exclusive than the Pickwick or Boston, although practically unknown except to the city's elite. The secretive Crescent Club is the most commanding, non-government organization in the city, said to control everything from local elections to sewage disposal. Inheritance is the only way to gain entrance, and the Club excludes blacks, Jews, and women. The president of the Crescent Club is Gaylon LeBlanc.

Gaylon left the Crescent Club at ten o'clock, returning to his house on the far end of Bourbon Street on foot. He liked to walk even though a deformity of birth had left his right leg an inch shorter than his left, and had rendered his right foot slightly more than a mass of misshapen bone and muscle.

With the exception of his foot, Gaylon could outlast a marathoner although his unique athletic ability leaned more toward weight lifting or heavyweight wrestling than running.

Despite his robust health and fitness, his deformity had left him embarrassed about his physical image. Because of this, he usually wore dark clothes.

At eleven at night, he stood at the front door of his million-dollar house, listening to the raucous sounds of the all-night party coming from further up Bourbon Street. Laughter peeled down the narrow thoroughfare, echoing off damp puddles, rotting brick and old frame structures. Bourbon Street was the first section of New Orleans to start recovery after Katrina. This was partly because of topography, and because of the stubborn mindset of the multifarious people inhabiting the Quarter. Gaylon was one of the people that never evacuated.

He glanced at the sky, straining to see the moon through an ephemeral glow of neon wafting from the strip joints, jazz clubs, and cheesy tee-shirt shops up the street. A steamy cloud creeping in from Pontchartrain finally moved away, revealing a full, golden moon. Before leaving his house, he checked his messages one last time, finding nothing that couldn't wait until morning.

After donning a black cape from the hall closet, he locked the door behind him and started up Bourbon Street, toward the lights and sound, soon moving through throngs of all-night revelers that thought the short man with a noticeable limp seemed perfectly normal in his sunglasses, bowler hat and black flowing cape that kissed the sidewalk. At least his appearance was normal for Bourbon Street. The cigar in his mouth remained unlit. A drunken female student put her arms around his neck, bestowing a sloppy kiss on his cheek.

"Strong shoulders," she cooed. "Bet you'd feel fantastic in bed, Mr. Bear."

Gaylon grinned as she moved her hands slowly down his back in appreciation. Hooking her elbow through his, she danced him around in a full circle. The girl's group grabbed her arm, pulling her away. Someone in her group had seen or sensed something that had frightened him inexplicably. Gaylon realized there were people with additional sensibilities. He had them himself. When the young man with long brown hair turned for a last, apprehensive look, he smiled and waved to him.

After wiping lipstick from his cheek with the back of his glove, the girl's touch still warming his back, he strode away. When he reached the lights of Canal Street, he went two more blocks before crossing the wide boulevard, busy with foot traffic even at almost midnight. Camp Street quickly darkened as he hurried away from Canal. Humidity and darkness soon engulfed him. He didn't mind. The dampness cleared his head, and he liked the dark.

Almost no traffic traversed Camp at this hour. He continued for five minutes before melding into the shadows as a police car made its way up the street. A derelict, drunk on Tokay, pressed a tin cup against his leg as he approached. He stopped, took the cup from the drunk, and crushed it in his palm, unworried the person's wine-soaked brain would remember him in the morning. The drunk swung at his legs with his cane only to have it wrenched from his grasp. Gaylon snapped the wooden cane with one hand, dropping the two pieces into the hapless man's lap.

"Bastard," the drunk called out as he walked away.

The alcoholic's reply brought a smile to Gaylon's lips. He proceeded west on Camp Street, seeing an ever increasing number of street people, drunks and derelicts back dropped by complete moonlight. Most moved in groups, and all had one thing in common; they were too stoned or inebriated, or both, to pay the man in a dark cloak much attention. He soon reached Lafayette Park, also known as Lafayette Square.

The small area sat among various government buildings—most notably Gallier Hall—and live oaks towering over crumbling brick walkways. Statues of some significant local citizens occupied the square but oddly not Lafayette himself. Gaylon had other things on his mind. He was waiting for someone, a street person he had observed during several such midnight visits to the Park. Tonight was different. Tonight he would do more than observe.

Gaylon sat on a park bench and waited. Unlike most normal humans, street people were reliable, tending to follow the same pattern every day, and every night. He waited there for one street person in particular, someone he knew everything about. More deeply, he had a personal connection with every street person. Something he'd never explained to anyone.

Although Sandra Tillson was only fifty-two, her years of drug and alcohol abuse painted her as much older. Gaylon had watched her for weeks as she pushed her shopping cart along the sidewalk, picking food from garbage cans and panhandling out-of-town visitors that ventured too far from the usual tourist haunts.

Sandra Tillson's habitual mental illness had destroyed her marriage, and her life. Her husband, who she never bothered divorcing, had taken custody of their only son. The principal at the school where she had taught had finally wearied of her arriving drunk, the musty stink of bourbon on her breath. After firing her, she never saw Sandra again.

It didn't happen overnight. At some point, she'd joined the nether world and began living on the streets, accepting handouts, becoming an unknown, even to herself, and not caring. Gaylon liked this. He waited patiently, fully intent on taking advantage of her mental incapacity. As a stray dog rifled a nearby trashcan, his wait ended.

Moonlight filtered through outstretched oak branches swaying in a damp breeze. He could see Sandra clearly through the moving montage of flickering illumination. So could the noisy dog and any other person in Lafayette Park that night. Gaylon realized as much. He also knew that Sandra would leave her cart by the buildings on the park's east side and squeeze through a narrow opening leading to the back entrance of a neighborhood café.

Thinking the recess behind his property secure, the owner often left the back door unlocked. Slender Sandra had discovered an opening into the recess, and used it almost every night to steal food from the café, careful even in her mental instability to take only scraps so that her intrusions would continue to remain unnoticed.

Knowing Sandra's routine, Gaylon scaled the brick wall with some difficulty and dropped silently to the other side. He had five minutes to spare as he waited in the darkness, his heart rate accelerating to an aerobic pace. He thought he heard the rustle of her filthy dress as she entered the passageway between the buildings. He wasn't sure because of the background noise caused by the nearby howling dog. A moving shadow coming toward him sent his heart racing even faster.

The hidden nook visually masked his impending attack. It was not enough. Someone would notice the distressed scream of a woman, even at midnight in Lafayette Park. Gaylon knew as much. Sensing his victim more than seeing her, he waited until he smelled her unwashed body and acrid breath. Then he acted. With practiced movement, he wrapped the garrote around her neck, twisting the noose just enough to silence his victim without rendering her unconscious. He wanted her aware, fully aware of everything he was about to do to her.

Sandra Tillson was about as tall as Gaylon although thin almost to the point of emaciation. He had little trouble lifting her by the garrote around her neck such that they stood, their faces almost touching, and her mouth open, twisted, and silent. Heat lightning flashed above the buildings, briefly illuminating abject terror in her dark eyes. She struggled, but the lack of oxygen to her brain left her with only the power to flap her arms. It was then she heard her last words, her epitaph whispered by Gaylon.

"See you in the graveyard."

Gaylon took his time with Sandra Tillson, although there was no need to hurry, his killing ground secluded and the woman unable to cry out. The experience left him ecstatic. His last kill had been less than perfect, a slow-moving police cruiser causing him distress and dismay, not to mention having to deal with the brute, Stampler. This one was perfect. He had kept the woman alive until the last precise razor cut. This time he had even taken an extra trophy.

Two hours had passed when he left his victim. Plenty of darkness left to return unnoticed to his house. After checking one last time for physical evidence he may have overlooked, he climbed the brick wall and re-entered the darkness surrounding Lafayette Park. The moon had turned from yellow to white, and he stared at the bloated orb. Suddenly unable to contain himself, he emitted a long, piercing howl that echoed off Gallier Hall.

As the plaintive cry died in his throat, something struck him from behind, a force strong enough to drive him against the brick wall. The impact knocked him senseless for a moment, and he shook his head, trying to reconnect with reality, when his attacker plowed him into the wall again with a massive body blow.

Gasping for breath, he swung his fist, hitting a jaw that barely budged. Struggling to regain his balance, he grabbed his massive attacker's large neck, held on with all his strength and squeezed.

Chapter 9

Heat demons rose up from the pavement as Tony and Tommy exited their car on Camp Street. It was another steamy day in New Orleans as a streetcar rattled by on St. Charles. Tony didn't notice. Thumping the roof of the car twice, he headed for the murder scene waiting for them behind the door of the little café. They weren't alone.

Beat cops and detectives, along with forensic investigators and photographers crowded the enclosed patio behind the tiny eatery. Between them, a battered body rested as the killer had abandoned it. The look in the dead woman's open eyes left a lasting reminder of the terror she must have felt during her last moments. Tommy and Tony joined Dr. Bernard as he made notes on a pad.

"Jesus," Tommy said. "She took quite a beating."

The woman's limbs seemed skewed in consciously unattainable positions, her torn skirt yanked up over her breasts and tattered underwear dangling on a twisted ankle.

"Looks like someone beat the holy hell out of her," Tony said.

"Massive bruising, contusions and razor cuts," Dr. Bernard said. "Our man kept her alive for quite some time before offing her."

"Cause of death strangulation?" Tony asked.

"You got it," Dr. Bernard confirmed. "She has a prominent ligature mark around her neck, and she doesn't look like she put up much of a struggle."

"The killer ambushed her. Knew her habits," Tony said. "He looped the wire around her neck before she saw him, and then toyed with her like a cat with an injured mouse."

"Shit, then we got the wrong man locked up downtown, or else a copycat."

"Shut up, Tommy. That's the last thing we need," Tony said.

Tommy paid little attention to Nicosia's admonition. He had just noticed that Donna Fonteneau and Paul Portie were working the scene. Intent on her job, she didn't see Tommy's inane grin as he waved, trying to get her attention.

"You say something, Tony?"

"No. I was scratching my ass," he said, pushing past Tommy to get a better look at the body. "How you doing, Donna?" he said.

"Good. Who you got there with you?" she said, giving Tommy a wink.

"Donna, you got a horrible taste in cops. Do we have an I.D. for the victim yet?"

"We found a locket. It has a picture in it of the victim, and a man, maybe her husband. The inscription identifies the woman as Sandra Tillson."

"The woman Stampler attacked at the Camp Street Mission," he said.

"Guess we don't have to worry about questioning her now," Tommy said.

"Any semen, skin, or hair samples? Any clues at all?"

Donna shook her head and said," Nothing Tony. Not a thing."

"Impossible," Tommy said. "No one's ever committed a crime without leaving at least one clue."

"This one did," Donna said.

"Yeah, well he's starting to piss me off," he said.

"Lieutenant," a beat cop called from the door of the little restaurant. "We found something out in the park."

Tony and Tommy backed out of the patio and followed the officer outside and down the sidewalk to Lafayette Park. They elbowed their way through the gaggle of curious rubberneckers, all eager to get a glimpse of the murder scene behind the yellow crime scene tape. A hectic reporter shoved her microphone in Tony's face.

"Do you know the identity of the murder victim, Lieutenant?" Before he could answer, she added, "Is there a link with last week's murder?"

Tony pushed the microphone aside, ignoring the pretty reporter's question, and kept walking. She probably already knew more than he did and only wanted his reaction for the noon news. So would Chief Wexler, he thought. The realization caused his early-morning beignet to do a flip-flop in his stomach.

After stepping over yellow tape and approaching the murder scene, crowd noise quickly disappeared, replaced by the silence of a beginning investigation. Forensic investigators, photographers, and detectives held sway near the old masonry at the eastern edge of Lafayette Park. Seeing Tony and Tommy, a police officer motioned for them to join him.

"Find something interesting?" Tony asked.

"I'd say," the man said.

The officer pushed through the shrubbery surrounding the courtyard. Their path led to a bare space between masonry and shrubs. Shadows beneath the shrubs masked the body, making it almost invisible until they were practically on top of it.

A large, white male stared open-eyed toward the sky his body reposed as if asleep. He might have been at rest except for the acute angle of his neck. The man's open mouth and his swollen, blue tongue told Tony, even before seeing the marks around his neck that he had died from strangulation. They stood gaping at the lifeless body of a man they both recognized as Jason Stampler. His facial features appeared more normal in death than when he was alive.

"How the hell did he get loose?" Tony asked.

Tommy was already on his cell phone, calling to find the answer. "A woman that said she was his mother showed up at the hospital. She convinced the night orderly and guard to let her into Stampler's cell to see him."

"They let her in? You kidding me?"

"Yeah, and neither of them seems to have an explanation."

Tony's resultant grimace was obvious to everyone in the crowd of onlookers. "Please explain to me, exactly, how she got away with Stampler, and how the hell did she take out the guard?"

"He's not really sure, but thinks she drugged him somehow."

"Just peachy."

"He said Stampler was smiling and acting perfectly normal after a few minutes with the woman."

"Unbelievable," Tony said, shaking his head in disgust.

"It blows the hell out of our theory," Tommy said.

"And raises more questions than answers," Tony said. "Have someone call on Stampler's mother and find out if she is responsible for springing him."

"You're right about this raising more questions," Doctor Bernard said as he elbowed past Tony and Tommy and knelt by the body, touching the victim's neck. "We got a positive match on Stampler's DNA. He is the man that raped the first victim."

"Well kiss my ass," Tony said. "How was he killed, as if I can't see with my own eyes?"

Bernard chuckled. "You already know the killer strangled him with his bare hands, Lieutenant. Before long, you'll be taking my job."

"Not likely, Doc."

"We must be dealing with King Kong," Tommy said. "What else?"

"No voodoo markings," Bernard said. "No bruises or contusions except for the neck."

"Your conclusion?" Tony asked.

"You're shafted," Bernard said. "Stampler's DNA matched the person that raped the first victim. Someone else killed Sandra Tillson, and then killed this person with his bare hands. I'm glad you're the detective on this case and not me."

Tony closed his eyes and massaged the pulsating vein near his temple. When he opened them, he took a long, scanning look around the park.

"What's the story about this area?" he said.

"Come on, Tony. You been here a thousand times. It's Lafayette Park."

"I know where I'm at. That isn't what I mean. There's a relationship with this place and the two murders. I can't quite put my finger on it. You a history buff, Doc. What's the story on Lafayette Park?"

"Well," Bernard began slowly. "The Graviers, a wealthy Creole family, had a plantation near here. It was in 1788, I believe, when a fire destroyed much of the city. Many of the residents wanted to move from the French Quarter. The Graviers obliged them, subdividing the plantation and selling off lots. The subdivided squares now bear the names given them by the Graviers. Magazine Street has warehouses. Poydras was an investor."

"And Camp Street got its name from the Graviers' slave camp," Tony said. "Now I remember. This is where they kept their slaves."

"So what's that supposed to mean?" Tommy asked.

"That's where voodoo came from. Slaves brought it with them from Africa."

"It was banned for years because the city's fathers were afraid it might start a revolt like the one they had in Haiti," Bernard said. The practice of voodoo intertwined with local beliefs and religion. Slave owners finally allowed their slaves, and free people of color, to have their ceremonies in the squares around town. They were open to everyone. Many whites, both poor and rich, often attended. Some even took part."

"Is this one of those ceremonial spots?" Tony asked.

"Don't know, but I wouldn't be surprised," Bernard said.

Tony glanced at a pigeon sitting on the statue. "Did the ceremonies coincide with cycles of the moon?"

"Probably," Bernard said. "Why do you ask?"

"Because last night the moon was full," he said, making his way through the yellow, crime scene tape and back to the car.

"Wait a minute," Tommy said. "I didn't get a chance to say bye to Donna."

"Catch her later. We got places to go. Sister Rose's Mission, down the street," Tony said, forgetting the car and continuing along the sidewalk.

Tommy hurried to keep pace with Tony's short legs as he proceeded down the street to Sister Rose's mission. They found the large hall almost empty. Still two hours before the lunch line opened, most of the mission's inhabitants were out on the streets. An old man with a mangled broom pointed to the stairway when Tony asked him where he might find Sister Rose. They heard voices as they neared the top of the stairs. It was Sisters Rose and Agnes.

Sister Rose was wearing the same plaid dress as before. Sunshine reflecting on her red hair through the window revealed a wisp of gray invisible in normal light. She was consoling a distraught Sister Agnes. Neither woman noticed Tommy or Tony. Sister Agnes was sobbing uncontrollably.

"Sorry to interrupt. We've had more murders. This time over in Lafayette Square."

Sister Rose nodded. "We know, Lieutenant. News travels fast along Camp Street."

"Then you already know the names of the victims?"

Sister Rose nodded again.

Not failing to overlook how distressed Sister Agnes was acting, Tony said, "I have a few more questions, but I can come back later."

"Please come in," Sister Rose said, wiping Sister Agnes' eyes with the red shawl draping her shoulders. "Go to your room, Agnes. I'll join you later."

"You gonna be okay?" Tony said.

Sister Agnes nodded, and then covered her face with her own shawl. Tommy, Tony, and Sister Rose watched her go.

"You want to ask me more questions about Sandra Tillson and Jason Stampler, Lieutenant?"

Still breathing hard from his brisk walk from the murder scene and the steep flight of stairs, Tony gulped for air.

"I'll get to that later. Right now, I'd like to know if your mission is associated with any organized religion."

"We have little support except for the good people that choose to help us." She glanced away as a door slammed, the muffled sound echoing down the hall. "Please excuse Sister Agnes. I'll answer your questions."

"We didn't mean to upset her," Tommy said.

"You didn't. There is a truckload of potatoes arriving at two, and our donations are always a little short this time of year. No problem, though. We'll just send them back. I'm sorry Lieutenant. I know our potatoes aren't a problem of yours."

"The killings," he said, staying focused. "They seem somehow related to the practice of voodoo. Have you noticed anyone around the mission with anything possibly connected with that particular practice?"

"Such as?"

"Amulets or hex signs, anything suspicious?"

Sister Rose seemed taken aback by the question, folding her arms as if suffering from a sudden chill. "We're tolerant of all religious beliefs although we only accept Christianity here. I haven't noticed anything suspicious."

"Thank you Sister," Tony said, fumbling for his wallet and finding his last twenty. "I know this won't pay for a load of potatoes. Maybe it'll help."

Sister Rose took the money without fuss and watched with folded arms as they backed off and started down the stairs. This time it was Tommy in the hurry, and he waited outside on the porch for his partner. He jumped when a delivery truck backfired in the street behind him.

"What's the deal with the voodoo questions? You think they know something about the murders they aren't telling us?"

"I think the killer must live around here someplace, probably within walking distance. Maybe the killer even came from the Mission. He may have a tattoo or wear a voodoo amulet. I'm looking for something that would peg him as a weirdo." Tony stopped in the shade of a building. When he caught his breath, he said, "We're in over our heads with this voodoo thing. It's time we got some outside help. Remember the guy Donna mentioned from the article about in the Picayune?"

"Yeah."

"I know him," Tony said.

"Who is he?"

"A disbarred lawyer who grew up in a wealthy family, here in town. He knows everybody worth knowing, and probably would be King of Rex by now except. . ."

"Except what?" Tommy asked.

"He got a divorce from his debutante wife, started drinking heavily, and threw one of his wealthy clients out a window."

"He killed one of his clients?"

"The only thing damaged was the man's bruised ego. They were on the ground floor, and there were shrubs outside the window. Still, the man came from one of the city's best families—even more so than Thomas did. They saw to it he lost his position with the upper crust, and his license to practice law."

"And then what happened?"

"He hit rock bottom and wallowed around in a drunken stupor for about a year. He finally quit drinking. Far as I know, he's never started back again."

"What's he do for a living now?"

"What he does doesn't actually have a name. Wyatt knows everything and everybody in this city. He knows the location of all the buried bones or at least who to call to find out. He helped a few friends. Before long, word spread. People started going to him when they needed to find something or someone, or have something done others might find unpleasant. He lives on the second floor above Bertram Picou's bar on Chartres Street."

Breathing heavily, Tony stopped to rest when they reached the car. The murder investigation was in full swing as he opened the door and crawled in behind the wheel.

"You okay, Fat T?"

Tony ignored the nickname. He had something else on his mind.

"Hell no, I'm not okay. I thought we had the murderer behind bars and the case solved. Now all we have is a lot of misleading information and no motive, unless it's somehow voodoo connected."

"And that's why we went back to the mission?"

"I have a feeling about that place I can't quite put my finger on yet. One thing I know for sure."

"What's that?"

"Sister Rose and Sister Agnes are covering something up."

"Like what?" Tommy asked.

"Not sure. All I know is Sister Agnes wasn't crying over a lost load of potatoes."

Chapter 10

Full moon in the Big Easy and Picou's Bar rocked with all the regulars, and scads of tourists wandering in from the usual crowd on Bourbon Street. Bertram Picou was in his element, waiting bar and entertaining a bunch of drunk Texans. As he worked, mixing countless gallons of pink hurricanes and cherry margaritas, he steadily consumed his own bottle of Cuervo. No one seemed to notice Tony and his younger sidekick meandering through the crowd. They found me at my usual booth.

"How you are, Cowboy?" Tony said, shoving in beside me.

"Tolerable. And you?"

"Like a maggot on a fresh body. This is my partner, Tommy Blackburn."

"How are you, Tommy? Like a cold Dixie?"

As Tommy's smile spread over his rugged face, I raised three fingers. Shirley, Bertram's server and current squeeze, saw my cue from across the crowded bar. She brought us two Dixie's and an icy glass of lemonade. Tommy ignored the chilled glass Shirley brought with her, taking a long pull directly from the green and white can instead.

"Fat T says you got a finger on the pulse of the town, Mr. Thomas."

Tommy's use of his partner's nickname earned him a glare from across the table. I barely suppressed a grin.

"Call me Wyatt. I've known Tony for fifteen years, and he's never said anything like that to me. He must need a favor."

"You know me too well, Cowboy," Tony said. "Got a minute?"

I had a date within the hour. I was meeting Mama, ostensibly to talk about our business activity. Still, Tony didn't appear in the mood for a rain check. As a perennial troublemaker, I wasn't in a position to ignore him.

"I always have a minute for two of New Orleans' finest," I said. "What can I do for you?"

Tony rested his elbows on the table and leaned forward. "You've heard about the murders up by Jackson Square?" I nodded. "We think voodoo is somehow involved." He waited a moment, looking for some sort of reaction from me when he mentioned voodoo. Seeing none, he quickly continued. "Since you seem to be the local darling on the subject now, we thought maybe you might be able to help us."

Tony removed a piece of paper from the inside pocket of his sports coat, unfolded it and slid it across the table toward me.

"What's this?" I asked after glancing at the strange symbols scrawled on the paper.

"Voodoo hex signs," he said. "We thought you might tell us what they mean."

"I'm afraid that rumors of my knowledge concerning voodoo are greatly overstated."

"Come on, Wyatt, we're drowning here. If you don't know what they mean, I know you can point us in the direction of someone that does."

I could feel Tony's obvious tension. It didn't matter. I would do anything to keep from involving Mama in police business. Folding the paper covered with hex signs, I put it into my own coat pocket. "No promises. I'll see what I can find out."

Tony slumped in the booth, relieved at my words. Tommy had finished his Dixie, and I motioned Shirley to bring him another. Neither man seemed to notice the noise of the crowd or the hot licks of the zydeco band performing on Bertram's small stage.

"Fill me in on what you know," I said. "It might help to identify the hex signs and shed some light on the situation."

Tommy glanced at Tony as if waiting to get tacit approval before proceeding. After getting the nod, he sipped his beer and then began.

"The murderer surprises the victim, wrapping a garrote around their neck before they have a chance to put up a fight. He applies just enough pressure to keep her alive, conscious, and unable to fight or call for help. He cuts her clothes off, probably with a straight razor. One of the victims was raped and sodomized. Both had hex signs carved into their flesh, likely with the same razor. He also takes body parts, souvenirs. The murderer left no physical evidence, no blood, or semen on the last two victims. What do you think?"

Tommy's reference to the last two victims confused me. Sensing there was something more they weren't telling me, I stored the information and let the matter slide for the moment.

"Sounds as if he has four hands," I said.

My words caught Tommy's attention. "You think he's got an accomplice?"

Tony stared at me, obviously waiting for my reply. "Serial killers sometimes work in pairs. The Hillside Strangler Case comes to mind. Still, one man could have done it alone. The murderer could have used a device on his garrote to keep it taut. Something like a thumb screw. If so, he could tighten it to whatever pressure he desired and let go of it without worrying about releasing the pressure. The victim would be powerless, and the killer would have his hands free to do other things."

"This guy's good," Tommy said. "How do you know so much about serial killers?"

"I practiced criminal law. The only way to be a successful criminal attorney is to think like one. Only problem is, it can become an occupational hazard if you aren't careful."

"Maybe we should consult with Mr. Thomas on all our cases."

"Maybe you should shut up and let him do the talking," Tony said.

The two bickered like an old married couple and neither seemed to notice or take offense at what the other said. When a balloon popped behind us, Tommy flinched.

"Been shot at lately?" I asked.

"Last spring," Tommy said. "I took a stray bullet in the

leg. How did you know?"

"Wild guess," I said.

Tony was through with small talk. Frowning, he asked, "Are you familiar with the Camp Street Mission?"

"What about it?"

"There are actually three victims. They were all street people, living in or around the mission."

"Three victims? The paper only mentions two bag ladies. What's the story on the third?"

"We're keeping it quiet. The third victim was a thirty two year old bi-polar male, six-foot-four, two-twenty."

Tony had thrown me a curve ball, though somewhat expected, from his earlier comment. I still had to think about what he had just told me for a moment.

"Was he also killed with a garrote?"

Tony glanced at Tommy before answering. "The murderer strangled him with his bare hands; no mean feat because it took four of our men to put the victim in a straight jacket when we had him incarcerated."

"You had the victim in custody?"

Tony winced as if I had slapped him. "He was our prime suspect until yesterday. Someone claiming to be his mother showed up at the police psych ward. She somehow drugged the guard and nighttime orderly and escaped with our suspect."

"Pretty serious mistake," I said.

"Don't worry," Tony said. "Heads are going to roll over this."

I nodded; refraining from saying, I hope one of those heads isn't yours.

"So you think he was an accomplice?" Tommy asked.

"Maybe, but it could also be just a pure coincidence. How do you know your murderer is responsible? Someone else could have killed the man."

Tony didn't immediately respond, waiting for Shirley to bring a fresh round of Dixie Beer and lemonade. A scuffle between a local and a tourist had started on the dance floor. The sax, guitar, and accordion drew quiet until Bertram separated the two men, throwing the local out for the night. I grinned, knowing the expulsion wasn't permanent. The man's only real problem was his wife of thirty years, awaiting her husband's return home with crossed arms and severe frown on her face. When the tussle ended, Tony continued.

"The last two victims were killed less than fifty feet apart. Time of death was the same. I believe in coincidence to a point. This wasn't a coincidence. The same person killed both victims."

I had to agree with Tony's opinion. "Why do you think the third victim could have been an accomplice to the murders?"

"Because of the brutality of the first murder, it appeared we were dealing with a much larger man—someone like Jason Stampler, our third victim. And something else," he added. "Jason Stampler raped and sodomized the first victim. We got a positive DNA match."

"Whoever killed Stampler must be a fairly large person himself," I said, ignoring Tony's bombshell piece of information.

Tony shook his head. "Except for what we found in Stampler's hands—a small hat and little glove. Our technical department now thinks whoever killed Stampler is only five eight to five ten. He wouldn't have to be large if he controlled his victims with a garrote, but that doesn't explain the brutality of the first murder."

"Too bad he didn't leave any physical evidence," I said.

Tony grinned. "I didn't say that. I said he didn't leave any physical evidence on or around his first two victims. Jason Stampler must have taken him by surprise because he had smeared blood on his shirt that was neither his nor the second victim's. He also had skin under his nails. On top of it all, he left a footprint, size eight. We now have the blood type, DNA and shoe size of the person that killed Jason Stampler. All we have to do is match it to the murderer."

"So what you have is a small murderer with strength enough to kill a large, extremely strong, bi-polar man with his bare hands. Someone that also preys on alcohol handicapped females and has a penchant for practicing voodoo."

"Females that are both former English teachers," Tommy said.

"Damn," I said with a smile. "What else could you add

to the mix?"

Tommy and Tony both smiled. "Hell, it's a riot, all right," Tony said. "If my ass wasn't hanging out from here to Baton Rouge, I'd be laughing right now along with everyone else."

"I feel your pain, Lieutenant," I said. "I'll have a close look at these symbols and do some thinking about what you told me."

Tommy slugged the rest of his Dixie as Tony, his own Dixie untouched, slid out of the booth.

"Thanks, Cowboy," he said. "You got a way of cooking the roux down to just the right consistency without burning it." He paused. "Say, what do you know about Sister Rose?"

"Like what?"

Tony placed his hands on the edge of the booth, resting his weight on his arms. "Like I said before, I got a hunch the Mission is somehow involved in the murders. I thought you might give me a connection. I guess if anyone in town knows about Sister Rose, it's you."

"What I know about Sister Rose, you've probably already read in the papers."

"You're not a lawyer anymore and Sister Rose isn't your client, Cowboy. There's someone killing people here. If you know something, tell me about it."

Tony had touched a nerve. It was true. Even after several years, I couldn't stop thinking like a lawyer. That was in my past now, and I responded accordingly.

"I don't know if the Mission or Sister Rose is connected with the murders. I do know about Sister Rose. She was married to a U.S. Senator. She had a drinking problem, and it caused a rift between her and her husband."

"Who was her husband?"

"Senator Whitney LeBlanc.

"You shitting me?" Tony said. "Sister Rose is Rose LeBlanc, former wife of United States Senator Whitney LeBlanc?

"She left him, along with a child, disappearing for some time before reappearing as Sister Rose. The rest you know or can figure out."

Tony slid out of the booth. "Thanks, Cowboy, you've been a big help," he said with a backward wave as he and

Tommy pushed through the crowd and exited Bertram's bar.

I was glad they had gone. Mama had called earlier, asking me along for a visit to her favorite blues club. Somehow, I got the feeling the invitation included more than just a discussion of our business. I'd always had an eye for Mama, and even the remotest possibility that she may also be attracted to me had sent my imagination into a full-blown tumble. I had counted the minutes since she called. I waited until Nicosia and Blackburn were gone before going upstairs. Despite my excitement at meeting Mama, I had other things on my mind. I needed to check on Bob before I left.

My cat's emaciated condition had grown progressively worse. I had taken him to the vet who had suspected worms. Another week had passed, and the worm treatment had not cured his problem. Despite his nagging about the cat, Bertram mixed up a Cajun concoction of honey and olive oil that he swore would take care of the problem. I was on my way upstairs when Celeste walked through the door, waving when she saw me.

As much as I liked the attractive, young woman, her sudden appearance put a crimp in my plans for the evening. Confused, I returned to the crowded bar, grabbed her elbow, and led her to my booth.

Chapter II

Gaylon grimaced when he got out of bed the morning after his trip to Lafayette Park. His head throbbed, and his muscles ached. When he rubbed his head, crusted blood covered his palm. What's worse, the linens on his bed looked as if a large animal had died there. With his pain somewhat lessened by a jolt of adrenaline caused by the sight of his blood, he yanked the sheets off the bed and hurried them outside to the trash.

Thinking better of what he had done, he extracted them from the trash, stuffed them into the brick fireplace, and started a fire. His housekeeper, Mrs. Keener, was due at any moment, and he didn't want to explain the bloody bed linen. He removed his clothes and tossed them into the flames, then hurried down the hall.

Gaylon resided on the far northeast end of Bourbon Street in what the locals called a shotgun house. Such houses were the norm in certain parts of New Orleans' Vieux Carre. If you fired a shotgun through the front door, the projectile would go through the back door without hitting anything. They didn't look like much on the outside. Inside, they were all but palatial mansions, and Gaylon's no different. A simple rectangle, the house was probably worth a million dollars or more because of its location. Like most of the structures in the Vieux Carre his house had survived Hurricane Katrina

He felt much better when he exited the bathroom some twenty minutes later. He doctored his wounds and swallowed a painkiller. After returning to the fireplace, he found Mrs. Keener prodding the smoldering remnants of his sheets and clothes with a cast iron poker.

"I thought the house was on fire," she said.

Mrs. Keener was probably forty-five, but her graying hair and stooped appearance made her look much older. Her dark face seemed laced with lines of worry. Gaylon had never seen her smile. Not that he particularly cared. The only time they conversed was when he was giving her specific instructions on what he needed done around the house.

He sensed she was frightened, or maybe just intimidated by him. That was okay with him as he certainly didn't want anyone meddling in his affairs. In this moment of uncertainty, he realized it was probably time to end her services. He glanced at the smoldering fireplace, touching a finger to his face when he noticed Mrs. Keener staring at him.

"An accident while sleeping," he said, remembering the fingernail marks on his face.

Mrs. Keener shook her head and turned away. She could see the scratches on his face, neck, and scalp weren't self-inflicted. It didn't matter because she knew better than to contradict her employer. During her first time on the job, Mrs. Keener, hoping to break the ice, had tried to tell a joke to her new boss. Gaylon had listened with folded arms. She had finished the punch line with a stuttering voice and was sure he would fire her when he turned and walked away without exhibiting even as much as a faint smile. She now realized he had no sense of humor and little tolerance for what he considered sass.

"You want me to polish the wood floors when I finish the rest of the cleaning?" she asked.

Instead of answering her question, he pulled a wad of bills from his pocket, peeled three hundred dollar notes, and handed them to her.

"You don't need to do anything now. I'm thinking of taking a trip to Europe, and I won't need you until I return. I'll call you when I do."

Mrs. Keener took the money. She direly needed the job but knew better than to argue. "Should I leave my cleaning supplies here?" she said.

"Take them with you. I'll call you." He glanced at his watch. "Lock up before you go. I have a ten o'clock appointment across town."

Gina Mae Keener couldn't suppress her tears as she watched him close the heavy door behind him. She waited until he'd hailed a cab before calling her son Andy. He was young, and she needed his help with her mops, brooms, and cleaning supplies. The three hundred dollars LeBlanc had given her would support them for a while though she knew it wouldn't last. Right now, she also needed her son's moral support and his youthful enthusiasm. Although Andy was old enough to drive a car, they didn't own one. It was too far from their little house on Terpsichore to walk. Mrs. Keener barely suppressed her tears when she called her son.

"Find your Auntie Elaine and see if she'll drive you over."

Ingrained with a strong work ethic, Mrs. Keener mopped and polished LeBlanc's beautiful, oak floors while she waited for her son and sister to come. She was sweating from exertion when she heard them knocking on the back door.

"Come on in," she said. "I'm the only one here."

Andy Keener and his Aunt Elaine entered the house in awe, gazing around at the trappings of wealth they'd never dreamed of. Mrs. Keener began to cry when Andy finally spoke.

"What happened, Mama?"

"I lost my job, baby. Senator LeBlanc is going to Europe, and he don't need me no more. I don't know what we'll do now."

Aunt Elaine watched as son Andy consoled his distraught mother. "It's all right, Mama. I can get that part time job flipping burgers at the White Castle."

"You'll do no such thing. You're a senior now, and need to study and graduate high school. I won't allow you to do anything else."

Gina Mae Keener hoped she wasn't speaking idle words. Older sister Elaine grabbed her elbow, pulled her to her bosom, and patted her back gently as she wept.

"Henry and I can lend you a little more money," Elaine said.

"I've taken more than you can afford already. We'll live. I'm almost relieved to get out of this place. That man made the hair stand up on the back of my neck."

Neither Andy nor Aunt Elaine had ever met the reclusive former senator, and couldn't guess at the reasons for Gina Mae's contempt for the man that bordered on disgust.

"We can have another garage sale, Mama. We made almost two hundred dollars on the last one."

"Andy, we already sold almost everything we had. There isn't much left we can do without."

Gaylon's floor was still damp as Gina Mae's eyes. Elaine and Andy packed up the aunt's old beater with cleaning supplies then waited on the back porch as Gina Mae left her house key on the kitchen table, and prepared to close the heavy door behind them.

"Wait, Mama," Andy said. "Let me take a quick look through the rooms. I may never get to see such a grand house again."

Unlike many parts of the country, New Orleans taxi drivers are friendly and talkative. Gaylon's driver was no exception, keeping up a constant patois as he drove his passenger across the seemingly endless Pontchartrain Bridge. Gaylon paid no attention and refused to respond to the driver's questions. The cabby didn't seem to mind, or require a response.

Gaylon maintained a residence on the north side of Lake Pontchartrain, known locally as the north shore. Little more than a fishing camp, the four-room house had a long dock that jutted out over the lake's shallow water. Hurricane Katrina had wiped out most of the many similar structures on the Lake. Without bothering to wait for the insurance money, he had rebuilt his cabin with funds from his Baton Rouge checking account—one of many that he maintained.

Gaylon had no close friends and no pressing appointments. He knew no one would miss him for a few days while the scratches on his face and neck mended. He watched as the yellow cab turned around and headed back toward the city. He made sure no one was watching before unlocking and entering his camp house.

The room was stuffy. Salt air blew in from the lake as he opened a few windows. Two gulls down by the shoreline raised a ruckus as they carped over a dead fish floating in the surf. Gaylon didn't notice. Removing a keychain from his pocket, he unlocked the bedroom's heavy door and entered, then carefully shut it behind him. With all the windows heavily draped, the room was dark. After flipping the light switch, he waited for his eyes to adjust to the dimness of the low-watt bulb.

Glancing around the room, he drew a deep breath and allowed himself to relax for the first time that day. On the walls were newspaper clippings of several previous murders. Some grisly object floated in a jar on a nearly empty bookshelf. After rifling through a case of jars in a corner, he selected one small and one large, and then filled them both with alcohol. He carefully arranged them, and then removed a rubber bag from his jacket.

He dropped two objects into the two jars, smiling for the first time as he watched mangled flesh slowly spread. In the first jar was a nipple, in the second a severed hand.

Chapter 12

Tony and Tommy had just gone out the door when Celeste made her entrance into the dissonance of Bertram's bar. I hurried downstairs to get her before some drunken Texan interceded and led her to my favorite booth in the dark recesses of Bertram's bar. I slid into the booth beside her, unprepared for what happened next.

Celeste had a strange look in her beautiful eyes—a feline expression I'd never seen before. After engaging me in a lustful embrace, she kissed me in a way that was anything but brotherly. Her warm tongue probing the inside my mouth sent my heart and mind reeling. Her actions puzzled me because our relationship had been all business until that moment. Still, I didn't push her away.

"Wyatt, I missed you. I can't believe how strong and brave you were last night."

"Your dad saved us, not me."

"You certainly didn't run away," she said, trying to suffocate me in her soft arms. "I think I love you, Wyatt Thomas."

I had to smile, the words of the comely, young woman sounding more like an enamored sixteen-year-old than a Doctor of Psychology.

"Never say anything like that to an old man. We have a way of capitalizing on the passions of younger women."

"Who's old? You can't be more than thirty five."

"Thanks. You're almost six years off," I said.

She grabbed my elbow and squeezed. "No problem. I've always liked older men."

"I'm not that much older. Am I?"

"Just kidding. I'm thirty."

"But your dad must be. . ."

"Seventy six," she said. "I was conceived between wives, during a memorable trip to New Orleans."

"Yes," I said, recalling Maurice's recollection of the subject. "Well remember your dad's experience, and take heed because New Orleans is can be a powerful aphrodisiac."

"Maybe you misunderstand my intentions," she said. "I said I love you. What I mean is I'm in lust for you. I intend to let nature take its course."

Celeste's lusty words took me aback, and my snappy response surprised even me. "Though I think you went too close to Marie Laveau's grave, you're invited to my room anytime you feel like pursuing your lust."

"Said the spider to the fly," she said, brushing my cheek with a soft palm.

Celeste's incredible warmth heated me to the melting point. My mind was still contemplating my meeting with Mama. It's not a date, I told myself.

She kissed me full on the mouth when I said, "I didn't know you were coming. I'm meeting Mama Mulate."

"A date?" she asked, her lips pressed into a sultry pout.

"Only to discuss business."

"Then can I come along?"

"It would probably be boring for you."

"I don't mind," she said.

Maybe I was wrong about Mama's intentions. Maybe she did only want to discuss business. My head told me no, but the beautiful young woman pressing so close to me that I could feel her heartbeat prompted me to forget the lovely voodoo priestess—at least for the moment.

"Let's take a cab, and go see Mama. If you're still horny when we return, we'll talk about older men and younger women."

After releasing myself from Celeste's arms, I helped her out of the booth and led her outside. I was still feeling guilty about ignoring Bob and his health problems, but decided to worry when I returned home.

Celeste and I took a taxi to a little café and blues club in the Warehouse District called Musique Azur. In addition to voodoo, Mama had a penchant for blues music. We found her sitting in a corner table devouring raw oysters and drinking Dixie. Celeste was wearing a short skirt, expensive shoes, and skimpy, lime green halter-top. Probably not the usual clothing you'd expect your psychologist to wear. Her appearance failed to go unnoticed by Mama who was not expecting me to come with another woman.

"You remember Celeste from the wake. I asked her to join us."

"I didn't know you were bringing anyone."

Ignoring Mama's irritated tone, I said. "It's okay, there's plenty of room."

Mama seemed almost jealous that I'd brought Celeste, maybe less than a surprise to me. I ignored the tension Celeste's presence had apparently created. She hailed the server and inserted herself in the chair between Mama and me. When the server arrived, Celeste ordered a dirty martini.

As my eyes adjusted to the dimly lit nightclub, I noticed Celeste was not the only woman at our table in a sexy outfit. Instead of her usual pinstriped suit, Mama's floor-length dress was simple and almost as translucent as a nightgown. It hung loosely by silken straps from her otherwise bare shoulders. Bouffant tresses draped her neck, highlighting a plunging neckline. An ornate, gold necklace covered the enchanting crease in her ample cleavage, much of which lay exposed by the daring gown. She was a sensation with bracelets of gold on both wrists, topped off with feather earrings dangling from her ears. I wasn't the only one that noticed. Celeste turned the back of her chair toward Mama, kicked off a shoe and began rubbing her foot against my leg. Deciding to make the best of a tenuous situation, I scooted my chair away from her.

After making a show out of ignoring Celeste's obvious advances, I helped Mama eat the oysters, and then ordered a dozen more. Celeste declined, making faces and sipping her martini as we ate. The singer, an Irma Thomas wannabe, would appear a little later. Until then, the club was relatively quiet, the acoustics perfect for conversation. After my conversation with Tommy and Tony, I had much to ask

Mama. A discussion of the recent murders seemed to get both women's minds off each other, at least for the moment.

Celeste listened raptly as I recounted my visit with the police. "I read about last night's murder in the paper this morning."

"Two murders, actually," I said, drawing a blank stare from Celeste. "The police are keeping the second one quiet."

When I handed the hex drawings to Mama, she glanced at them briefly. "They're drawings of vevers, symbolic designs formed on the ground in the peristyle at the beginning of a ceremony. I'm sorry," she said, seeing blank looks on our faces. "In Vodoun practice, a peristyle is an open sided temple, with several entrances, used for ceremonies. A mambo or houngan draws the vevers with flour, pulverized brick, or gunpowder—whichever powder is suitable for the ceremony. They are meant to invoke a particular loa in order to ask him, or her to perform a specific purpose, or to act as a go-between with another spirit entity."

"What are mambos and houngans?" Celeste asked.

"In the Vodoun religion there are three stages of initiation—kanzo, sur pointe, and asogwe. The kanzo, or worshipper, is the lowest level of initiation, and that is usually as far as anyone goes. The sur point is someone further initiated on the teachings of a particular loa for the goal of becoming a mambo, a high priestess of Vodoun, or a houngan, a high priest. I am a mambo. The asogwe is the ultimate human authority."

I could see by Celeste's dropped jaw and large eyes that Mama's claim had awed her. I was interested in what she had just said.

"You're sure these symbols were made by a houngan, someone initiated into the second stage of Vodoun?"

"Yes, it was probably someone with an intimate knowledge of our religion. I don't know if that means a houngan or a mambo."

"What would lead you to believe they might be?" I asked.

"Each vever identifies a specific loa and has a meaning specific to a particular houngan or mambo. This meaning is both personal and ephemeral, hence the use of powders that quickly vanish. Vevers summon loas, the gods of Vodoun, for specific purposes. They may have similar meanings but are all as different as the drawing skill of the mambo or houngan drawing it."

Celeste's eyes widened when I said, "These vevers were carved with a razor into the chests of murdered women. Is it possible their killer is a houngan?"

Mama shook her head. "It is possible, but all these vevers can be found on a search of the internet. Still, the tracings on this sheet create a specific pattern. A particular pattern a non-sur pointe would not likely know."

As Mama and I pondered the meaning of the symbols, Celeste became suddenly more animated. "Even though I know nothing of voodoo, I am a psychologist. I'm quite familiar with psychopathic behavior."

"Your point is?" I asked.

"This person may have a thorough understanding of voodoo. Still, these murders could have nothing more to do with voodoo other than a madman's attempt to resolve some past trauma, either real or imagined, he feels he has."

"The motive could be revenge," Mama said.

The singer and her backup band came on stage and began warming up. Something about Mama's words rang true, although I didn't know exactly why. We let the conversation simmer, ordering gumbo and more oysters, eating and listening reverently to the singer named Tante Hilda, belting her renditions of several blues standards. Though she wasn't Billie Holiday or Irma Thomas, her voice projected well. Patrons applauded appreciatively when she finished her first thirty-minute set.

Someone was smoking a cigar, and wispy vapor hung in an aromatic cloud over our table. Tante Hilda's music, the smoke, and three martinis Celeste had imbibed combined to render her into a New Orleans, mellow mood. By now she'd removed both shoes, had a contented smile on her pretty face, and was reclined in her plush, velvet chair. Her smile remained when I continued my conversation with Mama about the voodoo killer.

"Do you know Sister Rose, the woman that runs the Camp Street Mission?"

"Not personally. Why do you ask?"

"All the murders occurred near the Mission, and all the victims were street people that frequented it, either for food or shelter. Lieutenant Nicosia thinks there might be a connection. He questioned Sister Rose and her assistant Sister Agnes. He feels they may be covering up something."

"You mentioned a third victim," Celeste said.

I told them about Jason Stampler, explaining why the police were keeping it secret. From the look on her face, it seemed I had Celeste's newly found respect. The server was slow. The tray of oyster shells, sitting on the growing pool of water formed from melting ice, was still on the table in front of us. Mama poked at an oyster shell with her fork.

"Like what?" she asked.

"He doesn't know. I thought you might. Also, all the murders occurred during a full moon."

"That's not normal," Mama said. "Most evil is done during a new moon, when there is only a little light to illuminate the malevolence."

Mama's comment was enough to arouse Celeste's attention. "Not normal for a practitioner of voodoo, maybe. Certain psychopaths often become extremely agitated during full moons."

"Celeste is correct," Mama said. "The murderer's knowledge of Vodoun doesn't mean he is a houngan and is performing the killings for some ritual reason."

"Exactly," Celeste said. "Voodoo is likely connected in some way to his murderous impulses. If we knew the killer's motivations, we'd be on our way to catching him."

"Don't let Lieutenant Nicosia hear you talk like that. He'll deputize you and not allow you to return to Starkville until he catches his man," I said.

The server finally arrived to remove the rest of our oysters and gumbo, and to refill our drinks. From Celeste's slurred words, I was afraid she'd already had too many. It didn't matter. Mama, a woman that never seemed to get drunk, would give us a ride home in her Bugeye Sprite. The piano player had returned to the stage and was already filling the room with mellow chord progressions. Tante Hilda, the guitar and bass players would soon return. I needed to ask Mama a few more questions before they began their next set.

"The murderer took trophies, a nipple from a female victim, and the hand of the man."

Mama leaned forward in her chair. "He took a hand?"

"Yes, the man's right hand."

She frowned as she took a deep breath, and then exhaled slowly. "That's not good at all."

"Why? What's the point?"

"Vodoun has many gods and goddesses, and two key elements, Rada and Petro. The Rada element is most merciful, Petro more aggressive. Baron Samedi is a Ghede loa that specifically watches over graves and is custodian of the crossroads where spirits cross into this world. He wears a top hat, black coat, and sunglasses, even at night. He also smokes a cigar. He is the loa that intercedes if one needs to communicate with the dead."

"Lovely."

Ignoring Celeste's comment, Mama continued. "Baron Samedi will always strive to shake your hand after he speaks with you. If you offer it, he will take it. Those that understand this and wish to speak to him anyway always use the forearm of a cow in place of their hand. When this is done, Baron Samedi will take the cow's foreleg and not the person's hand."

I failed to grasp the full explanation of what Mama had just told me. From Celeste's puzzled look, neither did she. "What are you getting at?" I asked. Tante Hilda was just beginning to sing, and I barely heard her answer.

"The murderer is no houngan, or even a kanzo. There are two possibilities. He could be a psychopath, like Celeste says, that thinks he's Baron Samedi."

When she paused, I asked, "What's the second possibility?"

In a whispered voice I could barely hear above the music, she said, "Maybe he actually is Baron Samedi."

Chapter 13

With the small club filled to capacity, Tante Hilda finished her second set to resounding applause. Several dirty martinis had done more than mellow Celeste's mood. Now her chin rested on her knuckles, her elbows on the table.

"I think we better take Celeste back to her hotel," Mama said.

Celeste protested when I grabbed her hand. "One more set. I can't remember when I've had so much fun."

"Come with me to the ladies room," Mama said.

She helped Celeste to her feet, steering her, through the crowd, to the even darker hallway in back.

Ten minutes passed, and I'd just decided to check on them when they returned to the table. They were both smiling. Celeste appeared sober, and she grabbed my hand.

"Mama knows a jazz club even better than this place. It's barely midnight. Let's check it out."

I readily agreed, happy that she had not passed out in the bathroom. Mama had parked her Sprite just outside the door. A panhandler was guarding it dutifully. She gave the disheveled man a dollar for his troubles.

When she noticed my disapproving glance, she said, "Don't want him to overdose on my tip, now do you?"

"I don't see any danger in that happening."

Mama and I had a good laugh as we climbed into the tiny two-seater. Celeste didn't join in our frivolity. Whatever voodoo potion Mama had given her hadn't lasted long as she immediately went limp, falling asleep in my lap. Mama cranked the little four-banger, squealing the tires as she pulled away from the parking spot. Without asking, she drove me to Chartres Street to the front of Bertram's bar.

"Celeste is too drunk to go anywhere else. I'll take her home with me, and we'll talk with you tomorrow."

"Funny," I said. "She seemed fine when we left Musique Azul."

Mama had both hands clamped firmly on the sports car's little steering wheel. She was staring straight ahead when she said. "She's asleep because she had too much to drink and not because of anything I gave her if that's what you're implying. That girl cannot hold her liquor, and she is too young for you anyway. You should be ashamed of yourself."

Mama's words caught me by surprise. "Why Mama, if I didn't know better I'd think you were jealous."

"Pure nonsense," she said, gripping the wheel even harder.

"Mama, I know you have prepared potions for many things. Can you make one that would cause a crazy person to seem normal?"

Mama thought about my question for a moment before answering. "For a short while, but not forever. Why do you ask?"

"Just wondering," I said. "Could any mambo or houngan prepare such a potion?"

"All mambos and houngans aren't as knowledgeable as I. They would have to be quite powerful," she said.

"Thanks for the info, Mama," I said, smiling to myself at her conceit. "I better go now." I took a single step toward Bertram's before turning around and resting my palms on top of the passenger door. Mama finally smiled when I said, "By the way, I think you're the most gorgeous woman in the Big Easy tonight."

I watched them disappear into the night before entering Bertram's doorway. Slowly drawn notes from a lonely sax wafted on a damp breeze from nearby Bourbon Street. A horn from a tugboat on the river briefly joined the refrain.

Bertram had no backup bartender. When he got tired, or the crowd thinned to the point he was no longer making a profit, he just shooed everyone out and closed the bar.

Buddy's wake had apparently sapped his supply of energy, his place already closed for the night. I found him sitting behind the bar. The bar was dark, but he wasn't entirely alone, his collie, Lady curled up on her bed at his feet. She wagged her tail to acknowledge my presence before returning to sleep. I pulled up a stool and joined them.

"What's up, Cowboy? You look like someone just stole your favorite puppy."

"I had a date with two gorgeous women."

"And didn't hit it off with either one?"

"Not the problem. In this case, two were less than one because I didn't end up with either lady."

"How old you are?" Bertram asked in his best Cajun accent. Without waiting for my answer, he said, "That old and you don't understand women yet?"

He grinned and poured lemonade and a shot of Cuervo.

"I suppose you do?"

"Hell, I've been married more than once and every one different as night and day. Shirley slapped me tonight and said she's done with me." He tapped my lemonade glass and downed his Cuervo after saying, "Here's to you, Cowboy."

"Thanks. I've known Mama for years, and never knew she had any feelings for me."

"Mama Mulate?"

"Yes."

"She's a looker, that one and smart too. You could do a lot worse. Who's the other lady?"

"You know who she is—Celeste Duples, the daughter of my client from Mississippi."

"Mama Lou, she's a looker too."

We were getting nowhere talking about women. Both of us had plenty of practice on the subject, although neither had ever passed the course. It hadn't stopped us both from enrolling, semester after semester.

"Say, Bertram," I said. "What do you know about Sister Rose and the Camp Street Mission?"

"Probably the same things you do."

"What made her go off the deep end?"

Bertram didn't have to consider before answering. "That crazy husband of hers."

"Senator Whitney LeBlanc was crazy?"

"I don't mean he was crazy. He was a drunk and one of the biggest womanizers in Washington, and that is going a ways. He was a mean drunk. Word has it he beat his wife and even a few of his girlfriends. Because he was just about the most powerful person in Louisiana, his colleagues and cohorts kept it covered up."

"He and Rose had a son," I said. "Whitney LeBlanc raised the kid when Rose disappeared. What's the story on that?"

"Rose finally got tired of the beatings and affairs and filed for divorce. LeBlanc made sure she left the marriage with the clothes on her back and not much else. He got custody of the son, Gaylon, something that didn't happen often in those days, though it shows just how much power he wielded around here."

"I didn't know the circumstances."

Bertram poured himself another shot, killed it, and slammed the glass against the bar. "Something else a lot of people don't know is the son was adopted, at least by Sister Rose."

"What do you mean?"

"Whitney LeBlanc was the real father, but Rose isn't the real mother. He had fathered the child during an affair with his assistant. You probably know her as Sister Agnes."

"You're kidding me."

"No, I'm not. Agnes was not only Whitney LeBlanc's longtime assistant. She was also Rose's best friend. Rose knew about the affair, and was more afraid of losing her relationship with Agnes than her marriage to LeBlanc."

"I've never heard that story. Are you sure about it?"

"The kid was never actually adopted, at least legally. Even without seeing the birth certificate, I'd bet a bottle of Cuervo Gold that it lists Rose as the real mother. I got it from a good authority that LeBlanc pulled strings and had the records changed."

"Amazing," I said. "What's the status now between Sister Rose and Gaylon LeBlanc?"

"Whitney tried to poison his son's head toward Rose. Didn't work. He spent time with her in the summers, and lived with her for a while after Whitney died."

"What's the deal with Sister Agnes in all of this?"

"That's the odd one. Agnes hung close to Rose and LeBlanc as long as they were married. She was like a second mother to Gaylon. She stayed with Whitney long after the divorce until his death and her drinking got the best of her. She ended up on Camp Street with Rose. Rose took her in and dried her out, and they've been together ever since."

"One more thing," I said. "Do you know if either Rose or Agnes was ever involved in voodoo?"

Bertram rubbed his chin. "There were rumors about the Senator. Rose never moved from New Orleans while LeBlanc served in the Senate. He had a bachelor pad in Washington, and I heard he liked to throw voodoo ceremonies for his friends. Most people thought it was a joke, like Nancy Reagan consulting fortune tellers and such."

"What about Agnes? Did she live in Washington while Whitney was there?"

"Under the same roof," Bertram said. "I guess that's how they got so cozy in the first place."

"Guess so," I said, finishing my lemonade and storing Bertram's info on Sister Rose, Gaylon, Whitney LeBlanc, and Sister Agnes in particular, until later. "How do you know so much about everything around here?"

"You can't be a Big Easy bartender for twenty years without hearing more stories than you can shake a stick at. You'd be surprised what customers tell you after they've had a few."

Bertram was wrong about that. Nothing much surprised me about the Big Easy anymore.

"Thanks for the info. I need some sleep, and I'll see you in the morning."

"No problem," he said. "I'll put the lemonade on your tab."

Bertram had a long memory. I knew that he wasn't kidding about the lemonade, at least figuratively speaking. As he poured himself another shot, I left and went upstairs. Was Sister Agnes somehow involved with the murders near the Camp Street Mission? If so, could she mix a potion that would make a mad person seem sane? I had no time to come up with a plausible answer.

I found Bob at the end of my bed. When I tried to pet

him, he quickly jumped to the floor and stalked outside to the patio. Par for the course, I thought. I was batting a thousand recently when it came to my flawed personal relationships, even with my cat. Like Mama, Bob was letting me know it.

Chapter 14

Early next morning, Bertram awakened me by banging on my door. "Hey, Cowboy, wake up in there. There's someone downstairs looking for you."

"Not a bill collector, I hope?"

"No bill collector. Someone you'll want to see."

Bertram left without telling me the visitor's names, so I pulled on my pants and shirt I'd worn the night before, slipped on my shoes without worrying about socks, and headed downstairs. Bob was off roaming, so at least I didn't have to feel guilty about not giving him some treats and paying attention to him.

It didn't seem to matter much until I learned my visitor was Celeste. She also had on last night's outfit, her makeup a mess. She was sipping one of Bertram's specialties, a Bloody Mary, and she frowned when I scooted in beside her.

"Wyatt, I'm sorry about last night. I just had to apologize in person."

"You have nothing to apologize for."

"I acted like a fool. Why didn't you tell me you were seeing Mama Mulate?"

I started to deny Celeste's assertion, and then thought better of it before I spoke. "Did Mama tell you that we're seeing each other?"

"She didn't have to. It was obvious the moment we walked into Musique Azul."

Tires screeching outside the door signaled the beginning of rush hour, armies of workers descending on the C.B.D. Celeste seemed unaware. I took her hand and gave it what I hoped was a reassuring squeeze.

"Mama and I are just close friends. That's the only connection we have. The only one we've ever had."

My words brought an unexpected response. After hesitating a bit before pulling her hand away, she said, "I don't believe you, and my feelings are hurt because you kept your deep feelings for Mama from me."

"I promise that's not true," I said, reaching for her hand again. This time she yanked it quickly away and crossed her arms tightly against her chest. "Let's go to dinner tonight, just the two of us. We'll talk about this, and anything else you want."

Celeste at least thought about my offer before telling me no. "Mama is giving me a grand tour of the city's nightlife tonight."

"Oh? Where is she taking you?"

"Girl's night out," she said. "I don't know where we're going. If I did, I wouldn't tell you."

I'd only known Celeste a short time. Although I was already fully aware of her intelligence, it didn't seem to matter. I wondered if the gulf separating us was too deep to cross. I had little time to ponder the idea as Bertram arrived with another bloody Mary for Celeste and coffee for me.

He didn't help matters when he said, "Watch out for Cowboy here. He knows more pretty women than Elvis did, and he's about twice as slippery."

Celeste recoiled again. In my most sarcastic voice as Bertram returned to the bar, I said, "Thanks for your vote of confidence."

Bertram dropped a glass behind the bar and it bounced three times before breaking. Celeste drained the remaining drops of her first bloody Mary, pushed the empty glass aside and started on her second. Hair of the dog seemed to agree with her, and a silly grin soon appeared on her pretty face. She moved closer to me in the booth, giving me a bit of a nudge with her elbow.

"You are good looking," she said. "I can see why women like you."

"Don't believe everything Bertram says. In fact, don't believe a single word. Where's your father?"

"He has a business in Starkville. He'll be back this

weekend. I'm on summer break, and there's no reason for me to go home right now. What the heck! I may as well wait for Dad in New Orleans. See what transpires. Sometimes you can be too careful."

I waited until Celeste's stream of consciousness soliloquy ended before sliding out of the booth.

"I'll be right back," she said.

Bertram was crouched behind the bar, cleaning up broken glass. He gave me thumbs up and his best Cajun grin when he saw me glaring at him.

"Don't bring her any more drinks. I think she's still drunk from last night. Oh, and you had better call her a cab. I don't know how she got here. Doesn't matter. She can't return alone to her hotel."

"Don't worry Cowboy," he said. "Ol' Bertram here is looking out for you. I'll call that cab for her, but I bet you'd rather have her stay."

One thing I was sure of: Bertram was doing anything but watching out for me. Celeste had finished her Bloody Mary when I returned to the booth.

"Bertram's calling a taxi for you. If you're doing the town with Mama tonight, you'll need some rest beforehand."

"What I need is another Bloody Mary."

As if on cue, Bertram arrived with another drink, smiling and shaking his head when I gave him a dirty look. I refrained from preaching to her about the evils of alcohol. When the taxi arrived, I walked outside with her to make sure she got into the back seat. I knew the driver, one of Bertram's regulars. I gave him directions to Celeste's hotel, a twenty, and felt sure he would see to it she made it to her room in one piece.

"Thanks," I said to Bertram as I returned to the bar.

"Don't get all bent out of shape. It was a Virgin Mary," he said.

I pulled up a stool at the bar. "Remember what we were talking about last night?"

"You mean about women?"

"Exactly what I mean. I think I should go to St. Charles General Hospital and get an operation. When it comes to understanding females, a full frontal lobotomy might do me some good. Even my cat's mad at me."

"Hey, it can't hurt," he said. "And as far as that mangy cat, we'd all be lots better off if he'd just go back to where he come from."

"Thanks for your support. I'm going upstairs for a hot shower and change of clothes."

In an hour, I called Tony and told him what I'd learned from Mama. I didn't fill him in on what Bertram had told me about Sister Rose and her failed marriage to Whitney LeBlanc, nor did I tell him what I suspected about Sister Agnes. I wanted to talk to Mama about it first. In addition, I had a couple of other things I wanted to discuss with her.

Chapter 15

Tony was hanging up the phone when Tommy walked through the door.

"What's up, Fat T?"

It was still early, and Tony had heard his nickname only once so far that day. By noon, the occurrence would have become so ingrained he'd have blocked it from his mind, and let it go right over his head.

"Your ass if you don't quit calling me that," he said.

Tommy didn't apologize. "Who was that on the phone?"

"Wyatt Thomas. What's it to you?"

"Don't be that way, Fa—I mean, Tony."

"Where you been, anyway?" Tony asked, checking his watch. "It's a quarter after nine."

"I had a date with Donna last night. We didn't get in till late."

"That don't matter. Work hours are still work hours. Did you spend the night with her?"

"No, I didn't spend the night with her. Donna isn't that kind of girl. She knew a fancy restaurant out by Pontchartrain. We ate fried oysters then took a walk on the beach."

"Sounds real romantic. How's it going?"

"Slow. ain't even kissed her yet."

"Like you said, she's not that kind of girl. Even so, you can't expect breakfast in bed on the second date."

"At least I deserve a kiss."

Tony opened his mouth to give some more advice,

thought better of it and poured coffee instead. "Wyatt asked if we'd found the foreleg of a cow at the scene of the crime."

Tommy poured his own coffee. "How did he know about that?"

"Exactly what I asked him," Tony said.

"What did he say?"

"He knows we have to suppress a few things from the press. He wanted to know what else we were withholding from him."

"Did he come up with anything about why the killer cuts hex signs in his victims?"

"Yeah, we had a conversation about it. I heard more about voodoo than I ever need to know. He thinks the killer could be a voodoo priest, or even someone imitating a voodoo priest. There is a third possibility. The murderer might actually be a voodoo deity."

Tony's voice was flat, and Tommy didn't take him seriously. "He was kidding, wasn't he?"

"He wasn't kidding. According to Wyatt, one of the voodoo deities is Baron Samedi. Seems he's the one you call when you want to intervene with the dead. This particular deity usually takes on the physical manifestation of a man in sunglasses that smokes a cigar and wears either a bowler or top hat. He also wears a long black cloak over a dark suit or tuxedo."

"What a pile of shit," Tommy said, shaking his head and sipping the hot chicory-laced coffee.

"Maybe not. We found a bowler at the murder scene, and a cigar. And that ain't all," Tony said. "Whenever anyone familiar deals with the Baron, they bring along the hoof part of a cow's leg. They use it to shake hands with him to seal the deal because the he feels it's his right to take the person's hand in exchange for helping them."

Tommy had to think about what Tony said for a minute. "But the killer took Stampler's hand and left the hoof. Isn't that ass backwards?"

"Wyatt thinks we have a loony that believes he's Baron Samedi, or else is portraying Baron Samedi for some reason. He left the hoof because he knew someone would figure out the link."

Tommy refilled his cup. "Why can't we work on

something easy, like drugs or immigration?"

"My sentiments exactly," Tony said, refilling his own cup.

"So where do we go from here?"

"We find the killer before the next full moon," Tony said.

The water cooler was just outside Tony's office door. He and Tommy heard the familiar gurgle of a bubble rising to the surface as someone poured a glass. In a minute, the Chief entered. Both Tommy and Tony stood.

"Can I ask a few questions?"

"Come in, Chief," Tony said. "We were just discussing the Camp Street murders. Want some coffee?"

"No thanks. The wife only lets me drink decaf. Mind if I sit?" he asked, pointing at the empty chair next to Tommy.

"You bet," Tony said. "You want me to go down the hall for some decaf?"

"I'm okay. I'd like an update on the Camp Street murders."

Chief Wexler, replacing an overweight lifer that had never had an original idea, was in his third year as the leader of the 8th District. The former sheriff of nearby Covington, he was slight of build, beginning to go bald, and was soft-spoken. He rarely needed to raise his voice because he commanded the respect of everyone that knew him.

When one of his men or women was sick, hurt, shot, or in pain, Wexler was there to visit and provide support. He'd initiated too many positive changes to address, including the primary color of the police cruiser. His actions helped to boost his people's confidence.

Wexler's minions outperformed because they relished his approval without fearing his wrath—except as Tony had recently experienced, when things weren't going so well.

As he sat beside Tommy, Tony wished he had something more productive to report. Instead, he filled him in on what they knew, little that it was. When Tony had finished, Wexler grabbed a cup from the credenza.

"Maybe I'll have half a cup. Janice will never know." After returning to his seat, he said, "I'm glad you boys are handling this situation instead of me. What's your plan, Tony?"

"I want to place an undercover cop in the Camp Street Mission. My gut tells me the key to the murders is someplace close."

"Thanks for the update, and stay on it," Wexler said. He finished the coffee before walking toward the door. "The last thing we need is the press picking up on this story and running with it. It would boost tourism like a shark attack off Miami Beach, and we are just beginning to recover from Katrina. By the way, how's Lil and the kids?" he asked.

"Lil is fine, except she has a bit of that empty nest thing. My youngest son graduated and left home last year," Tony said.

"Tell Lil I said hi," he said. Before walking away, he paused and looked at Tommy. "I hear you and Donna Fonteneau are dating. Anything serious I should know about?"

"We're just friends," Tommy said.

"It's all right," Wexler said, raising his hand in a gesture of approval. "I like keeping things in the family."

Tommy waited for the Chief's footsteps to fade away down the hall. "You didn't tell me you were thinking about putting someone undercover at the Camp Street Mission."

"That's because I just now thought about it," Tony said. I want Paul Portie to do it, even if he isn't in our department. He understands enough about voodoo that I think he would recognize anything suspicious he saw."

"He seemed pretty strong about steering clear of anything to do with voodoo."

"Paul's a cop. He'll do what we ask him to do, and what's good for the force."

Tommy started to speak. He shook his head instead and poured another cup of coffee.

"Better catch up on my paperwork, or I'll be late tonight for my date with Donna," he said with a backward wave as he started for the hallway.

"Yeah, well don't let the door hit you in the ass on your way out," Tony said.

Chapter 16

Even after several days, Gaylon was still sore and stiff. After brewing a pot of coffee, he drew a long hot bath and soaked until the water turned tepid. Still achy, he emptied the tub half way and refilled it with hot water, his muscles feeling much better when he finally left the bathroom.

He toweled himself off as he walked into his bedroom, stopping to glance at his reflection in the mirror. Almost fifty, he could have passed for twenty-five. He had the body of an Olympic weight lifter, the result of years of free weight repetitions and steroid use. He didn't worry for long about firing his house cleaner. Just as well, he thought. Too much was happening in his life that he must never reveal to prying eyes.

He had always been a recluse since his days as an only child. Agnes, the woman that had raised him, was his confidant and closest friend. She had initiated him into the ways of Vodoun, and he had practiced that belief as long as he could remember. Secretly, of course. Vodoun gave him enormous power. It also had doomed him to a life of privacy and seclusion.

Since becoming a freshman senator, one of the youngest ever elected, he'd been an inveterate journal keeper. Nothing had changed. Like most nights, he sat at the computer in his bedroom and wiggled the mouse of his new computer. A thief had recently entered his house through an open window, stealing his old one.

He wasn't worried about someone reading his diary because he had always been careful not to reveal actual names. To the casual observer, it might seem as a work of fiction. He was more worried that a thief had rifled through his house. Like most victims of a crime, he felt violated. When the computer powered up, and light flooded the screen, he grabbed his head with both hands.

Headaches that consisted of laser sharp pain just above his right eye had returned. Like so many times before, the severe pain drove him to his knees. He remained for ten long minutes, banging his head on the hardwood floor in a futile attempt at relieving the searing pain coursing through his skull. When he finally regained his feet, a wicked smile had replaced the grimace on his face.

Gaylon strode to his closet as if nothing had happened, selecting a black silk shirt and black trousers. He dressed in front of the closet mirror, pulling up dark socks and lacing black shoes polished to a reflective shine. Tonight he fastened his shirtsleeves with pure gold cuff links. He also had a solid chain of gold around his neck, complete with a massive gold cross. After adjusting the cross of gold, he donned a tuxedo jacket, a new bowler, and dark sunglasses with white pearl frames. When he finished dressing, he lit a cigar and left the house.

Gaylon lived several blocks northeast of the tourist section of Bourbon Street, and he started in that direction at a healthy gait for a man with a noticeable limp. He heard the music and crowd noise long before he got there. Tourists and citizens alike knew Bourbon Street for the bars, strip joints, and jazz clubs. Laissez les bon temps rouler proclaimed a sign outside a bar. Let the good times roll. That was what New Orleans nightlife was all about, and what tourists came to see and experience. Drinking to excess and the widespread loss of inhibitions was what he planned to use to his advantage.

The street was crowded with midweek tourists, locals, and college students. The noise had reached a near-intolerable din, from car horns blaring at drunken jaywalkers, to tourists yelling and throwing beads out of second-story balconies. Music of every genre floated from the open doors of nightclubs populating both sides of the narrow street.

Bourbon Street had survived Hurricane Katrina, and it

was the first piece of New Orleans to reopen for business. The city had survived, none of the revelers thinking about the weather. When someone tossed a string of beads to him, he smiled and tipped his hat to them. When he gave them to an inebriated co-ed, she pulled up her tank top and showed him her breasts. Such was a common occurrence on Bourbon Street, and no one on the crowded sidewalk paid much attention, not even a beat cop. Neither did Gaylon. Music coming from an open door across the street drew him. The sign said Bourbon Street Jazz Club.

Gaylon pushed through the crowded room to the ornate bar in back. He found an empty stool and ordered a rum daiquiri. The rumpled bartender either didn't notice his bizarre costume, or else didn't care. He'd seen it all before and just wanted to go home. The janitor, cleaning up broken glass from an unruly patron, did notice and reacted abruptly.

The frightened man dropped his broom, wheeled around in a hurry and slammed into the wall behind him. Locked in place by Gaylon's smiling stare, he began to shake. The shake quickly dissipated into palsied tremors. When he opened his mouth to speak, nothing came out. Gaylon turned when someone touched his shoulder and the frightened man took the opportunity to slip away into the kitchen. The band was playing *When the Saints Go Marching In.*

The person that touched him was a gorgeous, brown-haired woman with large eyes. The charm on her necklace proclaimed her name as Celeste. When she spoke, Gaylon realized she was tipsy from too much alcohol.

"You must be Baron Samedi?"

"Why yes I am," he said. "How did you know?"

"Mama Mulate describes you to a tee," she said, hiccupping, and then grinning.

The puzzled look on Gaylon's face faded, quickly changing into a smile. "You know Mama Mulate?"

"Yes, do you?"

"Of course I know her. She's a local mambo with strong reputed powers."

Celeste beamed at his description of Mama. "Does she know you?"

"Every believer knows Baron Samedi. Unfortunately, we've never met in person, or in spirit, I should say," he added with a wink.

"She's in the ladies room. I'll get her. I know she'd love to meet you."

"No," he said, grabbing Celeste's wrist. "Not just yet. It's you I want to talk to. Please tell me, why are you here?"

"Mama's showing me some of the city's nightlife."

"Then you're not a local?"

"No, I'm from Starkville, Mississippi," she added.

"Are you here for pleasure or business?"

"A little of both, actually. I'm with my father, trying to find my grandmothers grave. We found it in the St. Louis No. 1."

"I know it well," he said. "It's near Marie Laveau's grave."

"Yes, but how did you know?"

"I'm the keeper of the dead. I know where everyone is buried," he said, matter-of-factly.

"You're good," Celeste said with a smile. "If you know so much, then what happened to my grandmother's body?"

"I can show you if you'd like. We can take a taxi to the cemetery where my powers are greater. I'll answer your questions. All of them."

The music had grown silent; the band was on a break except for the drummer who had launched into a frenzied solo that had the audience mesmerized. Celeste didn't notice, suddenly intent on the dapper man's intriguing invitation.

"Will you come with me?" he asked.

Celeste giggled. "I've had too much to drink, but not enough to go to a cemetery with a guy I just met. Especially one dressed like Baron Samedi."

Celeste had pulled her stool close to Gaylon's so she could hear him better above the noise of the club. He removed his sunglasses, cupped her face in his hands, and stared deeply into her eyes.

"Come with me and I will reveal a world you've only ever imagined."

Chapter 17

Mama loved the Bourbon Street Jazz Club, except for its bathroom. It was tiny, with only one stall. The band was on a break. Because of the wait in the bathroom, ten minutes passed before she returned to the bar. She hurried through the crowded nightclub, worried that Celeste may have already drunk too much to continue their night out. What she found was an empty chair. Their table was near the bar, so she hurried over to the attentive bartender.

"Do you know where the woman sitting here went?"

"Yeah, With a man wearing a tuxedo."

"She did what?"

"About five minutes ago. He was a strange one, even for Bourbon Street, dressed in a funny hat, dark suit, sunglasses, and a fat cigar. Sounds like he was going to take her to Marie Laveau's grave. I saw Richard, our cleaning person, talking to him."

Mama grabbed her mouth. "Where is Richard?"

"In the kitchen, last time I saw him."

Mama hurried around the bar to the kitchen's entrance, soon finding a little man cowering alongside a twelve-burner stove. "Richard, did you see the man in the tuxedo?"

He nodded and said, "Baron Samedi."

"You mean someone dressed like Baron Samedi?"

The faded tattoo on Richard's thin, brown arm flashed in the muted light as he shook his head. "It was Baron Samedi. He tried to shake my hand. I hid in here."

The chef and his busy aides didn't seem to notice the

exchange between Mama and the frightened cleaning person. They did notice when she grabbed a plucked chicken from a chopping block and ran out the door with it. Even after taking the chicken, Mama was not done with the Bourbon Street Jazz Club, rushing back to the bar.

"Hand me that bottle of rum." Something in Mama's voice caused him to comply immediately with her request. "Watch my purses. I'll be back."

With a dead chicken in one hand and the bottle of rum in the other, she pushed through the packed club, outside to the sidewalk crowded with late night revelers. It was after midnight, many of the people on Bourbon Street already drunk and rowdy. A woozy, young man wearing an orange, University of Tennessee tee shirt pinched her well-turned derriere as she hurried past. She noticed, but focused only on reaching the cemetery, she ignored it.

Traffic control prevented vehicle traffic down Bourbon Street at night. The cross streets remained open. Having visited many times, Mama knew exactly the location of Marie Laveau's grave. She hurried toward the St. Louis Cemetery No. 1, only four blocks north of Bourbon Street. A yellow cab passed her as she reached the intersection.

Although the taxi driver had no other paying customer, he was reluctant to stop for the gorgeous woman with wild eyes, not to mention the dead chicken and a bottle of rum waving over her head. She chased after him, screaming for him to stop until he took a right turn and disappeared up the street in a screech of tortured rubber.

Mama's Bugeye Sprite was three blocks away in the wrong direction. With little hope of hailing a cab, she hiked her long skirt over her knees and began running up the dark street toward the cemetery. She had left her cell phone in her purse, but had already decided not to call 9-1-1 and notify the police. She felt sure that if provoked, Baron Samedi would immediately dispatch Celeste and disappear into one of the cemetery's many darkened corners. She had to rely on her knowledge of Vodoun and powers as a Mambo to save Celeste.

Mama, among her many talents, had starred on the women's track team—eight-hundred meters, and the mile—at the University of South Carolina. She could have made the Olympics if she had wanted. She still jogged every morning, seven days a week, and was in excellent condition. The sight of her racing up Conti in a full-length skirt, her shoulder-length tresses trailing behind her as she waved a dead chicken, and a bottle of rum was an unusual sight. Luckily, there were no pedestrians on the sidewalk at that hour of the night.

Not even winded, she slowed when she reached the entrance to the St. Louis No. 1. She found the cemetery locked tight for the night but knew a private entrance. A well-worn pebble and broken shell pathway traced a moon-illuminated, circuitous route through the graveyard. It didn't matter that there were no streetlights because she knew the way to Marie Laveau's tomb in the dark. When she reached the grave, she saw the shadows of two people standing beside it. One was Celeste, the other Baron Samedi. Celeste had a red rose in her hand, plucked from a bouquet in a vase beside a nearby crypt, and a wire encircling her neck.

"Papa Legba, Papa Legba," Mama Mulate began to chant.

She was calling on the Loa of Doorways and Crossroads, trying to contact Baron Samedi. Celeste was still in a state of what amounted to suspended animation. Mama's chanting resulted in the hoped-for result with Gaylon/Samedi.

"For what purpose are you summoning me, Mambo?" he asked.

Mama moved toward the shadowy figure. "I've brought offerings; a fresh chicken and a bottle of the best Jamaican rum, oh wise one."

"Then show your respect and dance for me like a proper mambo," he said.

The moon was still bright, though no longer full. Mama placed the chicken at her feet, uncorked the bottle, and dribbled rum down her head and chest. Though there were no drums, Mama's lithe body began to pulsate to a silent beat, an ageless dance that was at once precise and sensual. Baron Samedi watched as she moved ever closer until she was nose to nose with him.

Picking up the beat, he began dancing the wild bamboula with her. Soon, they were both dripping with sweat. When the dance reached an explosion of unrestrained motion, Mama fell to the ground, rolling in the dust, and dirt like a sensual boa constrictor, her skirt hiked far up her long, brown legs.

Mama crawled to where she'd left the chicken, licking it with her long tongue. Then, after clamping it in her teeth, she slithered back to Baron Samedi's feet and dropped it there. Baron Samedi took the chicken, squeezing it in his hands until the bones cracked, before pulling the dead bird apart and waving the two halves in the air. Mama watched, chanting an ancient Dahomey poem as she rotated her head to the beat of the chant.

"Baron Samedi accepts your offering," Gaylon/Samedi said as he backed into the shadows. "Both of you, at least for now, may return to the realm of the living."

Mama waited until she no longer heard shell crunching beneath his feet before rushing to Celeste. The young woman's eyes were wide, a strange smile affixed to her pretty face. Gaylon/Samedi had drawn a vever in blood on her forehead. Around her neck was a garrote. It was still snug around her neck, locked with a thumbscrew.

She wanted to run. She didn't because Celeste remained in place, unresponsive to what had just occurred in her presence. Knowing she didn't have the right gris-gris to fight Baron Samedi's magic, she took the young woman's hand and led her along the muted pathway to an exit near the intersection of Conti and Basin Street.

Though Mama had no cell phone, Celeste still had hers. She realized as much when it began ringing. It was Maurice Duples calling.

"Celeste. Are you okay?"

"It's Mama Mulate, Mr. Duples. Celeste is in the powder room, and yes, she is okay. You want me to have her call you?"

"No, I had a strange feeling that something was terribly wrong. Please don't bother her. She'll think I'm a crazy old man trying to interfere in her life. Just tell her I called, and that I'll be back in New Orleans in a couple of days."

When Maurice hung up, Mama took the cell phone and dialed Wyatt's number; his phone rang four times before he answered.

"Wyatt. Celeste and I are near the St. Louis No. 1 Cemetery and I need you. Grab a taxi and pick us up. And please hurry."

Chapter 18

I'd just dozed off when the phone on the nightstand beside my bed rang. It was Mama Mulate, and she sounded terrified. After a brief explanation of what had happened, she gave me directions to where she and Celeste waited. I promised to be there in ten minutes. Quite a task as I was undressed, still half-asleep, and somewhat disoriented.

At least Bob had gotten over his snit. He was lying at the end of my bed and didn't awaken when I stroked him. It distressed me how skinny he'd become, and I promised myself I'd return him to the vet as soon as possible.

Bertram's bar and my tiny apartment were close to where Mama had made her call. I got there, in a cab, in less than fifteen minutes, and found Mama and Celeste waiting on the street. I immediately noticed that Mama was agitated and Celeste non-responsive. She showed no emotion as Mama herded her into the back seat. I also noticed the deteriorated condition of Mama's clothes.

"What happened?"

"Take us to the Bourbon Street Jazz Club," Mama told the driver without answering my question. "After I get our purses we'll go to my house. Then I'll tell you what just happened. You won't believe it."

Crafted from pure silk, Mama's dress was already revealing. Dirt and blood stained its thin fabric, ripped and torn in too many places to count. She also exuded the strong smell of alcohol but didn't seem to notice, or care. Though largely unsuccessful, as was the taxi driver who kept checking his rearview mirror, I tried to keep from staring.

When we'd gotten as close to the club as the cabbie could take us, Mama had him stop the car.

"Wait for us," I said, following her out of the cab.

Bourbon Street, after midnight, is like no place on earth. Nudity is common, hedonism rampant. It didn't matter because no one on the street seemed prepared for Mama's otherworldly appearance, her long black hair tousled, her clothes torn and dirty.

She was on a mission, and I barely kept up with her and her long legs. The band was on a break, and Mama caused quite a stir in the club as many eyes observed her march to the bar. The rumpled bartender reached under the counter and retrieved two purses. Mama fished inside, found a five, and handed it to him.

"What about the bottle of rum?" he asked as she started for the door. Mama stopped, found another five in her purse, and tossed it on the bar. "Wait just a moment. That bottle cost forty bucks."

Mama turned and faced the bartender, hands planted firmly on her hips. "You're either lying or else you're an idiot. That cheap bottle of swill almost got me killed. I gave you ten dollars, and that's twice as much as it's worth."

As Mama marched out of the jazz club, I handed the bartender two twenties. The last thing she needed was a trip to jail. I was too impatient to hear what had happened to her and Celeste to settle for that.

"Is that enough to cover it?" I asked.

"Hell yes," he said with a grin. "I haven't seen a sight like that in thirty years. I'd have paid her forty."

Despite his levity, he didn't return my money. Forgetting about it, I followed Mama out the door. She beat me into the cab, and I found her consoling Celeste. The wide-eyed cabbie quickly dropped us on a side street, next to her Sprite.

We left the noise of Bourbon Street and drove into the quiet darkness of Mama's neighborhood. I listened to boat whistles on the river as I followed Mama and Celeste into the house. Mama went directly to her gris-gris shelf, returning with a small bottle filled with an unknown powder. She opened the bottle in front of Celeste, dusted some into her palm, and blew it up her nose. Celeste blinked and shook her head, looking first at Mama Mulate, and then at me. Mama didn't stop to explain, and I didn't need an explanation anyway.

"Wyatt, I'm going to take a shower. Call the police and get them over here. I saw the killer tonight, and I'm too tired to tell the story more than once."

"At least tell me what you just did to Celeste," I said.

Mama stopped before reaching the door. "It was Baron Samedi. He zombied her. I didn't have a potion at the cemetery to counteract what he did so I had to wait until we got here. She's okay now and probably won't remember a thing."

"What's going on?" Celeste asked. "How did we get here?"

"A long story," I said, shaking my head. "We'll both have to wait for Mama to tell us what happened."

It was after two when I called Tony's house and woke him up. An hour passed before he and Tommy arrived, neither of them particularly attentive or happy. Their demeanors changed noticeably when I poured them cups of strong, chicory-laced coffee.

Mama soon joined us looking remarkably refreshed, considering the trauma she must have endured. Her sexy dress was gone, replaced by a floor-length, terrycloth bathrobe. Her long hair was still wet, and she was attempting to towel it dry. She winked and grinned at me when I handed her a cup of coffee.

We joined her in the parlor, and she spent the next half hour explaining what had happened. I hardly believed her story. Tony, Tommy, and Celeste seemed equally doubtful. We had finished the pot of coffee, and I went to the kitchen to start another. Having stopped jotting notes, Tony was talking to Tommy.

"Get someone down to Bourbon Street Jazz and get a statement from the bartender and cleaning person. Question everyone there and see if anyone else saw the man." Tommy went to the front porch to make a few phone calls while I refilled everyone's coffee. 'Why didn't you call us? We could have caught him?"

"I told you why, Lieutenant. Celeste was in danger. In my opinion, her life would not have been worth a plug nickel if patrol cars had reached the cemetery before me. I was her only hope."

"What if you were wrong?"

"I wasn't."

"That still doesn't explain why you waited nearly two hours to call us. We could have closed in on the area and caught the killer before he had a chance to get away. I'm not buying your account that he's a voodoo god and that he disappeared into the graveyard mist."

"You're right, Lieutenant. I probably should have called 9-1-1, if it hadn't been for my extreme duress."

Tony snapped his notebook shut. "Well it's too late to worry about it now." He glanced at his watch and said, "I'd like you to come down the station and confer with a police artist so we can get a picture of this guy to the news stations and police on the street."

"You certainly don't mean now, do you?"

"It's urgent, or I wouldn't ask."

"I'll change clothes," she said. "Maybe I should call someone to fill in for my eight o'clock class."

Tony drank the last drop from his coffee cup. "If we hurry, you can still make it."

Chapter 19

Four in the morning when Mama finished her rambling tale, Tony didn't bother returning home. He was lucky, he thought once again, to have such an understanding wife. Lil wasn't so lucky having a cop for a husband. He and Tommy gave her a ride downtown, and then waited patiently as she worked with the police artist.

"Thanks," Tony said when they finished. "I know you have classes to teach, and you probably need a little rest. Do you have a bit more time?"

"We've already spent the night together. What else can you ask of me?"

Trying not to think about it, Tony allowed the double meaning to drift slowly over his head. "I need you to do one more little favor for me."

He'd shaken her hand and suddenly realized he was still holding it. Letting go, he backed up a notch, placed his hands behind his back. Mama grinned. Although she had the same effect on most men, she always enjoyed seeing the power at work.

"You know I'm dog tired. It doesn't matter. I'll try to help any way I can," she said.

Mama's eyes were big and brown, and they locked Tony into a momentary spell. When he finally broke the stare and glanced away, he thought of his wife Lillian and felt guilty. Mama Mulate was a woman that could do that to a man. With some difficulty, he explained what he wanted her to do for him.

"I've had an undercover cop at the Camp Street Mission

for a few days now. I have a feeling the place is somehow associated with the murders. I'm getting an update tonight, and I think you might be able to help me make sense of it all. Can you meet us at nine, at Carlucci's Bar?"

"I'll try to make it," Mama said. "Give me the address."

To her surprise, Mama got through her eight o'clock class without a glitch. She didn't have time to change clothes, surprising her students by her casual appearance. Her eleven o'clock was also significant as she almost nodded off while reciting a passage from one of Elizabeth Barrett Browning's sonnets.

She remained awake, although virtually inert, during a three o'clock staff meeting. When she made it home at five, she found Celeste asleep in her bed, and thought briefly about lying down beside her. She didn't. If she took a nap, she might not wake up for her meeting with Tony. She made a pot of strong coffee and tended to her flowers instead.

Because of the subtropical rainstorm that had encompassed the city, the sky was already dark at nine that night. Rain poured from the rafters, spraying water in the puddles forming on the sidewalk. Tony glanced at his watch as he stood at the door of Carlucci's, waiting for Paul Portie to appear.

Mama had arrived just before nine, wearing sequined jogging clothes instead of the usual, business dress that marked her as a tenured professor. Still quite stunning, Tony had thought. After introducing her to Donna Fonteneau and the crew, he asked if he could get her a drink from the bar.

"A frosted mug will do," she had said. "Cold Dixie is about the limit of my alcohol needs tonight."

Thunder echoed down the empty streets. All the tourists were somewhere else, either at a restaurant, cozy bistro, or jazz venue. Any place out of the rain. Tony didn't notice as he waited for Paul Portie. His mind was concocting fantasies about the attractive Mama. Better stop thinking about her, he reasoned, or his wife Lillian might suspect something was wrong. Despite his reasoning, he couldn't shut down his fantasies.

Tony went outside and stood in the rain, waiting for Paul Portie because the bartender had failed to recognize the cop during their last meeting. Mike wouldn't let him into the bar until the Lieutenant had spotted the problem and interceded. Portie had looked and smelled, like a Camp Street wino. This time, despite his discomfort, Tony waited at the door until Portie finally showed up, some twenty minutes late.

Seeing the sticky Lieutenant in the doorway, just beneath the overhang, Paul smiled and extended his hand. Tony raised his own hands and backed away.

"Considering how you look and smell, I think we can forego the kiss on the check."

"Don't know what you're missing, Lieutenant."

"Oh yes, I think I do," Tony said, following him into the bar.

Mike did a double take when he saw Paul Portie. Paul's hair was even longer and dirtier than the last time.

"Would you guys mind sitting in the back, away from the rest of my customers?" he asked.

"Stow it Mike. This is police business," Tony said. He glanced at the table with the other cops and Mama, seeing their pitcher of Dixie was empty. "Bring us two more pitchers and keep them coming. On my tab."

"Yes sir, Lieutenant," Mike said, saluting.

"Everyone moved away from Paul Portie. "Oh, come on, you guys. I can't smell that bad."

"Yes you do," they chorused. "Stay at that end of the table."

Sergeant Carnahan tossed him a fat cigar. "Light that up. At least it'll mask your bouquet."

"Don't mind them," Tony said. "This is Mama Mulate. I asked her to join us. She's a voodoo expert."

Paul and Mama exchanged pleasantries as Paul filled his glass with cold Dixie. He downed the beer in one giant gulp and quickly poured another.

"A little thirsty?" Tony said.

"I'm not into T-bird or Mad Dog 20-20. The people I've hung out with never goes to the corner bar for a cold Dixie. I've been craving one for days now."

"Drink all you want. Mike's bringing more and I don't

think it'll ruin your performance at the mission."

"Got that right," Portie said. "Those people drink more rotgut in one night than most people in a lifetime."

Mike brought two pitchers. Tony noticed Donna was in an animated conversation with a young cop that had recently joined the force. Tommy must have already said something wrong because she had her back to him. His feelings obviously injured, he sat with his legs and arms crossed. He wasn't smiling.

"Mama's tired, Paul. Give us a quick breakdown of what's happening at the mission."

"Frankly, I've had a hell of a time getting to know anyone. Those people are less trusting than a pack of pit bulls and about as warm."

"They have reason to be unfriendly," Tony said.

"Maybe, but you'd think anyone could get a job if they wanted to. I'm not sure they're much better than a pack of dogs at the pound."

"Now wait just a minute," Mama said. "I don't think I like where this conversation is heading. Those people, as you call them, are human beings and deserve our respect. I cannot believe you look and smell like shit yourself, and yet you act like a superior being, even in the face of your best friends shunning you. How dare you! Those people deserve our help and support, and not your scorn."

Neither Tony nor Portie was prepared for Mama's outburst. "I'm sure Paul didn't mean anything," Tony said.

Paul Portie interrupted him. "I'm so sorry if I came across as a bigot. You become cynical when living on the street. I'm black myself, and my mother was a housekeeper. I empathize with the mission people. The only thing I can say in my defense is that police work tends to harden you around the edges."

Tony started to say something. First, he took a quick look at Portie. He wasn't smiling. Paul's rebuttal to Mama's criticism had duly chastised her.

"It's my turn to apologize. I jumped to a conclusion. I should have allowed you the opportunity to explain. I'm sorry. Please continue with your story."

Paul smiled and topped off their beer mugs. Everyone else had moved to the far end of the table, already deeply engaged in their own conversations. Tommy hadn't touched his beer and stared morosely at a Dixie poster on the far wall. Donna, busy talking with the young cop, continued to ignore him.

"There's something going on at the mission, all right," Portie said. "Even though it took me a while to make a few acquaintances, I now know that Christianity isn't all that's practiced there. Not everyone that lives in the mission is a wino. Many are just down on their luck and need a temporary place to live or grab an occasional meal. Some of these more coherent people are into voodoo. There is even a core group of practitioners."

"They're not even trying to hide it?" Tony said.

Mama wasn't smiling.

"I hate to cause so much controversy but have either of you heard of the First Amendment, and freedom of religion? Vodoun is a true religion. Last time I checked, I could go to Canal and call a service if I wanted. Am I wrong, Lieutenant?"

"Well, I've never thought of voodoo as a legitimate religion, but. . ."

"Yes?"

Tony stopped what he was about to say, his mouth open, and no words coming out. Finally, he managed, "I just never considered voodoo a religion."

"Then what do you think it is?" Mama said.

"I guess I never thought about it."

Mama didn't answer. Instead, she slapped him hard across the face. Realizing what she had done, she put her face in her hands and closed her eyes. "I'm sorry, Lieutenant. I'm tired and shouldn't have used you to take my fatigue out on."

Tony, almost as if he'd expected it, barely winced at the slap in the face. After a momentary glance at the other end of the table to warn the others to mind their own business, he finally spoke.

"You've had a hard twenty four hours. You don't need to apologize."

Paul Portie put down his beer. When he did, everyone turned away from Tony and Mama. They all knew the street-tough detective's reputation as a no nonsense cop and couldn't believe he had barely reacted to the slap in the face. Still, they knew better than to interfere.

Donna, her new friend, Doc Warner, Tim Carnahan, Tommy, and the rest of the people at the table had quieted, feeling the tension generated by Tony and Mama. Tony sat with his hand outstretched, wishing he were somewhere else. Instead of taking his hand, Mama hugged him.

"I'm so sorry, Tony. I can't even begin to explain how tired I feel."

"It's okay," he said, ignoring everyone's sudden amused expressions. "Paul, what's the next step?"

"There's going to be a ceremony day after tomorrow. All the members from the mission will be there. No one trusts me enough yet to tell me where."

Tony glanced at Mama Mulate. "You know anything about the Camp Street group?"

"No, I don't. Most of the practicing Vodoun groups have few members in common. I could ask around. I wouldn't even mind attending the ceremony."

"Too dangerous," Tony said. "The killer may be there and would recognize you."

Paul Portie began shaking his head. "I got a problem, Lieutenant. Attending a voodoo ceremony would go against my religious beliefs. You need to find someone else to go."

"Donna said you'd already attended a ceremony. What's the difference?"

"That was before I became a born-again Christian. I wish I could help you, Lieutenant. My church don't allow it. Please don't ask me to."

"Why don't you come with me, Tony?" Mama asked. "You're the best man for the job, and you can protect me if we encounter any danger."

"I don't know. Someone might recognize me."

"Nonsense," Mama said. "I'll fix you up so your own mother wouldn't know who you are."

Tony blinked. "Maybe you're right. If the murderer is there, I could put the cuffs on him, and our troubles would be over."

Mama grinned and leaned back in her chair.

"If you try to arrest Baron Samedi alone, Lieutenant, your troubles will just be starting."

"Then I'll figure something out."

Tony wondered what Lillian would think about him attending a voodoo ceremony with a beautiful voodoo priestess. His decision to keep that information to himself wasn't what had induced his guilt feelings—feelings resulting from his strong attraction to Mama. He hoped she didn't notice, but had a feeling she knew his every thought.

Mama had taken a taxi to Carlucci's and gladly accepted Tony's offer to take her home. When she opened the car door, he grabbed her hand and continued holding it longer than appropriate.

"You've been a tremendous help, Mama. Sorry we've had a few crossed wires."

Without answering, she kissed him before running to her front porch, through the rain that was now just a trickle. When she reached her door, she blew him another kiss. As Tony watched the lights go off in her house, his persistent guilt grabbed him by the neck and squeezed.

Chapter 20

A week had passed without hearing from Maurice. When he finally called, it took a moment for me to recognize his voice. Still in Mississippi, he informed me that he would return to New Orleans as soon as he concluded his business in Starkville. He wanted to know how I'd progressed in finding his mother's body, and if I had found out who had taken her place in the crypt. He was also worried about Celeste.

Encouraged by his latest thousand-dollar check, I told him there was nothing concrete to report about his mother, but I felt that it'd only be a matter of days before I'd have something. As for Celeste, I had to tell him there was nothing to report. Truth was she and Mama Mulate had partied together almost every night since our visit to the blues club. I knew this even though they had excluded me. I tried not to worry about it. As Bertram had wisely pointed out, the only thing worse than a jealous woman is two jealous women.

I'd finally managed to return Bob to the vet. The doctor looked worried when she checked his emaciated body. "We need to do some blood work. It will take a while to get the results. Until then, we'll put him on a high protein diet."

I felt somewhat better after our visit to the vet. Bob would be okay I told myself. I wasn't worried about what it might cost. My work was steady for a change, and Bob the only family I had.

Because of all the hoopla going on, I'd put off a trip to the Notarial Archives. The first city leaders were sticklers for detail and had kept meticulous records of every birth and death. They stored these records in the Notarial Archives. Like all archival repositories, ours is like a restaurant with a ten-page menu—almost too much information to process. Although Katrina had spared the archives, the storm had dispersed far and wide many of the people that had worked there.

In the Big Easy, there are many ways to obtain information if you know whom to ask. I knew of at least two sources in particular—Madame Toulouse Joubert and her faithful companion Armand. Since I was pressed for time, they were my quickest wealth of reliable information, and a much easier solution to my problem than spending three or four days in the archives.

I'd not seen Armand or Madame Toulouse in months, but I knew where to find them. They were usually at a little bar just off Bourbon Street called Allemands. Since neither Celeste nor Mama had called me with an invitation to join them, and my dance card was otherwise empty, I decided to visit Allemands that night.

There was a party going on in the French Quarter. Though it wasn't Mardi Gras, it didn't have to be. By now, the family tourists had all eaten and retired to their hotels for the night. Others were listening to jazz or drinking coffee and eating beignets at Café du Monde.

Most of the college students, off for the summer and visiting the Big Easy for a little I and I—intercourse and intoxication, and likely not in that order—were all within a four block radius of Bourbon Street. Probably every one of them was in an advanced state of inebriation. I realized as much as I turned the corner and started up Bienville. I found the world's largest block party even livelier when I reached Bourbon Street.

Noise on Bourbon continued as a distant peal by the time I'd reached Allemands. A celebration was in progress—a raucous affair attended by regulars, hip locals and more than a few tourists. Like many bars in the Quarter, it could have passed as a double to Bertram's place. I was only there to see Armand and Madame Toulouse, and ignored the laughing and joking around me. The two people I sought smiled and scooted over when they saw me.

"Wyatt, my man. How you doing?"

"Tolerable, Armand. You?"

"Smokin', man."

Armand was doing just that, and the pungent odor of marijuana mingled with stale air in the bar's dark corner. No one seemed to mind. I had known Armand for twenty years. I still didn't know his last name. Maybe Armand was his last name.

Armand was more than slightly eccentric. His shiny black blazer draped the black turtleneck sweater strangling his scrawny throat. His clothes looked uncomfortable, but he seemed aloof and unaffected. He also had glossy, black hair and a pointed goatee. Armand always wore black, his clothes pinning him as a throwback to the fifties—a stereotypical beatnik if such a creature still existed. He was not alone.

Armand's partner had crowded into the booth beside him, her velvet mini riding high up on thick, café au lait thighs. Madam Toulouse Joubert, an imposing black woman, was Armand's antithesis. She had coarse facial features, shoulders like a linebacker and a man's voice to match. Her bouffant hairdo was almost blonde and pointed toward the ceiling. She was a woman that loved bright colors, and her puffed lips were as red as freshly oxidized blood.

Armand and Madam Toulouse knew more about the Quarter, and old New Orleans, than any two people I knew. For many years, Madam Toulouse had worked in the Notarial Archives, her day job, in the basement of the District Court. The Archives provided her access to the detailed history of the city from its inception, and she had expanded on this knowledge through the years. Now, she could recite the membership rolls of the exclusive Boston Club and tell you the likely candidates to serve as the next King of Comus.

Armand, an expert collector and dealer of New Orleans art and antiquities, complemented her knowledge. He knew the wealthy and powerful in the Big Easy on a first name basis—many of whom would deny the association if asked. Together, Armand and Toulouse fashioned a formidable duo. I ordered us a round of drinks and briefly explained my situation. When I finished my story, Armand shook his head in sympathy before killing his shot of Johnny Walker Red.

"You should have called me earlier, Cowboy. I could have saved you some embarrassment. Duples is a contraction of the name Duplesses. I'm surprised you didn't already figure that one out after seeing their inscriptions on the crypt."

Madam Toulouse wrapped her large hands around her Hurricane glass and sipped the icy, pink concoction through a bright red straw. "Arthur and Megan Duplesses live on St. Ann. Arthur inherited his Daddy's fur business. He used to have a warehouse on Decatur when it was still a business district. Arthur took over, retiring about fifteen years ago with even more money than his father had left him."

Armand's dark mustache twitched with a crooked grin. "Arthur used to be a wild one. Only the years slowed him down. He and Megan don't get out much anymore."

"You know anything about Maurice Duples or his daughter Celeste?" I asked.

Again, Armand's mustache twitched, and he exchanged a knowing glance with Madam Toulouse. Madam Toulouse winked at me.

"Wyatt, you have a particular talent for seeking out people with the right answers."

"Then you know the answer?"

Armand and Madam Toulouse nodded in unison. Madam Toulouse leaned against the padded booth, crossing her long legs. "Maurice is the illegitimate son of Arthur Duplesses."

"You're kidding me. What did they do with the mother's body?"

"Nothing," Armand said. "It's still there. Nawlins folk always looked the other way when it came to trysts and affairs. Hell, everyone that is anyone, to this very day, has a mistress or two. No one even minds a man burying his mistress alongside his wife. Still, it would be inappropriate to put her name on the crypt."

"That's an absolute no-no," Madame Toulouse Joubert agreed.

Someone in the bar dropped a glass. When it exploded against the floor, I flinched. Madam Toulouse and Armand remained nonplussed. Noise from the crowd abated for an instant, then resumed to its previous discord. I tried to ignore the noise, contemplating what Armand and Madam Toulouse had just told me.

"Maurice Duples isn't going to like that bit of info. Do you know anything else about his mother?"

"She was one of the many mistresses that Arthur kept around town. His wife Megan is quite a woman to have put up with him all these years," Armand said.

"I remember the name Duplesses now. Wasn't he once the. . ."

"That's right," Madam Toulouse said. "King of Rex back in the forties."

King of Rex is the most coveted title in the Mardi Gras hierarchy of krewes. A krewe is a New Orleans' social club. The Krewe of Rex is one of the most, if not the most, exclusive krewe. Only the richest and most influential men are considered, and then only after a donation to the Krewe of Rex of at least a million dollars, so the story goes.

"Duples does have lots of money. I thought he earned it on his own."

"Nawlins rich folk often adopt their bastards and treat them like family. Since Arthur didn't embrace and acknowledge his son, there's probably a reason," Armand said.

"Such as?"

"Well, she could have been black, although most Creole families generally overlooked that little problem. Guess you'll have to figure out that piece of the puzzle on your own," Armand said.

When Madam Toulouse Joubert got up to go to the bathroom, Armand lit up another joint. They had either told me all they knew or else had decided to let me find out the rest for myself. Whichever, I knew my visit was at an end. Thanking Armand, I asked him to give my regards to Madam Toulouse, winding my way through the crowded, rowdy bar, I returned to an even rowdier party on Bourbon Street.

Chapter 21

I'd learned a lot from Armand and Madam Toulouse, but I still needed to add a few details before Maurice Duples returned to New Orleans. Celeste could fill in some of the gaps about her father if she, along with Mama, weren't still annoyed with me. The two had become fast friends. Celeste had moved out of her hotel room and was now staying with Mama. Mama was in the process of assisting Celeste in earning a Master's Degree in New Orleans nightlife. I decided to give Celeste one more chance.

"I can't remember why I'm irritated with you," she said when she answered her cell phone. "Mama's busy doing something else tonight so maybe I'll give you one more chance."

Mama had led Celeste on an advanced tour of many New Orleans' hot spots but had not yet shown her everything. There were still places to see. One such landmark was Dagobert's on Lake Pontchartrain. It was where I intended to take her.

Celeste and I had taken the streetcar from Mama's to the bus stop. It was a blue afternoon in the Big Easy, all overcast and misty but not enough to prevent Celeste and me from enjoying the bus ride down Lakeshore Drive. Dark clouds were moving up from the Gulf, and a stiff breeze was chopping Pontchartrain's surface into soapy-green froth. Boats still on the lake had taken notice and were lowering their sails. Making for shore under engine power.

Hurricane Katrina had destroyed many of the marinas and most of the boats on the lake. Still, there is a plethora of rich folks in this part of the world, and the old ways soon began reappearing. An anomaly of the storm, Dagobert's Restaurant had survived virtually unscathed—at least one thing fortunate for the citizens of New Orleans.

Celeste and I were the only passengers on the bus. The driver, oblivious to both of us, snapped his fingers as he sang along with the music from his headphone radio. After disembarking at West End Parkway, we watched the bus pull off in a cloud of diesel smoke. Luckily, for us both, I'd brought an umbrella.

"Where are we going?" Celeste asked.

"Dagobert's," I said as thunder rumbled overhead and fat raindrops began falling, slowly at first, and then faster and harder.

Celeste's expressive eyes were two shades darker than the storm clouds racing above us. A strong wind jostled tethered boats and slapped lines against furled canvas. It picked up as we approached Dagobert's near Lake Pontchartrain's marina.

New Orleans' cuisine is world famous, but the city has a secret of which Dagobert's is a part. It is a haven for fried-food junkies. You name it; they fry it in the Big Easy—shrimp, oysters, catfish, and hushpuppies—even top sirloin steak. The West End, on Lake Pontchartrain's bank, is where most citizens satiate their hunger for fried food. Dagobert's was arguably the best restaurant in the West End and had remained a prime destination for knowledgeable locals.

Steady rain left us both damp despite the umbrella as we pushed through Dagobert's oversized front door—just in time as the storm had reached monsoon proportions. We weren't the only customers that night with a craving for fried seafood. People jammed the entryway and no one seemed to mind getting a little wet while they waited. Maybe because the aroma of cooking seafood had locked them in place.

"There's an hour delay. You're welcome to wait in the bar," the door attendant said.

I pointed toward Dagobert's dark bar. "I see an empty table in back."

Berv Dagobert's forgiving wife Inez soon walked past

our table. I'd known her almost as long as the Dagobert family and had even dated her briefly in high school. Busy with the crowded bar, she didn't see me sitting there.

"Hi, Inez. No smile for an old friend?"

Recognizing my voice, she responded with a grin and a hug. After kissing my forehead, she drew even closer. Close enough that I could smell her perfume and feel the warmth radiating from her ample bosom.

"What are you doing here, stranger?" she asked. "I haven't seen you in a coon's age."

"Bringing a friend for fried New Orleans. Inez, this is Celeste Duples from Starkville, Mississippi."

Inez was all woman. Not quite fat but far beyond lean. She had dark, Cajun hair raked back into a severe bun, her loose-fitting clothes contrived to hide large breasts that apparently embarrassed her. She had piercing, green eyes, the color of Pontchartrain just before sundown. Her determined efforts to conceal her abundant physical attributes had failed miserably.

"Glad to meet you, Celeste. Keep an eye on Wyatt. He's quite the ladies man."

"Now don't be spreading lies," I said.

"I think I've heard this story before," Celeste said.

"Trust me, it's true," Inez said, cocking her head and winking at Celeste. "I'll tell Bervard you two are here. He'll want to meet your lady friend. He'll see to it you get a table with a lake view."

"Wonderful," Celeste said

"What are you drinking?"

"What do you suggest?" Celeste asked.

"Wyatt will tell you I mix the best margarita on the lake."

"Then that's what I'll have. And you, Wyatt?"

"Make it two," I said.

Inez knew me too well and asked, "With tequila or without?"

"One regular and one unleaded," I said.

Inez smiled and then hurried off behind the carved mahogany counter that had dominated the room for as long as I could remember.

"She's very pretty," Celeste said as thunder rattled the

windows, interrupting my thoughts. "You know everyone in New Orleans, don't you?"

"Not quite everyone. I have known the Dagoberts—Berv and his younger brother Perley—all my life. Perley has his own place on Poydras. I grew up with them, and their parents were like my own."

A circular deck facing the lake occupied two sides of Dagobert's. When it wasn't raining patrons sit outside, basking in warm weather and the slow anesthesia induced by Inez's famous margaritas. Now, the deck lay deserted, awash in rain and choppy water. Patrons crowded inside, in the bar and the main dining area, raising the noise level to Mardi Gras proportions. Because of the clamor, I failed to hear Bervard Dagobert walking up behind me. I didn't know he was there until he put his brawny hand on my shoulder.

"Wyatt, my man, how you are?" he said in his Cajun drawl.

Although about the same height, Berv Dagobert exceeded my age by more than five years and weight by fifty pounds. Over the years, he'd succumbed to a steady diet of his own fried food. Now his body had sunken to his belly, and his puffy cheeks seemed out of place, nestled between his dark, unruly hair.

"I'm well," I said. "Good to see you, old pal."

"Hey, who you calling old?" he asked with a grin. "Who this pretty girl you got with you? She your daughter?"

"Don't start with me, Berv. I'll have to take you out you to the barn, just like I used to, and kick your aging Cajun ass."

"Yeah," he said squeezing my shoulders. "I remember the last time you were going to kick ol' Berv's ass. You cried like a baby for a week when I got through with you."

"You must be thinking about someone else and not me? What I remember is whipping you like a redheaded stepchild."

"Boys," Inez said, returning with our margaritas. "If you don't settle down, I'll kick both of your asses. Miss Celeste here is a lady and doesn't need to be subjected to a couple of loud-mouthed windbags."

Berv and I were both laughing. "Sorry, Miss Celeste," he said. "I can't understand what a pretty lady like you is doing with a no good like Wyatt, but I'm glad you're here anyway. Your smile warms up the whole room and makes me almost forget about the storm outside."

"Watch him," Inez said. "He'll charm the pants off you. He did me, anyway, and he's just pure evil." Then she added, "These two have enough hot air between them to float the Titanic."

Ignoring his wife, Bervard said, "Hey, Wyatt, did you tell Missy here I cook the best damn seafood in New Orleans. What are you eating tonight?" he asked before I could answer his first question. "Don't tell me. I'll just bring a little bit of everything. It may be hell outside, but it's gonna be heaven in here tonight. I'll go clear a table and get you a view of the lake."

"This is lovely just where we are, and Inez is close enough for us to visit," Celeste said.

"She can be pretty nice when she wants to be," Berv said.

By now, Celeste was in the spirit, and Inez's margarita did nothing to erase the amused grin from off her face. New Orleans has that effect on people. Before Bervard left us alone at the table, he bent over and whispered in my ear.

"I got a little problem, Cowboy. Can you come up to the office before you leave and talk to me about it? Inez will keep your pretty girlfriend company."

He seemed relieved when I said, "Sure, I'll see you in a bit."

"Take your time and enjoy," he said. "I ain't going nowhere."

Inez had already brought Celeste another margarita, and she was working on it with abandon. When Bervard left our table, she said, "I just love your friends. Why didn't you tell me about this restaurant before now?"

"Stick with me, kid," I said with a wink.

Chapter 22

"I love it here," Celeste said. "The atmosphere is electric, and I don't mean the storm outside."

"New Orleans has lots more to offer than most tourists ever see. Many of the people here are regulars that started coming to Dagobert's with their parents."

"Maybe we can bring Dad when he returns from Mississippi."

"Actually, he's part of the reason I asked you here tonight."

Celeste's smile disappeared. "Oh?"

"One reason, at least. Not the only one. I've missed seeing you the last few days."

"Oh?"

"What I mean is I like you a lot."

"Oh?"

Realizing I was on the spot, I glanced around the crowded bar for support. "Where's Berv when I need him?"

"If you can't do better than that, I'm walking out the door this minute."

"And leave me with only fading dreams of the most gorgeous, intelligent woman I've ever met?"

Celeste's smile returned to her pretty face. "That's better. Who said only the Irish are full of blarney?"

Full of shit was more like it, I thought. Still, I could see I was scoring points. I needed all I could muster after the past week. I stopped a flower girl wandering through the bar and bought her a five dollar rose. I knew it was worth it when she blew me a kiss. I waited until we had finished our salad and third margarita without broaching the subject of her Dad. Luckily, she brought it up herself.

"Did you find out about my grandmother?"

"I learned quite a lot—things I couldn't ethically tell you if I were still an advocate. But I'm disbarred, and I think you need to know, so here goes."

I recounted the story I'd heard from Armand and Madam Toulouse Joubert, watching for her reaction, either positive or negative. Outside, the storm had abated for the moment, and Dagobert's air conditioning system worked overtime to cleanse the air of excess humidity. It was a losing proposition in New Orleans during the month of July.

"Your grandmother is buried in the grave we visited. She was Arthur Duplesses' mistress, and that means Arthur Duplesses is your biological grandfather. In New Orleans, it's okay to have your mistress buried beside you in the family crypt. Her name isn't there because that's unacceptable."

"You think my grandmother was some sort of social outcast?"

"I don't know. I need to speak with Arthur and Megan Duplesses. I'd like to find out before your father returns to the city."

"Yes," she said. "He's much too fragile to handle any bad news."

"You'd be the expert on that," I said. "Still, he's paying me to give him details about his past. I don't know what else I can do except tell him the truth."

Celeste remained silent, a distant look in her eyes. After a long pause, she said, "Maybe we should have Mama put a spell on him and make him forget the whole thing."

Although she was joking, it didn't seem like such a terrible idea. She laughed and slapped at me when I asked, "You think she would do that?"

The waiter soon appeared with a seafood feast befitting royalty—fried scallops, shrimp, crab, catfish, okra, and hush puppies. The batter on the fried okra was the best I'd ever tasted. I wanted to ask Celeste about her encounter with Baron Samedi, but the night was going so well I didn't dare. Apparently reading my thoughts, Celeste initiated the discussion herself.

"Mama isn't much fun lately. She is so deeply into the murder investigation. I told her I can't remember a thing. Doesn't matter. She won't let it go."

"You were almost the strangler's fourth victim. Mama saved your life. She earned the right to be concerned."

"Yes, and I really don't know what I can do to help her."

"We could try hypnosis."

Celeste's smile faded. "I've studied hypnosis extensively. I have been hypnotized many times as part of my psychological training. For some reason, the thought frightens me. I know that sounds inexplicable."

"No. You were in a deep trance when Mama found you. Baron Samedi apparently induced the trance. Perhaps the experience has left you anxious. I understand."

Celeste's smile reappeared. "I'm the psychologist here. I could have you put in jail for practicing without a license."

"I'm not practicing. Just blathering," I said.

"You might be right. Maybe I do have a subconscious aversion to hypnosis induced by my encounter with Baron Samedi. The event was apparently frightening and disturbing. I just don't remember it. Hypnosis could be the appropriate therapy. Do you know a skilled psychotherapist in New Orleans?"

She flashed me a silly grin when I said, "I can hypnotize people." Seeing her skepticism, I added, "I taught myself while I was in the Army. I learned the technique from a book I read at the Fort Polk library. Surprising what you can learn in the Armed Forces."

"You must be joking."

"I'm not. You know how simple the theory is. With a little practice, anyone can do it. I hypnotized your father to find out where your grandmother is buried."

"No way! Weren't you worried you might cause Dad irreparable damage?"

"I don't think so. Let me hypnotize you. I swear I won't leave you out there in cyberspace."

"I don't trust you to hypnotize me, and that's final."

"If you're willing to be hypnotized by a psychologist or psychiatrist, I'm sure we can find someone qualified to perform the task."

Celeste had a valid argument. I wouldn't like a

taxidermist operating on my heart or a taxi driver representing me in a court of law. The thought almost made me laugh because many doctors and lawyers are not much better at their job than someone off the street is. The same goes for every job out there, no matter how high or low up the totem pole.

Celeste must have felt she had hurt my feelings because she reached across the table, grabbed my hand. "I'm sorry. I didn't mean to offend you."

I kissed her fingers. "Hey if I were you, I wouldn't let me hypnotize you either. Still, we could have had some fun."

When Celeste yanked away from my grasp, I realized my offhand comment had set the night back on track. Her laughing even interrupted the people at the adjacent table.

"I didn't realize I'm having dinner with a comedian," she said.

The food kept coming until we cried uncle. Inez appeared as we finished our coffee. "Cowboy has some business with Berv upstairs for a few minutes. I'll sit and keep you company. Sam will bring us more coffee and a piece of the best key lime pie you ever ate this side of Florida."

"I won't be long," I said. Inez put her arms around my waist and rested her head on my shoulder. I pulled her closer. "What's the matter?"

"It's Berv and Perley. They're feuding, and I don't know what to do about it."

"Hell, they've never stopped doing that. What else is new?"

"It's different now. Since Mom Dagobert died, the boys hardly talk anymore."

"We'll talk about it later. Right now I better hear in person what Berv is all lathered up about."

A large window facing Pontchartrain backed our table. Outside, the sky was black. The storm had returned, stalled directly overhead. Fingers of lightning parted the night for a moment as I pulled loose from Inez and started upstairs.

Knotty pine paneling covered the walls of Berv's office, a leather couch proclaiming it as a man's room. It was adjacent to Inez's office, tiny by comparison. The place where all the real work happened. Inez attended to most of the details of running the restaurant. Unlike the gun cabinets and hunting trophies in Berv's office, file cabinets and old ledgers filled her little eight-by-ten. An open door provided direct access between the two rooms.

"Get comfortable," Berv said, fetching coffee for me from a pot on the shelf.

He poured a glass of straight whiskey from a decanter he kept in his personal wet bar before joining me.

"Now, what's the problem?" I said.

"It's Perley. He tried to burn the place down."

"You're joking."

"Ain't a joke," Berv said, his accent growing thicker. "Inez's office caught fire."

"What started it?"

"Perley started it."

"I asked how, not who."

"A frayed wire on one of them little, electric heaters women like to use to keep their legs warm. It sparked some papers in Inez's trashcan. Next thing we know, we got smoke pouring out the doors."

"And you think Perley frayed the wire on purpose and started the fire?"

"Got that right."

"What caused you to draw that conclusion?" I asked.

"Who else woulda done it? Perley was here all day, working on the books."

"Maybe no one did it. Sounds like an accident to me."

"That's what Perley claims. Says he was downstairs when it started. What'd you think he'd say?"

"More importantly, what did the insurance investigators say?"

"They couldn't prove nothing, and so they paid off on our claim."

"Then what's the problem? What reason would Perley have to burn Dagobert's?"

Berv downed his whiskey, returned to the bar, and poured himself another shot. Outside, the rain was ebbing although raindrops continued drumming the slate roof. Without asking, I helped myself to more chicory-laced coffee.

"There's more to this, isn't there?" I said. "Inez says you two are feuding."

Berv's big head slumped, his chin dipping in an almost imperceptible nod. "It's Dagobert's. Perley calls it quaint, out of style. Me, I just don't see it. Papa made this place famous frying oysters and shrimp the old way, not blackening them in a pan like we burned it accidentally and served it to the customer any-old-how."

"Can't you compromise?"

Berv stared at me as if I'd suddenly cast aspersions against the Virgin Mary. "Papa left me in charge," he said, stabbing his breastbone with his finger. "Just 'cause Perley studied under some fancy French chef downtown don't mean he knows how to cook any better than me. Till I die, we do it my way at Dagobert's."

"So that's all this feud is about?"

"Hell no, that ain't all. Wait till you hear what else he done."

Berv didn't have time to tell me as the baritone voice of his younger brother caught us both off guard.

"Still got a shell caught in your craw, big brother?"

Neither of us had heard Perley Dagobert enter the office. When he spoke, Berv's jaw dropped, along with his drink. Glass shattered against the hardwood floor, ricocheting off the walls and spraying splintered shards across the room. Red in the face, he started picking up the pieces.

"You get the hell out of here, man," he said.

"Keep your shorts on. After I get my stuff, I'm outa here."

"Then do it fast."

Perley was a younger version of his brother Berv only with darker hair and more of it. He also lacked the paunch that encircled his brother's waist. Berv loosened his collar as Perley retrieved a box in the corner, grinning when he saw me.

"How's it going, Cowboy. When you comin' to a good restaurant? I'm just down the street from the Quarter, on Poydras."

"I heard. Congratulations."

"Best Mirliton dressing in town. Bring your lady with

you. The dinner's on me."

Perley gave me a brotherly hug, picked up the box, and then slammed the door behind him without saying bye to his brother. Thunder rocked the windows, reminding us it was still ongoing as it shook us back to reality.

"You didn't fix me a free meal just so I would listen to you carp about the way Perley cooks. What else did he do?"

He kicked a piece of glass into the corner on his way to the wet bar. This time, he slumped into the couch, sinking down until his head rested on the armrest.

"Perley took out an insurance policy on the restaurant over a year ago. I just found out about it."

"You have to be kidding me, Berv. Because Perley is mad about the way you run the restaurant, he took out an insurance policy so he could burn it down and collect the money. Pardon my skepticism."

"I ain't paying you to think. What I want is for you to check it out and tell me the truth."

I'd known Berv all my life. His insinuation that he thought of me as little more than a hired gun stunned me. I poured another cup of Java, swallowing indignation along with the strong coffee.

"I'm as close to Perley as I am with you. I wouldn't do anything to dampen that trust. Not for any amount of money."

"Now don't get your dauber in the dirt," he said, feeling the air grow cold. "I wouldn't ask you to do nothing like that. I just need you to nose around some. Ain't nobody better at that than you and it won't be no slight on Perley."

I didn't have time to answer. A fire alarm blaring above the rain halted our conversation and prevented me from punching Bervard Dagobert's crooked nose. As the sound of the alarm blared through the cracked door, Berv's face went white. Even with his fifty extra pounds, he managed to beat me out the door and down the stairs.

Thick smoke, frightening diners jamming through the doors, billowed from the kitchen. Most of the restaurant's patrons had already huddled outside in the pouring rain. Berv didn't join them. Instead, he grabbed a fire extinguisher off the wall in the hallway and used it to spray a skillet ignited with hot grease. When trucks from the fire station arrived, nothing remained of the fire except soot and smoke. Despite minimal damage, the smoky blaze resulted in a mass exodus of diners from the restaurant. Celeste and I stuck around long after the fire trucks, and everyone else had all gone home.

The fire had a strange effect on Inez. She sat on Berv's couch, sobbing uncontrollably and hugging her knees. Berv had worked himself into frenzy, pacing around his office like one of the Siberian tigers over at Audubon Park. Celeste and I stood against the wall, propping it up and staying out of the way.

"I can't believe Perley would do this to me on Friday, my biggest night."

"Perley didn't do anything. It was a grease fire. It's happened a dozen times," Inez said between sobs.

She was right. Years of accumulated grease had saturated walls, wood floors and ceiling. By its very nature, Dagobert's was a fire looking for a place to happen.

"May-be," Berv said, drawing out the word. "But the fry cook said Perley stopped by the kitchen right before the fire started."

Inez calmed herself and poured three shots from the bar. "He just wanted to say hello."

"May-be. It still scared this poor little girl nearly to death," Berv said, taking the glass from Inez. He downed it and placed a comforting hand on Celeste's shoulder. "I'm driving these two on home now. Too wet for them to take the bus."

"No, you're not," Inez said. "You've had too much to drink. I'll take them. Take a nap on the couch till I get back."

"Check Perley out for me, will you Wyatt? Find out what he's got on his mind," he said as we walked out the door.

We followed Inez to her Maroon Expedition parked out back beneath the restaurant's only overhang. A good thing, as rain continued to fall in proverbial bucket loads. A newspaper swirled out of the darkness, and then was gone. Berv had not argued when Inez told him she was taking us home. He apparently had other things on his mind. It didn't take a rocket scientist to see she also knew it. Celeste crawled into the back seat and fell asleep almost immediately.

"You all right, Inez?"

"Making it," she said. "You don't think Perley set fire to Dagobert's?" she finally asked.

"Of course not. I think there's something going on between you and Berv. Am I right?" When she nodded, I said, "Why don't you tell me about it?"

My words brought another round of tears. Inez had made a strong roadie and had put it in a red, plastic cup. Before answering my question, she buried her nose in it.

"Berv is having an affair," she said

"Who says so?"

I saw them with my own eyes, right there in his office."

"Doing what?"

"You know what."

"Making love?"

"I'd call it screwing."

Her terse reply struck me like a sharp kick in the groin. "This is all a bit much. Maybe you'd better explain."

"After a visit to my mother's in Marrero, I realized I'd locked myself out of the house. Dagobert's had closed for the night, and Berv wasn't home yet. I drove over to get a key from him."

"Go on."

"The front door was shut tight, and I couldn't get anyone's attention when I banged on it. That's when I saw Berv's light on upstairs. I climbed the fire escape to tap on his window. When I peeked in, I saw them going at it, right there on the couch."

"You caught them in the act?"

A smile appeared on Inez's face. "I never seen Berv move so fast when I started banging on the window. His little whore grabbed her clothes, got dressed in the bathroom, and then ran downstairs to her car."

"What did Berv do?"

"I was bawling pretty bad. He made me a shot of whiskey and practically poured it down my throat. When I finally calmed down, he got on his knees and begged me to forgive him. Said he was sorry and wouldn't see her no more."

"But that wasn't the end of it?"

141

"No. He still has a thing for her, and I'm afraid he's going to leave me," she said, tears returning in a river flowing down her cheeks.

"Berv would never leave you."

"Yes he would," she said. "She's young and pretty. Everything I'm not. Wyatt, I'm so scared."

The rain had stopped when we reached Mama's house. Inez woke Celeste. "You're home, honey. I'll give Wyatt a ride to his place."

"That's all right," Celeste said. "I want to talk to him about a few things. Mama will take him home when she returns."

I could sense Celeste's suggestion wasn't part of Inez's plan. It didn't matter because Celeste wasn't taking no for an answer.

"You sure?" I don't mind a bit," Inez said.

"I'm sure. Let's go before the rain starts again."

I followed Celeste into the house, confused as to why she'd been so abrupt, almost rude, with Inez. I soon found out why.

"I wouldn't trust you alone with that woman. She had her hands all over you. You're staying right here with me."

It was getting late and Mama's Bugeye Sprite gone from its parking space outside. "Where did you say Mama is?"

"She didn't tell you? She and Lieutenant Nicosia went to a voodoo ceremony some place south of here."

Chapter 23

Light rain peppered the grass as Tony parked his car in Mama's driveway. Still dressed in his paisley tie and brown-checkered sports coat, he had absolutely no idea what to expect. Mama shook her head when she saw him and motioned for him to follow her to a room in the back.

"You can't go to the ceremony looking like that. Don't worry because I have a closet full of men's clothes. I'll find something suitable for you."

Tony didn't ask how she'd come to collect the men's clothes that filled the closet. Mama told him anyway.

"Remnants of past relationships and former boyfriends. Just my luck. The only thing I have to show for too many failed romances is a bunch of used clothes. I'm going to clean the whole room out one of these days."

"Why wait? The Salvation Army is just a phone call away."

"After tonight, I may do just that. Right now, we need to find something in here for you to wear."

Mama began tossing various garments on the floor behind her before finally deciding on a pair of baggy pants and a loose fitting African weave shirt embroidered with colorful designs. She handed them to him, along with a well-worn pair of sandals.

"I don't know about this," he said.

"It's perfect. I'll wait outside while you change and then we'll see how you look."

Mama was still dressed in her dark blue suit when Tony had arrived. After changing into the clothes, he returned to the living room. Mama had also changed. When he saw her, he stood with his mouth open, staring at the lovely woman dressed in a tie-dyed silk caftan with absolutely nothing on underneath. His response didn't go unnoticed.

"Put your eyes back in your head, Lieutenant. My outfit is acceptable for a respected mambo to wear at a ceremony."

"What about me?" he asked.

She turned to a mirror, draping and adjusting strands of beads around her neck.

"Your clothes look fine, although I think we need to apply some makeup to keep you from drawing too much attention. Come with me."

Tony followed her to a little bathroom. She pulled a stool up to the sink and ordered him to sit. Tony's hair was already dark. When Mama finished, his hair was more than black. It was dark black. She also applied a facial cosmetic that turned his skin several shades darker. She finished the costume by tying a red bandanna around his neck and placing a beaten straw hat on his head.

The bathroom's lighting exposed her body. That wasn't all that excited him. She brushed against him several times while applying the makeup—close enough that he hoped his baggy trousers did not reveal how her proximity affected him.

"You look like one of the brethren now. Just shorten your verbiage. A few grunts and nods will do." Tony almost choked when she added, "That's how I like all my men."

"You got a real way of putting things," he said.

Warm summer rain continued outside Mama's house.

"We'll have to put the top up on the Sprite. Your police cruiser would attract too much attention."

The roofs of older British cars are often difficult to raise and lower, Mama's Bugeye Sprite no exception. Tony was out of breath when they finally got it secured into place.

"Guess it wouldn't hurt me to shed a few pounds," he said.

"Nonsense. You look good."

"Then why does everyone call me Fat Tony?"

"Nicknames have a way of sticking sometimes. You may be a little overweight. You're certainly not fat."

"You think?"

"No way. If you ever want to get totally svelte, just let me know. Mama's got a spell or a potion for almost everything."

"You got something to lose weight that really works?"

"You don't see any fat on me, do you?"

"No ma'am I don't," he said.

As they headed south in the rain toward Jefferson Parish, thunder shook the car, momentarily curtailing their conversation.

"That was close," she said.

"A miss is as good as a mile," Tony said. "Tell me a little about what we're in for tonight."

"This is all complicated, and there are many things that even I do not know. Voodoo, as most Americans call it, has its roots in Western Africa, the center of the slave trade. When the slaves came to the new world, they brought with them elements of several religions. They married and intermingled with the local Indian people and found that many of their core beliefs were similar. Elements of Catholicism were also added."

"Yeah, yeah," he said. "Hocus pocus, zombies, and all that."

Mama turned her eyes from the road and glared at Tony. "I thought you were genuinely interested in what you're going to see tonight and what it represents."

"I want to catch a murderer, not watch someone drink chicken blood."

Mama slammed on her brakes so violently, the car kicked up mud as it powered onto the shoulder, soft and slippery from hours of rain. After doing a one eighty, they slid to a stop, just before smashing into a giant oak. Mama grabbed the passenger handle and pushed open the door.

"How dare you. I would never mock your religion. How dare you mock mine! Get out, now. You can walk back to New Orleans. I won't suffer a fool."

Mama's outburst took Tony quite aback. Suddenly realizing how utterly disrespectful and hurtful his remarks had been, he would gladly have walked back to New Orleans in the pouring rain if he could have only rescinded his words.

"I'm sorry. I see now how passionate you are about the

subject. I'm Catholic and the last person to persecute someone else's beliefs. Forgive me?"

Mama's tirade was far from finished. "People that believe in voodoo, as you call it, have suffered much more than persecution. Fear and misunderstanding of the belief has resulted in the near extermination of the believers. They persist, even today. Don't you realize this is more than hoodoo and gobbledygook?"

"I apologize. I'll never be so stupid again. I promise. My day was horrible."

Mama heard something in his voice that caused her to take a deep breath and lean back against the steering wheel. The passenger door was still wide open, rain blowing in on them. Tony didn't seem to notice, and neither did Mama.

"Tell Mama," she said.

"I had to watch an autopsy today. The victim was a thirteen-year-old runaway, raped, sodomized, and murdered in the most horrible way. I just can't get it out of my head."

"We all have our demons, Lieutenant Nicosia. Fortunately you don't have to contend with yours alone."

She fished around in the tiny glove box until she found a small vial of white powder. Tapping a small amount into her palm, she rubbed her hands together and bent close to Tony's face. Before he realized what was happening, she blew the dust up his nose, grabbed his ears, and yanked his head. After chanting a few words in some African tongue, she drew a vever on his forehead with the white powder that had sprayed on his face. His mind reeled a moment. Then, as if a bright light had shined on his brain, the day's lead-weighted events lifted off his shoulders, suddenly and totally. Nearby thunder rocked the small car as Mama restarted the engine.

"Close the door."

"I don't know what you just did. Don't make no difference, though. I'd promise you a permanent job if you'd just follow me around all day with that stuff you just blew up my nose."

"Nothing more than herbs and potions, Lieutenant. All healers possess them."

"Hey, what happened to Tony?"

"You just refrain from making any more absolutely ignorant comments and maybe I'll warm back up."

"I'm sorry. Please forgive me."

"Okay, but like I tell my students, you're on probation until you prove yourself."

"Where is the ceremony taking place?" Tony asked.

He wanted to add, in case I have to call for back up. Having learned his lesson, he refrained.

"We are on our way to a secluded spot near Bayou Rigolettes, on the road to Barataria Bay."

Mama was finished trying to teach a reluctant student and continued along the lonely, blacktop road in silence. Tony, on the other hand, had just had an epiphany. Logically, he knew he could explain what had just happened in different ways. The fact remained she had ridded him immediately of an enormous psychological burden. Tony was a devout Catholic. Still. . .

"You said that voodoo has roots in Catholicism."

"Yes, I did say that."

"Now look, I said I'm sorry,"

"Are you sure?" she asked.

"Positive."

"Okay then. Vodoun and Catholicism are similar in many ways."

"Go on. I'm listening," he said.

"Catholics have their saints, human beings anointed years after their deaths because of some miracle or act of extreme kindness they had performed during their lifetime. They believe individual saints have specific powers to intervene directly with God on behalf of the living."

"And?"

"They pray to these saints for intervention and create elaborate icons to remember them. Vodoun has its loas, spirits that can arrange for specific purposes with God. Each loa is represented by a vever, or symbol."

"My poor dead mother would roll over in her grave if she heard the comparison you just made."

"There are similarities in all religions. Have you read the Golden Bough?"

"Never heard of it," he said.

"Most people haven't. The book goes into considerable

detail on the similarity of all beliefs and religions. Check it out. It'll surprise you."

As the rain suddenly grew even heavier, Mama had to turn off to the side of the road to keep from running into the ditch.

"You were about to tell me about tonight's ceremony when I got out of line."

Mama turned off the engine, crossed her arms, and cocked her head toward him.

"You sure?"

She smiled when he said, "I'm listening to every word you say."

"Lasyrenn is Loa of fishes and queen of the ocean. The mambo orchestrating tonight has considerable powers. She will be instructing a new initiate."

Mama waited to see if Tony would make a face. He didn't.

"Go on with the story," he said.

"According to hearsay, the mambo disappeared for three years. When she returned, her skin was whiter, hair longer, and straighter. Supposedly, Lasyrenn had taken her to the bottom of the sea where she lived while the spirits instructed her. Her story gradually became known."

"You don't sound convinced," Tony said.

"I think she may have taken advantage of a popular folktale to strengthen her power and influence."

"What's this woman's name?"

Thunder clapped overhead as Mama answered. "Her name is Mambo Aghnee."

Chapter 24

When the rain had subsided a bit, Mama continued along the blacktop, this time at a much slower speed to avoid hydroplaning into the ditch. Her body language indicated Tony had regained her good graces. As flashes of lightning illuminated the cab of the car, he could feel the thaw.

"Tell me about the case. Maybe I can help," she said.

"The three victims were homeless, the two females both murdered in a ritualistic fashion. All lived near the Camp Street Mission. Slow strangulation with a thin piece of wire killed the two women. The murderer strangled the male with his bare hands. Oddly enough, the male victim was our prime suspect in the case."

"Why did you suspect the murdered man?"

"His history of violent behavior. He'd once attacked his English teacher and both female victims were former English teachers. Problem is, he was also a victim."

"I see," Mama said. "A mystery wrapped in a conundrum."

"Something like that," Tony said. "We found a bowler hat, cigar, and flashy sunglasses at the scene. That's compatible with your description of the man that attacked Celeste."

"Baron Samedi," she said. "Wyatt told me the murderer took a hand and left the foreleg of a cow in its place."

"The way Wyatt explained it to me, this Baron person should have ended up with the cow's hoof. Tommy, my partner, said it sounds ass backwards."

"Unless the murderer left the foreleg as a clue."

"Or to make us think he's someone that he's not," Tony said.

"The person that enticed Celeste away from Bourbon Street was Baron Samedi, and not someone disguised as him. Of that, I am sure."

"Mama, I'm having trouble absorbing this spiritual stuff and such. I can't deal with a ghost here. I need a killer that's an air-breathing human being."

"He is Tony. In Vodoun, we deal with the concept of possession. Spirits often possess the bodies of the living. Possession causes them to do things they would not ordinarily do. You will see this at the ceremony tonight. These possessions are usually initiated by mambos or houngans."

"You mean someone could be directing the murderer?"

"That is exactly what I mean."

"Great! I can see the confused looks in the eyes of the jury right now. Every defense attorney in the city will be clamoring to represent the killer. Hell, the case is already so convoluted that I could get him off myself."

Again, the rain became so intense that Mama pulled to the side of the road, put the car in neutral, and engaged the emergency brake. This time, she kept the engine running because the roof and windows of the little car were so porous there was little chance of asphyxiation.

"It'll work out," she said.

"I hope so. Now finish your story about tonight's ceremony."

"Each Vodoun ceremony is unique, meant to invoke a particular Loa to negotiate with Bon Dieu. Our faith has three stages of initiation. Most worshipers never go beyond the first level. The next requires much more time and effort to achieve. Mambos and houngans are initiates of the second level. The third level is, quite simply, the most powerful practitioner of our faith on the earth."

"And who is that?" Tony asked.

"That's a secret even I don't know."

By now, the ground was saturated and heavy rainfall streamed across the road with large fish flopping around in the middle of the narrow thoroughfare. It seemed to be raining fishes. Tony worried the intensified storm would result in canceling the ceremony.

"This could go on all night," he said.

"Have faith," Mama said. "The rain will cease long before the activities begin."

"If you say so," he said.

He began to notice her perfume—an enchanting fragrance further enhanced by the sweet, subtle scent of her warm, damp body. Like a double shot of straight whiskey, it quickly intoxicated him.

"The ceremonies are often quite sexual as Vodoun is the religion of common people. Poor people of the world have no place in their lives for puritan mores and morality. Life is not all flowers and fairy tales, it's also bladder wrenching fear, utter poverty, and rotten meat. Will you be okay?"

"I've been around the block a time or two."

"I'll bet you have. What do you think is the most appropriate gift for the Queen of the Sea?"

"Fish, I guess," he said.

Mama laughed aloud. "Never offer Lasyrenn fish. Appropriate offerings are sweet, white wine, mirrors, and perfume. It was a reasonable guess."

As Mama predicted, the rain soon abated and finally stopped altogether. They still had a problem. When she put the car into gear, the rear wheels spun in the mud. They were stuck. Tony got out and rocked the car, pushing as Mama applied the gas. Luckily, the vehicle wasn't heavy, and the pavement close by. Still, he was out of breath when he reentered the car.

"You're way too young to be wheezing like that after a little exercise. I have something to increase your strength. You're going to need all you can muster before the night ends."

She reached into her purse for a vitamin bottle filled with capsules, popping one into his mouth.

"What is it?" he asked.

"Yohimbe. An extraction from the bark of an African tree. Warriors used to drink yohimbe tea before going into battle. It has psychotropic properties. Simply put, it alters perception, emotion, and behavior. It was the first drug approved as a treatment for sexual dysfunction. Unlike

Viagra, it does more than make you erect."

"Like what?" he asked.

"Puts you in the mood. Makes you want it like a rutting stag."

"Do you get it from Africa?"

"You can buy it over-the-counter at practically any drugstore."

Since Mama had made clear the herb only works on male subjects, he wondered why she kept a bottle in her purse. He didn't need her drug because he was already hot for the gorgeous voodoo mambo. While taking a hard corner, Mama reached over and grabbed his thigh for support. When her electric touch brought him to an almost instantly erection, he began to worry.

The car's top that had been such a bear to raise and secure was a pussycat to lower. The rain had finally ceased, and Mama unlatched the top, laying it behind them as she drove.

"Never did like these things," she said.

Mama exited the main road and took an even narrower blacktop that led into a thicket of trees, bushes, and vines. An armadillo ran across the road in front of them. Minutes later, the pervasive rhythm of Congo drums, echoing through the draping shadow of live oak and Spanish moss, encompassed their senses.

"Mambo Aghnee will have a mistress-of-ceremony. Her name is Estelle. There is also a group of servers dressed in white. Most of the worshipers will only be onlookers. Some will even become possessed."

Between the yohimbe and magic powder Mama had blown up his nose, Tony's head had begun to hum. Though he couldn't explain the feeling, he knew it was a mental high more powerful than he'd ever experienced. The herbs, Mama's perfume, damp night air, and the steady drumming had transported him to a different plane of reality. Worse, he'd almost forgotten the main reason he was there in the first place. He remained in his seat after Mama parked and got out of the car. Opening the passenger door, she grabbed his hand.

"Are you ready?"

He had a silly grin on his face as she nudged him gently

out of the bucket seat. It no longer worried him that she might see the obvious bulge in his pants. Mama simply smiled as she led him to the peristyle illuminated by torchlight. The brethren had already started gathering, many sitting cross-legged in a circle around the peristyle, their bodies swaying to the beat of Congo drums.

Chapter 25

"Being a mambo has its perks," Mama said. "There's something important I have to tell you. It's possible you may be asked to perform in the ceremony."

Her statement normally would have sent Tony running to the comfort and safety of the car. Tonight was different. He was different.

"How will I know what to do?"

"You'll know," she said.

The heavy rain had passed, heading south toward the Gulf. Humidity remained carrying with it the dueling fragrances of perfume and night blooming hyacinths. The mingling aromatic scents further lifted his already elevated libido. As he and Mama swayed to the music, the tempo of the three drums began to change. A cloud of smoke, billowing from the far side of the peristyle, appeared after a loud pop. The smoky cloud remained near the ground as humid air prevented its rapid dissipation. With everyone's attention rapt, a young woman appeared followed closely by three women dressed in white.

The woman named Estelle, Mambo Aghnee's La Place, danced slowly to the rhythm of sultry drums. Attractive Estelle had the body of a college athlete. Gris-gris and charms draped from chains around her neck, decorating her white dress. Her legs, exposed to mid-thigh, were the color of coffee lightened with extra cream. Bouncing cornrows framed her face and expressive eyes.

The servers carried a hidden stash of offerings for the Loa Lasyrenn. Estelle took a bottle of white wine from one woman and danced to the poteau mitan, a post in the ground acting as the altar. Removing the cork, she poured a few drops on the post. Dropping to her knees, she began writhing like a serpent. When she finally returned to her feet, she grabbed the neck of her dress with both hands and ripped it open to the top of her dark pubic hair. After pouring the rest of the wine down her chest, she caressed her breasts with the bottle. Sinking to her knees, she continued her snakelike dance.

The serpent dance caused the audience of fifty or more people to sing, sway, and moan, many joining in with their own writhing movement. Estelle crawled on her belly to her servers, retrieving from them dove feathers and a mirror. Something unusual happened this time when she deposited the offering at the poteau mitan.

The audience gasped as the loud pop of another explosion sounded. A second thick cloud of smoke billowed up from the far side of the peristyle. From the cloud of smoke, another woman appeared. It was Mambo Aghnee, her arms outstretched to the heavens, right hand clasping a rattle made from a calabash gourd.

Mama Aghnee's flowing hair reached her waist. Instead of black as Tony had expected, it was a striking shade of blonde. Her pale skin seemed almost as though it had never seen the light of day. Her knee-length mantle of loosely beaded seashells made no pretense of covering her otherwise nude body. In that obscure age somewhere between early forty and seventy, her legs and torso could have passed for an athletic twenty-five year old. The youthful-looking mambo had neither scar nor blemish on her body. Her finest asset kept the crowd from spending too much time staring at her body. If she locked you with her eyes—limpid blue, color of the sea pooled in Bahamian coral grottos—it was hard to break the stare.

Mambo Aghnee danced around the perimeter of the peristyle, shaking the rattle at her servers and the rapt audience. She circled three times, and then moved toward the poteau mitan. dropping to her knees, she produced a bag containing powdered eggshell from beneath her beads. Pouring the eggshell into her hand, she used it to draw Lasyrenn's vever in the dirt. Everyone watched until she completed the masterful drawing, the symbolic meaning known only to her.

Mambo Aghnee pivoted on her knees, facing a bit of the peristyle that she and her La Place had oriented. Swaying observers parted and the servers appeared, between them a young woman with an angelic smile and nude body. They danced her to the awaiting Mambo Aghnee.

Something about the striking mambo seemed vaguely familiar to Tony. Awash in the beat of drums, Mama's perfume, and flickering torchlight, it failed to register as something important. The breaking and ebbing waves of dancers and performers engulfed him. Like the rest of the crowd watching the ceremony, he was only intent on the actions of the naked initiate and Mambo Aghnee.

After the servers and Estelle had oriented the initiate, Mambo Aghnee began dancing around her, shaking her rattle. Estelle and the servers placed offerings at the poteau mitan and on the body of the initiate. The young woman was soon dripping with perfume, honey, and white wine.

Matched by Mambo Aghnee's frenetic movements, the drummers changed the rhythm of their instruments. The faster she danced, the more sexually overt her gestures became. The crowd responded, mimicking every move and mannerism the animated mambo made.

A collective gasp surged through the mass of swaying bodies following someone's shrill scream. Almost on cue, a dozen observers began rolling on the ground, their bodies, and limbs writhing in a burst of uncontrolled motion. Mambo Aghnee's actions were similar, although wilder and more animated.

The possession had begun. Having accepted her offerings, the loa Lasyrenn had finally appeared embodied within the molten shape of Mambo Aghnee. Sultry and brazen, Lasyrenn/Aghnee pulsated through the faithful, humping their legs, stimulating them with the sexually explicit use of her lips, tongue, hands and body. Her lewd behavior prompted more possessions. Those possessed rolled, squirmed, squealed, and cried on the ground beneath her bare feet.

As Lasyrenn/Aghnee passed among the true believers, they opened a pathway toward the vever, the poteau mitan, and the loa's newest initiate. Tony watched the blue-eyed woman mount the young initiate and hump her like an excited stallion. When the simulated, although quite explicit action ended, Lasyrenn/Aghnee stretched to her full height and pointed to the woman she straddled with her legs.

"Ainsi sort-il," she shouted.

"Ainsi sort-il," the dancers replied.

Estelle and the servers helped the young initiate to her feet, and then pulled a white dress over her head. One of the women brought an ivory bowl that she and the others used to clean the initiate's head. Following the ceremony known as Lave Tet, they led her away into the trees. Although the initiation had ended, the ceremony was not yet complete.

Mama's drugs had already altered Tony's perception of reality. No reality remained. As if on cue, the drumming intensified as every reveler crowded into the peristyle. He had the vague sense of Mama dancing around him, her caftan pulled down to her waist to reveal her bare breasts. It all seemed natural as she pulled him into the crowd.

Tony's spirit had entered a wild, bacchanalian dream as Lasyrenn/Aghnee singled him out of the crowd. She danced toward him, her muscles flexing, skin glistening with sweat. When he reached for her, she smiled and pulled away, then moved even closer, blowing in his ear and licking his eyeballs as she played with his nipples through the coarse cotton fabric of his shirt. Soon, she squatted atop him, humping him in a lascivious manner.

Lightning flashed overhead, joining the fireworks already ignited in Tony's brain, his reality suddenly altered beyond breaking. After turning the wildly excited Lasyrenn/Aghnee on her back, he spread her legs and began humping her as if a man possessed. He was possessed. Crowding around him, they began chanting Ghede, Ghede, Ghede.

Finished with Lasyrenn/Aghnee, Ghede/Tony rose to his feet and saw Mama. Stalking her, they launched into a game of cat and mouse as interpreted by dancing and movement that was both ritualistic, and sexually explicit. Ghede/Tony finally caught her, rolling her in the dirt beneath him, her shapely legs pointing toward the darkness.

Mama's skirt lay crumpled on the grass, her shapely

legs spread wide and inviting, her eyes wild with desire. Ghede/Tony needed no encouragement. With tongue hanging from his salivating mouth, he lowered himself between her legs and had his way with her.

Chapter 26

With the ceremony still ongoing, Mama enlisted two strong men to help her carry Tony back to her car. Having passed out with a large smile on his face, he was okay. Not requiring his services as a driver, Mama didn't attempt to revive him. She just turned the car around and headed toward city lights on the far horizon. They had only gone a few miles when, groaning and holding his head, he regained consciousness.

"Where are we?" he asked.

"On our way back to town. Are you okay?

Tony hand went to his forehead. "Someone must have kicked me in the head when I passed out. I think I'm about to die."

Mama grinned. The rain had long since passed and ephemeral stars filled the heavens above them in the open car. Air rushing past his face made him feel better, and then ill. One moment he felt as if he were about the throw up, the next second the feeling would pass. Mama fished inside her purse.

"Take two of these and a shot of this."

She handed him some pills and a small bottle containing dark, amber liquid. "What is it?" he asked.

"Aspirins and a shot of Wild Turkey. They are both beneficial for a hangover. Together, I'm sure they will fix you right up."

Tony swallowed the aspirins, chasing them with a healthy slug of Wild Turkey. "Jiminy," he said. "What I won't do to solve a case. Too bad, I can't remember a thing that happened. Except. . ."

"Yes?"

"Did you and I? Did I. . . ?"

"Have wild sex with practically everyone at the ceremony?"

He rubbed his head and took another long pull from the bottle of Wild Turkey. "Maybe I don't want to know."

"Do you?" she asked.

"I have certain vague memories although the whole experience is more like a dream to me. I don't even remember leaving the ceremony."

"That's because you passed out. I had to get someone to help me carry you to Betsy here."

Tony groaned and continued sipping the Wild Turkey. "I'd feel lots better if I knew I didn't do something terrible like kill someone, or something."

"You killed no one. The Loa Ghede possessed you and used your body. I can assure you it performed admirably for the Loa. You, however, did nothing and have absolutely nothing to be ashamed of."

"I'm hearing two stories here," he said. "What exactly did my body do?"

"You, personally, did nothing because your mind was out of gear, so to speak. Your body did some things, I presume, of which you have little or no memory. Is that correct?"

Tony blinked. "I only have the vaguest recollection of much of anything. The last thing I remember is Mambo Aghnee's dancing going from wild to even wilder. She could make a Vegas lap dancer blush with her moves."

"Not her moves, Lasyrenn's. The Loa Lasyrenn possessed her body. It was Lasyrenn that performed the ritual humping of the initiate."

"Ritual humping, huh?"

"Tony, I know the ways of Vodoun are strange to you."

"That's for sure. Who is this Loa Ghede you say possessed me?"

"Ghede is part of the Gede family of spirits. They are guardians of the dead and masters of the libido. Ghede is interested in all aspects of human frailty. Since he is the Lord of Resurrection, he is also involved in death. Ghede is death. He's also the phallic deity, often pictured with a giant hard-on."

Tony moaned. "This is cutting too close to home. Are you sure I did nothing wrong? I'm a pretty straight guy, you know?"

"That you are," she said with a smile. "And you did absolutely nothing shameful."

He grabbed his forehead and groaned, torn between not knowing what he had done, if anything, and feeling guilty about potentially doing something he couldn't remember.

"I may just have to cross you off my dance card, Mama before I get into really big trouble."

"Just don't worry that pretty little head of yours about it," she said.

Tony closed his eyes, letting her words waft over him. He quickly fell asleep. When he awoke some time later, he realized the aspirin and Wild Turkey had brought some relief. They had arrived in Mama's driveway, and she was shaking his shoulder.

"Wake up, Tony. We're home."

"Speaking of which, home is where I better go."

Mama laughed again. "Have you looked at yourself in the mirror lately? You go home like that, and your first twenty years of marriage will be your last twenty. Better come into the house and sleep it off on my couch."

Tony sensed the wisdom in her words. He remained sitting in the passenger seat until she came around the car and opened the door. When she reached for his hand, he grabbed her instead and pulled her close. For a long moment, he gazed into her limpid, brown eyes.

"We're friends, right?" he asked.

"Yes."

"I had a strange dream when you woke me. It worries me. Please tell me one more time. Do I need to feel guilty about something?"

"Not with me you don't."

"What about Lillian?"

"Tony, you experienced an altered state of consciousness. In my religion, we believe in the crossroads, a place where the spirit world can cross over and join the living. The peristyle was at the crossroads tonight and much more than just handshakes exchanged. What you saw and did was no more real to you than a waking dream. They are, in fact, both as real as you or I."

"You mean. . ."

"What I mean is maybe neither of us really exists, except in the blink of an eye."

"And I didn't do anything wrong?" he asked.

"Give it a rest. We are not responsible for actions beyond our control. You do not even remember what happened. How could you be guilty of anything?"

She kissed his forehead before turning toward the front door of the house. He opened his eyes and called to her. "Wait. Did you see anyone from the mission you recognized?"

"We both did," she said.

"I don't recall seeing anyone that I know. Who are you talking about?"

Mama blew him a kiss and turned back toward the house. "Mambo Aghnee is Sister Agnes."

Chapter 27

I was lying on Mama's couch, listening to river sounds through an open window when she and Tony arrived. I'd not slept since Celeste and I had returned from Dagobert's, mainly because Mama's fat cat Bushy wouldn't stop kneading dough on my chest. Whenever he stopped for a minute, his partner Cliffy would take his place. Cliffy was also a large cat. I could hear Mama and Tony conversing as she rattled the keys in the lock. She didn't have to worry since it was unlocked.

"Wyatt, you scared me half to death," she said when she flipped on the light and saw me on the couch. "What in the world are you doing here?"

"I could ask you the same thing, and from the looks of your clothes and Tony's makeup, I'd say I'd be in for an interesting answer."

He was in no mood for lively banter. "Don't start in on me, Cowboy. I've had a long night."

"I can see. You two look like the star performers in an L.A. sex party."

My words must have hit too close to home. He'd started for the door when Mama grabbed his elbow and stopped him.

"Wyatt, if I didn't know better, I'd think I just heard a ring of jealousy in your voice."

Mama's assertion wasn't far from the truth. My mind had concocted all sorts of stories about where the two, Tony dressed as an African dandy and Mama in the most revealing outfit imaginable, had been until four in the morning. Light reflecting through her caftan made her look even more sexually charged than if she had on nothing at all. What's worse, she saw me staring at her, and needed no power as a mambo to see what was on my mind. When Celeste heard us talking, she appeared at the top of the stairway.

"Oh Mama, look at you. What a babe!"

Mama ignored her and went to the kitchen. Tony and I followed, as did Celeste, also dressed scantily in a little wisp of nothing, aqua blue peignoir.

"Lieutenant Nicosia, is that you?" she finally said.

I grinned, and Tony turned red, "Doing a little undercover work." Seeing my smile and realizing his double meaning, he said. "Get off my back, Cowboy."

"I didn't say a word."

"Stop it," Mama said. "I'll make us a pot of coffee and then we'll tell you where we've been. Course you two might do the same for us," she said, glancing at Celeste's revealing peignoir.

While the coffee brewed, Mama went upstairs. Returning after a quick shower, she was wearing a posh, terry-cloth bathrobe, her long hair still wet. She seemed in no hurry to dry it, other than for an occasional dab with a large towel.

"You're next, Tony," she said, pointing to the room where she had outfitted him with clothes for the ceremony. "There is a shower, fresh towels and the water is still hot. I put your clothes in the sink. We'll wait till you return for explanations."

We sat in the kitchen, drinking strong, New Orleans coffee. Mama lit a candle, and we waited in silence, amid relative darkness, for Tony's return. When he did, even in the candle's flickering light, I could see by his dyed hair that he'd have some explaining to do when he finally made it home. Being single sometimes has its blessings.

I didn't let them remain silent for long. "Our curiosity is properly whetted. Tell us what you and Tony were up to tonight."

Mama began. "Tony's had an undercover man at the Camp Street Mission. He reported that some of the people practice Vodoun. They had a ceremony tonight, and we checked it out."

Tony seemed relieved that Mama glossed over the details of the ceremony. After telling us an abbreviated version of the story, she finally allowed that the presiding mambo was none other than Sister Agnes. It took me a moment to consider this piece of information. Once I did, I decided it was time to tell them what I knew about Sister Agnes.

"Bertram told me something about Sister Agnes. Seems she worked as Senator Whitney LeBlanc's assistant. They carried on a long-term affair, and she is the real mother of Gaylon LeBlanc. According to Bertram, Whitney was a devotee of voodoo, and they often had ceremonies for their friends in Washington. Gaylon still thinks Sister Rose is his mother and maintains a relationship with Sister Agnes."

Tony asked, "Is there more?"

"I think the woman that had Jason Stampler released from the hospital was Sister Agnes. You said the night attendant told you he began acting perfectly normal soon after the person claiming to be his mother arrived. Mama tells me that a voodoo mambo could have accomplished this sudden personality change with a potion."

"And why didn't you tell me all this before now?" he asked.

"This is the first chance I've had."

"I don't see how this case could get any weirder," he said, rubbing his head and staring at the black stain that came off in his hand.

"I do," Celeste said. "Wyatt would like to hypnotize me to help me recall details of meeting Baron Samedi."

Tony and Mama gave Celeste a look.

"Are you going to let him?" Mama asked.

"I'm a psychologist. I would never let a non-professional hypnotize me, even if they were capable of doing so."

"Even though Wyatt isn't a psychologist, he is a professional," Mama Mulate said. "I'm sure he wouldn't leave you hanging out there, or irreparably damage your psyche."

"I'm not worried that he would do either of those things."

"Then let him do it." Mama said. "Maybe you'll remember something that will lead us to the killer. Why not give it a try?"

Mama's question visibly agitated Celeste. "Privacy. My innermost thoughts are personal to me."

Tony couldn't help getting into the act. "Wyatt isn't interested in your innermost thoughts, are you Cowboy?"

"Maybe just a little," I said, "It doesn't matter though. I swear I'll only questions that pertain to Baron Samedi. Mama and Tony will stop me if I try to get out of line."

"You have my word on that," Mama said.

Celeste hesitated. "I don't know. It's asking a lot."

"This Baron Samedi character could have killed you," Tony said. "We need to know who, and why before he does it to someone else. If Cowboy here gets out of line, I'll cold cock him."

When Celeste buried her face in her hands and began to weep, Mama grabbed her and made soothing sounds. "It's okay, child. We won't force you to experience something you find so painful if you're that frightened."

Celeste cried on Mama's shoulder for five long minutes. When her sobbing finally ceased, she sat back in her chair, crossed her arms, and swallowed heavily.

"Okay," she said in a voice so low we barely heard it. "Let's do it."

Chapter 28

Despite her fear of hypnosis, Celeste proved a quick study. She entered a trance, her head, and eyes noticeably droopy, almost from the moment I started. I had her full attention, along with that of Tony and Mama.

"I want you to watch the flickering flame and listen to my voice and relax. I am going to help you return to the night you and Mama went to the Bourbon Street Jazz Club. Are you there yet?"

"Yes," she said, the word spoken dreamily.

"What are you doing?"

"Sitting at the bar, waiting on Mama. She's in the ladies' room."

"What's going on around you?"

"The club is crowded. The combo is playing, everyone into the beat and rhythm. Someone comes in the front door and makes his way to the bar. He is wearing a black tuxedo, bowler hat, and flashy, white plastic sunglasses. He has an unlit cigar clamped in his teeth. He seems strangely familiar."

"How so?"

"He looks exactly as Mama had described Baron Samedi."

"Are you frightened?"

"No, he is smiling and looks quite dashing and debonair. I want to talk to him. Before I can, a cleaning man bumps into him, and looks as if he is going to pass out. He jumps back, and I can see his terrified eyes. He even calls the man Baron Samedi."

"Does the person with the cigar accost the cleaning man?"

"No, he just smiles as if he appreciated the recognition, and then extends his hand for the man to shake. The frightened man backs off and hurries into the kitchen. When I touch the person in the tuxedo, he asks me where I am from, and if I am here on business or pleasure. I tell him about our excursion to the St. Louis No. 1 Cemetery to find my grandmother's grave.

"I know it well," he says, "It's near the tomb of Marie Laveau's."

"How do you know about my grandmother's grave?"

"I'm the keeper of the dead. I know where everyone is buried."

"What happened to grandmother's body?"

"I can show you if you'd like. The graveyard is where my powers are greatest. I'll answer all of your questions when we get there."

"Maybe I've had too much to drink. Not enough to accompany a person I just met to a cemetery. Especially one dressed like a voodoo deity."

"Then what happens?" I asked.

"He removes his sunglasses, cups my face in his hands, and stares into my eyes.

"Come with me and I will reveal a world you've only imagined."

Celeste paused, and I asked, "What happened when you reach the cemetery?"

"I follow him straight to my grandmother's grave. He knows exactly where it's at."

"The woman's bones are in the tomb and were never moved. She was a whore that used to work in the bars down by the river."

"I asked him, are you sure?"

"I can show you."

"He's slipping wire around my neck. I have the feeling that I am about to die. For some reason, I am not frightened.

"Is he black?" I asked.

"No, he's white, not tall. His complexion is fair and his hair almost blonde. And when he walks, he has a pronounced limp."

"How old is he?"

"No older than forty and is in unusually good physical condition. When I touch his shoulder I can feel it is thickly muscled, as is his neck."

"Now what's happening?"

"Mama arrives. She seems agitated and out of breath as if she had run a long distance. She is carrying a dead chicken, a bottle of spirits. She dances for Baron Samedi. When she offers the gifts to him, he seems pleased. Mama is rolling around on the ground and pouring spirits on herself. Baron Samedi seems placated. He takes a rose from a vase beside Marie's tomb, places it in my hand, and then turns into a raven and flies away."

"Are you sure?"

"Yes."

Celeste's story was finished. Her eyes had fully closed, head tilted forward, chin on her chest. It was time to reawaken her.

"When I snap my fingers you will awaken fully. You will feel terrific and remember only what you want to remember."

Celeste's eyes opened. A long moment passed before Mama put her arms around the younger woman and cradled her to her bosom.

"Are you all right, child?"

"Yes. What's the matter with everyone," she said with a smile.

Tony took Celeste's hand, giving it a reassuring pat.

"You corroborated Mama's description of the man and provided some information that we didn't have. You said the man walked with a limp. That's not something Mama or the cleaning man told us."

"A flood of memories is filling my head. I must have repressed the meeting with Baron Samedi," Celeste said.

"And why is that?" I asked.

"Baron Samedi knows who Mama is. He told me she was a highly respected mambo of some power. The way he said it makes me think it was not in an admiring way. I have the feeling he means us harm. He tried to kill me. I think he may return and try to finish the job."

"There is much danger around," Mama said.

She went into a back room, returning with an armload of various objects. She gave pouches filled with unknown substances to Tony, Celeste and me.

"What is this?" Celeste asked.

"Gris-gris. Put them around your necks and do not take them off. They will protect you from spells someone may try to cast. Also wear these amulets."

She gave us each an amulet engraved with a specific vever. Celeste and I put ours on. Tony just shook his head.

"I'm a police officer. I can't wear these."

"Yes you will or I'll cast a spell on you myself," Mama said. "Here's something else for you. Take one in the morning before you eat."

"What is it?" he asked.

She laughed and said, "Just call it Mama's voodoo diet." She handed him something else, a small vial. "Tell your partner to tap some of the powder into the drink of the person he desires."

"Love potion number nine?" Tony said.

Mama nodded. "Don't make jokes. It is powerful stuff. Now put on your gris-gris. Someone could kill any of us."

"Not on my watch, he won't," Tony said. "I'll call for twenty four hour surveillance of the house, and undercover officers to keep watch from nearby when you're not here. I promise, the next time you see the maniac it will be in a police lineup."

"Thank you so much, Lieutenant Nicosia," Celeste said, giving him a hug.

Mama made a second pot of coffee. When we finished drinking it, Tony said, "I'll flip you for the couch, Cowboy."

"You take it. I'll catch a cab back downtown."

"You sure?"

"I've already warmed it up for you," I said.

Mama brought him a pillow and blanket before retiring upstairs to her room. I called for a cab and went out on the front porch swing. Celeste joined me. Early morning traffic was already moving along nearby St. Charles Avenue, tugs and tankers lining up on the river. The morning was cold and damp, and she snuggled closer for warmth.

"What frightened me more than anything about the encounter with Baron Samedi is that he knew about my grandmother. What I mean is that he clearly knew about her."

"Are you sure?"

"He even knew her first name. I thought I would die of shame when he told me she was a riverfront whore."

Despite my skepticism, Celeste's story comported well with that of Armand and Madam Toulouse Joubert. They'd said there must be a strong reason Arthur Duplesses didn't accept Maurice as his son. Being a prostitute was a compelling reason for one of the city's elite, and I wondered how Maurice would react to the news.

"There's something unnatural about Baron Samedi. It frightens me more than I can tell you. It's as if he were here with us right now."

"No one's here except you and me," I said. "Baron Samedi, or whoever he is, is just a man. A deranged man, I will grant you. Not a god or deity."

Celeste drew closer, staring dreamily at passing car lights. She grasped my arm tightly and rested her head on my shoulder. "There's something else I didn't tell Lieutenant Nicosia," she said.

"Oh?"

"I recognized Baron Samedi. I mean the person he actually is. Though I can't quite place him, I know I've seen him before."

"How do you know him?"

"I don't know. For the life of me, even though I'm searching my brain, I cannot come up with the answer. I only know he seems very familiar to me."

Chapter 29

Bob was waiting on my bed when I finally made it home. He allowed me to touch him twice before jumping to the ground and scratching at the patio door. I opened the sliding glass door and watched him walk out on the second story balcony overlooking Rue Chartres. He ate a few sparing bites when I opened a can of high protein cat food, and I noticed how skinny he'd become. It caused me to remember that I needed to call the vet and ask her the results of his recent blood test.

Leaving the patio door open, I took Bob's position on the bed and closed my eyes, not waking until I heard Bertram's booming voice at the door.

"Hey, are you breathing in there? Someone downstairs wants to see you. Some of us have to work, even if a certain tomcat kept me up half the night wailing like a banshee in heat."

I ignored Bertram's comment about Bob. "Give them a beer on my tab. I need a shower to clear the cobwebs."

"Your tab's already busting at the seams. Maybe you should try clearing it every once in a while."

Bertram was mumbling as he stomped down the stairs. Twenty minutes later, I made it downstairs. Maurice was waiting for me at my usual booth.

"Sorry," I said. "I had a late night, and I'm not moving very fast this morning."

"No problem. Bertram makes a mean Bloody Mary, and I thought I would split a gut when he told me the story about chasing muskrats on Bayou Teche."

I hadn't heard that particular story and vowed not to ask. Maurice looked natty in a light blue, summer blazer that went well with his silver hair. His expensive trousers and Italian loafers would have cost many men a week's pay. His clothes didn't seem to matter when he peeled off ten hundred-dollar bills from a wad in his blazer pocket and handed them to me. Torn between returning them to him, I suppressed blurting out the truth about his mother. I did neither, excusing myself for a moment to take the money to Bertram.

"Subtract whatever I owe you and hold the rest for me, will you?"

Bertram was many things. Dishonest was not one of them. Despite his carping about how much I owed him, I knew he'd only take the actual amount I owed him. The rest, he would put in his safe that he kept behind the bar. Maurice was working on his second bloody Mary when I returned to the booth.

"Thank you for saving my daughter from that madman. If anything ever happened to her, it would kill me."

"Thank Mama for that. She risked her life to save Celeste, and I only came along later."

"I appreciate what both of you did. I'm sending Celeste back to Starkville for her own safety. She doesn't need to be here. I won't feel safe until she's back in Mississippi."

"Have you told her?"

"Not yet."

"Lieutenant Nicosia has promised around the clock protection for Celeste and Mama Mulate. There's no reason to think they were targeted, or that the attack was anything other than random."

I was not entirely convinced, and apparently neither was Maurice. "They can both identify the man. He'll try to kill them before the authorities arrest him. I won't let Celeste be the bait in some police trap."

The man from Mississippi had thrown me a curve ball. He knew more about life and human nature than I had given him credit. I couldn't disagree with his argument.

"Maybe, but Tony would never use Celeste and Mama as decoys."

"You know that for a fact?"

"I think I do," I said.

"Maybe you don't know Lieutenant Nicosia as well as you think you do."

I didn't immediately answer, wondering what he knew, or thought he knew about Tony. A car's tires screeched, outside on the street as it swerved to miss a pedestrian.

"He's never lied to me," I said.

"Has he ever used you?"

I let the comment go unanswered. "I understand your concern, Mr. Duples."

"It's Maurice. I'll just feel better when Celeste is back in Starkville. Do you have news for me?"

After worrying how I would tell him about his mother, I was ready to change the subject to something not quite as stressful as Celeste's encounter with the murderer. Following my visit with Armand and Madame Toulouse Joubert, I had paid a visit to the Notarial Archives. I now knew the story of his mother's short life, at least most of it.

"Your mother's name was Beatrice, and she was only twenty eight when she died of consumption. Her maiden name was Fant, She moved to New Orleans, along with her parents, in 1907 at the age of two. Your grandfather was a dockworker. He and your grandmother had eight children. Your mother left home when she was fifteen, working at many different jobs in order to make a living. She met Arthur Duplesses when she was only eighteen, and they maintained a relationship until your mother died ten years later. Arthur Duplesses is your father."

Maurice Duples stared at me, slack-jawed. Seeing his glass was empty, I motioned Bertram to bring him another. Maurice waved off my request and made one of his own.

"Jack Daniel's, neat, and you may as well bring the bottle with you."

Bertram brought a bottle of Jack Daniel's and a large glass of lemonade for me. After pouring a generous shot, Maurice downed the bourbon in one swallow, and then poured himself another. I began to realize the man was manic, and I was about to earn every penny he had paid me.

"If Arthur Duplesses is my father, where is Mother's body, and why is the name Megan Duplesses carved on the crypt instead of Beatrice?"

"Your mother's remains are still in the tomb. Your mother and Arthur Duplesses weren't married. Megan is Arthur's wife. Your mother lived with them until she died. When she did, they sent you to stay with your Aunt Marnie, your mother's sister, in Starkville. Didn't your aunt ever tell you anything about your mother?"

"When mother left home, Aunt Marnie was still young. She knew no more about her than I did."

"Arthur Duplesses sent your aunt money the entire time you were growing up. He even paid for your college. He and his wife are still alive, in New Orleans."

"But he never let me know who he was, or called me on the phone, or even sent me a birthday card."

"He wouldn't have sent money every month if he didn't love you."

"Don't sugarcoat the situation. Today I learned I'm a bastard, my mother buried in an unmarked grave, and that my real father has never cared enough to call me. What could be worse?"

I sipped my lemonade and decided not to tell him.

"You said my father and his wife are still alive. I want to meet them."

"I don't think that's such a brilliant idea. They are both well into their nineties. Your visit could cause lots of distress."

"No more than the heartache I've felt all these years. I want to see them. Do you know where they live?"

"Not far from here, on St. Ann's."

"Will you take me?"

"Yes, I'll make an appointment with them."

"When?"

"Tonight, if they will see us."

Though my words seemed to soothe him, I worried that if he kept drinking Jack Daniel's he would pass out in his hotel room long before dark. Maybe that wouldn't be such a terrible idea. It seemed appropriate that Celeste accompany us to see her real grandfather.

Business in Bertram's bar was slow. Seeing our conversation was at an end, Bertram brought over his personal bottle of tequila and joined us. Maurice was one of those rare persons who never appeared drunk. He became alert and began smiling again when Bertram continued his tall tale about Bayou Teche. I took the opportunity to excuse myself.

"If they are receptive, I'll make an appointment with Arthur and Megan Duplesses. I'll get back with you soon as I find out."

I desperately needed another couple of hours of sleep and left the two chatting in my booth as I headed back upstairs to claim them.

Chapter 30

I called Arthur and Megan Duplesses. They agreed to see Maurice, Celeste and me that night at nine. I left a message for Maurice that I would meet him at his hotel. He'd already left when I got there. Celeste arrived in a taxi as I walked out the front door.

"Where's Dad?"

"He must have gone without us. Let's take your cab. It'll be faster."

"Where to?" the driver asked.

"Bourbon and St. Ann's. And please hurry."

Although the Duplesses' house wasn't far from the hotel, I had a strange feeling every minute saved in getting there might be useful. We found the front door open and we entered without knocking. We found Maurice Duples braced against the wall, the ensuing scene worse than I'd suspected.

Maurice was pointing his Luger at an old man in a rattan wheelchair. A purple Afghan draped the man's legs, and he seemed oblivious to the pistol pointed at his chest. His crooked grin looked eerily similar and every bit as deranged as Maurice. He waved his gun at us in a menacing fashion. Remembering the scene at the cemetery, I pinned Celeste against the wall. The old man spoke, returning his attention to the center of the room.

"You wanna kill me? Go ahead. I'm ninety-six next month," he said, giving one of his useless legs a hard slap with the flat of his hand. "I already done more living than any three men. Nothing you do can take that away."

"I'll kill you, all right. Soon as you tell me why you

moved my mother's body."

Arthur Duplesses squinted and leaned forward in the wheelchair, assessing the likelihood that the person with the gun was someone he knew.

"You crazy? Who are you, anyway?"

"Maurice Duples. My mother's name was Beatrice, but you already know that."

Arthur Duplesses' rheumy old eyes glimmered with sudden recognition in the light of the overhead bulb. He began to laugh. "You about a dumb one, you. You mama was a whore I met one night out on the town. I only took her in 'cause I felt sorry for her lazy ass."

"You're a liar."

"Don't call your daddy a liar."

When Maurice opened his mouth, no words issued. Outside the open door, a horse-drawn carriage clomped by on the street. The distant howl of a dog baying at the moon over by the Iberville Project put an exclamation mark on the old man's words.

"What the hell are you jabbering about, old man?" he said.

"Don't look so surprised," Duplesses said. "You think your name was Duples all these years? What kind of dumb name is that? You mama was my whore, and you're my bastard boy."

His grip on the Luger wavered, but for only a moment. After glancing at Celeste, he returned his gaze, and the barrel of the pistol, toward the old man.

"My mother was no whore. Now I want to know what you did with her body."

Duplesses howled with laughter, and it quickly drew into a dry, hacking cough. "She's right where we put her back in the thirties."

"Then why isn't her name on the crypt?"

"Whores don't have their names carved on gravestones. Your mother was a whore, dumb ass."

The old man's words were more than Maurice could handle. Grabbing him by the collar, he prodded the barrel of the pistol into his temple.

"Take back what you said about my mother. Do it right now before I blow your brains out."

Duplesses laughed again. "You gonna kill me? I told you, I'm almost ninety six-year old. You got more to lose than me, 'cept you too stupid to realize it."

I got between Celeste and her father. "He's right, Maurice. You know the truth now. Killing this old man will serve no purpose."

"You're wrong, Mr. Thomas. It'll make me feel lots better."

"Daddy, Wyatt's right. Killing him will only get you thrown in jail. Please drop your gun and let him go, I beg you."

Maurice dragged the old man out of the wheelchair and slapped him across the face. It just made him laugh harder.

"You about a dumb one, you know that? You must have got it from your mother's side 'cause you damn sure ain't got any Duplesses' brains. Thank God, I never let that crazy wife of mine change your name. She wanted me to. I had to break her damn nose to shut her up."

"The last nose you'll ever break," Maurice said, slamming the old man back into the rattan wheelchair.

Celeste had seen enough. Rushing past me, she grabbed her father's arm and tried to pull him away from Arthur Duplesses.

"Please, Daddy, stop it," she cried.

Duples shook her away from his arm and grabbed Duplesses' collar again. This time he stuck the barrel of the pistol in the old man's mouth. The old man showed no fear, continuing to taunt his agitated son.

"Bastard boy, bastard boy," he mumbled, the barrel of the pistol obstructing his words.

"Stop it, Maurice," I said. "He's not worth it to you. Think of Celeste. Now you know what happened to your mother. Killing your father won't bring her back."

The old man chortled at my plea, and it quickly turned into another fit of coughing. When his seizure abated, he started to speak again but never got the words out of his mouth. Instead, someone behind us, an old woman, barked a command.

"Let him go, Maurice, and back away."

He reacted quickly as if he somehow knew the woman's voice. Letting go of Duplesses' collar, he took two steps backward. Just in time as a mighty blast rocked the room, knocking the old man out of his wheelchair and blowing him against the wall. When Celeste and I regained our senses, we turned to Maurice. His eyes were wide and his mouth open. Both barrels of a twelve-gauge shotgun had blasted Duplesses. A gray-haired old woman dressed in tattered silk dropped the smoking gun.

"He's the bastard, not you. I should have killed him years ago. He kept your mama and others like her. Never gave a whit for my feelings or theirs."

After letting the shotgun slide to the floor, Megan Duplesses crossed the room to where the stunned Maurice, again braced against the wall, waited. When she touched his cheek, he dropped the pistol to the floor.

"Mama?"

"Yes, Maurice. I want you to know, your real mama's still in that tomb. The old man just had her bones pushed to the back of the vault. I loved you like a son and begged Arthur to let me keep you after Beatrice died. He answered by breaking my nose and kicking out my front teeth. He sent you to Mississippi, and I was too frightened to go and get you. Son, will you ever forgive me?" she asked, tears welling in her eyes.

Maurice put his arms around the old woman and began to weep. Celeste joined him. I hurried to the phone and dialed 9-1-1.

Distant sirens sounded minutes after I called for help. Megan Duplesses hugged both Maurice and Celeste then pulled away from their embraces, rushing to her dead husband.

"He did love you, at least in his own crazed way," she said. "He sent money every month and paid your way through college. He thought I didn't know. It's the only decent thing he ever did in his life."

She knelt and kissed her husband's cold cheek a last time before clutching her heart, gasping once, and sinking to the floor beside him. Celeste, her father, and I rushed to help her until the E.M.T.s arrived to the blare of an ambulance's siren.

Tony gave me a go-to-hell look when he and the N.O.P.D. made it to the scene. Between stilted explanations, deftly omitting why we were there in the first place, I spirited Maurice's pistol off the floor and into my jacket. Arthur and Megan ranked high among the city's elite. I knew Tony would find a way to overlook the fact that the old man had died from an intentional shotgun hole in his belly. His death, subsequently resulting in Megan's untimely heart attack, would go down as accidental.

Other than some puritanical need to punish Maurice for his temporary insanity, I saw no reason to involve him further in Duplesses' death. New Orleans is the home of few Puritans, and I certainly was not one of them. The ambulance rushed Megan Duplesses to University Hospital where they placed her in critical care. Celeste and Maurice would be there when she came out from under anesthesia. On the way to the hospital, Celeste informed me the real reason I covered up for her father.

"The X I made on Marie Laveau's tomb. I wished that my father would find out about his family so his terrible memories would stop driving him crazy. And I wished for a happy ending."

A crowd had gathered outside the townhouse on Bourbon and St. Ann. Gunshots, police cars, and ambulances have that effect on people. Someone that lived on nearby Rue Bourbon watched the commotion from the sidewalk across the street. Someone that had other plans for Celeste's happy ending.

Chapter 31

Gaylon stood outside the townhouse on St. Ann, watching as an ambulance arrived to take Megan Duplesses to University Hospital. He waited with the gathered crowd as Wyatt Thomas hustled Maurice and Celeste Duples out the front door. As the crowd dispersed, he hailed a cab and followed them to the hospital.

Gaylon had nothing nice to say about Wyatt Thomas. He knew that the know-it-all troublemaker and the mambo Mama Mulate were dangerous meddlers, and he took extra care that no one saw him. The French Quarter detective stayed with the Duples until the hospital had admitted Megan Duplesses to critical care. Once they did, he left them alone for the night. Gaylon missed none of this.

Father and daughter remained in the waiting room as he lurked nearby, hoping Celeste would take a trip alone down a darkened hallway. Baron Samedi had reprieved her life once before. This time he was in charge with no intention of being as generous.

The waiting room remained open all night although critical care allowed no visitors into the ward after nine. Gaylon didn't know the plans of Celeste and her father, but he intended to stay close by until he found out. With the waiting room crowded with concerned families, he knew he'd have difficulty remaining unnoticed. Sitting across the room from them, he hid his face behind a Times Picayune he found in a chair.

At nine, most of the people in the waiting room retired to somewhere else for the night. As the waiting room thinned, Gaylon took the opportunity to visit the men's room. As timing would have it, Maurice and he were in adjacent urinals at the same time. The reaction he felt was exquisite, the secret knowledge and absolute power he possessed sending a feverish shiver up his spine.

A U.S. Senator from Louisiana for a single term, he was aware people still recognized him on the street. To conceal his identity, he had donned faded coveralls, dark glasses and a ski hat pulled over his ears. He looked like a common laborer. Enough so that Maurice Duples didn't acknowledge his presence. Realizing that Celeste was alone while Duples was in the bathroom, he hurried back toward the waiting room, quickly realizing she'd gone somewhere else.

The hospital cafeteria had closed for the night. The only place remaining to get a Coke or candy bar was from the concession area in the basement, at the end of a long hallway. Deciding to go for coffee, she'd taken the elevator to the basement. She found the corridor poorly lit and deserted. The cafeteria workers had all gone home. Finished with the basement, floor janitors had moved up to the next floors. With no cafeteria, and no hospital rooms in the basement, Celeste found herself all alone.

Unable to locate Celeste in the waiting area, Gaylon assessed the situation. A middle-aged woman stood at the pay phone, and all the chairs and couches were empty. She had gone to the bathroom, or downstairs to the basement for coffee, he reasoned. Hoping for the latter, he hurried to the elevator down the deserted hallway from the critical care waiting room. Instead of going down, he took the elevator one flight up.

There were only four ways into the basement. Critical care was near the center of the hospital, and only a single utility elevator went to the basement, along with an adjacent stairway in case of emergencies. A second bank of elevators and a stairway near the concession area led up to the main portion of the hospital. Celeste had used the elevator and planned to return to the visitor's room the same way she'd come. The main bank of elevators would take her far from the critical care area. Too far, he decided. She wouldn't be up for sightseeing.

Upon reaching the third floor, he found it dark and

deserted. This portion of the hospital served primarily as storage and workers rarely visited at night. He'd brought along a phone book from the Critical Care waiting room. Stepping out of the elevator, he jammed the book in the door. When the doors tried to close, a sensor encountered the heavy book and started a round of metallic-sounding opening and shutting.

With a little luck, he thought, service would not discover the glitch for hours. This would leave Celeste with no way back to the critical care floor except by way of the stairs. Gaylon followed the narrow staircase to the basement. Only one utility light dimly illuminated the stairs, and he covered it with his sock hat. With the stairwell darkened, he peeked out the door, seeing no one there.

Celeste hurried down the long corridor, uneasy at being the only person in the basement. The concession area was at the far end of the hallway. The break room had metal reinforced, heavy glass windows on two sides. A glass door provided the only entrance into the room filled with soda, candy dispenser, and hot drink machines. Drastically lowered fluorescent lighting saved energy, and only dimly lighted the room—along with the ephemeral glow of candy and soda machines.

Though the coffee machine wasn't empty, she could see from the dark liquid pouring into her cardboard cup that it wasn't fresh. Having no better option, she paid for a second cup of coffee. When the whirring sound ceased, she listened intently a moment, thinking she'd heard someone coming down the hallway. She finally decided she was mistaken. Cradling the two steaming cups against her chest, she started back down the hall.

Celeste's shoes had thick, rubber heels and the distinct sound they made echoed down the long empty hallway. Halfway to the elevator, she stopped at the women's restroom, pondering whether to go in or wait and use the facilities upstairs. She reached for the doorknob, and then hesitated. The empty basement seemed far too dark and scary. Releasing the handle, she started again for the elevator.

After rounding the corner at the end of the long hallway, she pushed the button on the wall. From the light at the top of the unit, she could see the car was on the third level. After a moment, she pushed the button again. It didn't work. With the elevator locked on the third floor, she decided to try the stairs. When she opened the door to the stairwell upstairs, she found it dark and foreboding. Only barely able to see, she hesitated. Worse, she heard someone coming down the terrazzo hallway—someone moving with the uneven, shuffling gait of a man with a pronounced limp.

Celeste's heart began racing and she halted, frozen in place at the base of the darkened stairwell. She waited, staring through the tiny window in the door. Soon a man appeared. He wore neither bowler hat nor tuxedo, but Celeste knew who it was.

The man she recognized would have raped and killed her if Mama hadn't interceded. Mama was nowhere near, and Celeste would have to depend on her own wits for survival. She waited behind the door until the man reached for the door handle. When he did, she shoved it open with all the strength she could muster, striking him in the forehead and stunning him. As he stood there holding his head, she raced past him around the corner and back down the long corridor.

Celeste was ephemerally aware of someone following her as she sprinted down the hall. She knew she was faster than he was. It wouldn't matter if he trapped her against a dead-end. When she reached the elevators, she pushed the button, waiting briefly as the shuffling sound of a heavy man coming down the hallway behind her filled her ears. Not waiting, she grabbed the stairway door but found it locked. In desperation, she ran into the break room and pushed a candy machine in front of the door. Suddenly, all the lights went out.

Celeste couldn't see out of the concession area. She did know that someone outside could see in, the only remaining glow coming from the vending machines. Wedging herself behind one of the machines, she waited, heart pounding as someone tried the door. Finding it blocked by the candy machine, he put his shoulder into it. Celeste's blockade held but only for a moment. When Gaylon finally managed to kick the door open, his actions set off a distant alarm. Ignoring the blare, he began tearing into the small space, trying to find the woman he'd come to kill.

Although Celeste's mind screamed, she remained silent as he burst through the door. Totally focused on finding her, he tossed vending machines away in anger. When he saw her ankle, he grabbed it, yanking her toward him. She was waiting for him with the only weapon she had—the hard, rubber heel of her shoe.

Celeste lashed out with the shoe, banging it repeatedly against his face and head. Gaylon managed to fend off most of the blows with his hand, so she kicked him in the face with her other shoe. Breaking loose from his grip and scrambling to her feet, she raced for the door. Slipping on slick terrazzo, she crashed on her face, banging her head against the corridor's limestone wall. Blocking the pain, she scrambled on hands and knees, willing herself down the hallway, making it to her feet before he turned the corner of the concession area. Gaylon was right behind her, moving rapidly, and drawing ever closer.

Gaylon was fast, almost supernaturally fast. Celeste fell twice, and he quickly made up the distance between them. The elevator remained out of order, and she realized the dark stairway was her only chance for survival. She didn't hesitate. Tearing up the stairs, she tripped and racked her shin. Knowing she had no time to nurse the scrape, she scurried up the stairs, clothes ripped, elbows and knuckles bleeding. She found the first door locked.

Frightened, but not ready to die, she hurried up the stairs to the next floor, quickly finding someone had put an obstruction in the doorway. She pushed through only to discover the dark, hospital storage room. Sensing the passage led to a dead end, she sensed that following it could ultimately result in her death.

The phone book was in the elevator, the door still trying to shut. The killer might be waiting on the ground floor at the elevator door. Kicking the phone book into the hallway, she dived into the elevator and punched the button for the ground floor. For a long moment, nothing happened, and then the door shut and the elevator started downward.

Chapter 32

Celeste burst through the elevator door into the waiting arms of her father. Beside him were Tony and Tommy, surprised when they saw her torn clothes.

"The killer's in the basement," she said.

"We're covering all the elevators, stairways, and doors. My men are doing a floor-by-floor search. If he's still in the building, we'll catch him."

"How did you get here so quickly?" she asked.

She wanted to add, though not fast enough.

"When the Hospital alarm sounded, we came immediately. I knew you were here with your father and suspected the alarm was somehow connected. At any rate, we weren't far away."

Maurice hugged his unsettled daughter and patted her shoulder. "That's it," he said. "You're coming to Starkville with me tonight."

Tony shook his head. "Bad idea, Mr. Duples. Celeste is safe now. We made a mistake today. From now on, she'll have a twenty-four hour guard. I can't guarantee her safety in Starkville."

"You can't keep us here if we want to leave," Maurice said.

"Oh yes we can. Your daughter is a material witness. She's seen him and can positively identify him."

"She'd be safer in Starkville and can return when you need her."

"Starkville isn't that far away, and it would make his job easier. She stays here, and that's that."

"Are you using my daughter as a decoy?"

"I don't like your tone, Mr. Duples. The investigation into the death of Arthur Duplesses is pending if you get my drift. Your daughter is staying in New Orleans. So should you, if you know what's good for you."

"I'm calling my lawyer about this," Maurice said.

"You do that," Tony said. "Meantime, don't get in the way of my investigation. Got it?"

Maurice nodded. "There's nothing more we can do here tonight. Let's go back to the hotel."

"I've checked out, Daddy. I'm staying with Mama. I'll be okay."

"I'm warning you, Lieutenant. If that monster harms a single hair on my daughter's head, I'm going to have your ass in a sling."

"Relax, Mr. Duples. We'll take care of her. You got my word on it."

✎

Gaylon had followed Celeste up the dark stairway, exiting the stairwell to the third floor just as the elevator door closed. By now, his mental alarms were blaring. He'd kicked out a window facing the alleyway, cutting his leg on a jagged piece of glass when he piled out the opening. So intent upon escaping, he didn't notice the pain as he vaulted a fence and disappeared into the alleyway. He hailed a cab by waving a hundred dollar bill until a driver finally stopped. Once settled in the back seat he realized his leg was bleeding, and blood was seeping from the gash on his forehead.

"Where to, mistah?" the cabbie asked.

"Camp Street Mission."

A few blocks from the Mission, he had the cab pull over. The driver had glanced at him in the rearview mirror. From his troubled expression, it was likely the man recognized him and could see his blood-soaked pant leg and bloody forehead. When the cab stopped, he grabbed the man's neck and squeezed him until his eyes bugged out and he ceased struggling. To make the killing seem like a simple robbery, he rifled through his wallet, taking all the money he found. Leaving the back door open, he glanced around to make sure no one had seen him before starting on foot to the mission.

188

It was late, the weather mild. With no rain in the forecast, most of the homeless people were out on the street. Gaylon found the entrance to the Camp Street Mission ajar, the place practically deserted. Hurrying upstairs, he entered Sister Agnes's room without knocking. He found her sitting at the mirror, combing her long, blonde hair. His sudden appearance didn't surprise her. When she saw his bloody pant leg, she went to the bathroom and returned with scissors, a sponge, and a pan of hot water.

"What happened to you?" she asked.

"You don't want to know."

Sister Agnes sliced the pant leg and applied pressure to his leg wound until it stopped bleeding. "You need stitches," she said.

"No. Just get rid of the blood and tape it up. I'll be all right."

"What happened?"

"I tried to take care of one of the women that can identify me. She got away."

Sister Agnes finished cleaning his wounds, shaving the hair on his leg before applying iodine and taping the it tightly. After bandaging his forehead, she folded her arms and backed away.

"Thank you. I know where to come when I need help."

"I'm very angry with you," she said. "You know how I felt about Jason, and yet you killed him."

"He attacked me. I had to defend myself, or he would have killed me."

"I want you now, or I would kill you myself. Your wounds aren't serious. What did you come here for?"

"Your help, with the mambo and her friend. We both want to see them dead before they realize who I am."

"What is this mambo's name?" Sister Agnes asked.

"Mama Mulate," he said.

Sister Agnes began removing her clothes, unmindful of his presence. Going into the bathroom, she returned wearing a black chemise. She lit a single black candle in the center of a table and extinguished the lights. In various places around the room, she lighted incense. From a special shelf, she grabbed several bottles filled with various unspecified ingredients and placed them on the wooden table. After sitting in front of the candle, she stabbed the dagger into the table with the force of both her hands. Then she shook her long blonde hair and stared with a frown at the candle flame.

"Did you know that Mama Mulate was at the ceremony of my newest initiate?"

"I did not, and that troubles me. Does that mean she already knows about us?"

Sister Agnes didn't answer as she dusted combustible dust into the candle's flame. The powder ignited slowly as she measured it from her palm. For just a moment, the acrid odor of burned chemicals overcame the smell of incense. She stared into the flame as she dropped the powder. When it finished burning, she gazed at Gaylon.

"Mama Mulate may have all the answers. It doesn't matter because she hasn't put them together yet in a plausible sequence. She is assisting a police officer—a Lieutenant Nicosia. He has been here at the Mission twice asking questions. He was also at the ceremony with Mama Mulate. Ghede possessed him during the ceremony, so I know that he is vulnerable. Mama Mulate is different. She is a powerful and dangerous mambo and won't be so easy to be rid of."

"Then you must call on the powers of darkness," he said.

Fully transformed into Mambo Aghnee, Sister Agnes fetched a red bandanna from her collection and returned with it to the table.

"Lieutenant Nicosia wore this bandanna to the ceremony." She deftly tied the bandanna into the figure of a person and then placed it on the table beside the candle. "We must first learn if this Nicosia is protected by Ghede."

Mambo Aghnee began a chant as she drew a vever on the table with powdered bone extracted from the dried skeleton of a black rooster. She took Gaylon's hand and incised careful x-shaped marks in each of their wrists. With their blood commingled on the tip of the knife, she dropped it onto the vever. Smoke from the candle turned from gray to black.

"Accept our offerings, Ghede," she said. "Help us with your dark powers to avenge a wrong done to us."

Mambo Aghnee scooped up the powdered bone dripped with blood on the blade of the knife and held it in the candle flame. The flame went gold, and then blood red.

"What does it mean?" Gaylon asked.

"Ghede won't oppose us," Mambo Aghnee said, "But he won't help us either."

With that, she took the knotted, bandanna figurine and placed it where the vever had been. She used it to sever the bandanna figurine, and then dropped the two pieces into a jar of vinegar and goat's blood. The figurine bubbled violently before settling to the bottom of the jar. Mambo Aghnee capped it and returned to the table.

"Something is blocking the spell. It's late. I'll try again tomorrow."

Mambo Aghnee's room was small with little more than the table, two chairs, and the bed where she slept. Standing from the table she slowly pulled the chemise over her head, revealing her nakedness to him. Strolling slowly and suggestively to the bed, she climbed beneath the covers.

"What do you want me to do?" he asked.

"Join me. You killed the love of my life. Now, you must comfort me the way you used to."

Chapter 33

I spent the morning talking with my extremely concerned veterinarian, Dr. Olivia Riser. "Bob has Feline Immunodeficiency Virus, also known as F.I.V., a disease of the immune system similar to the human AIDS virus. The virus has three stages, Bob in the late second phase of the disease where the condition results in progressive destruction of white blood cells and dysfunction of the immune system. I'm afraid there's nothing we can do for him."

Dr. Riser's prognosis came like a sharp blow to the head. "You can't mean anything at all, surely?"

"Make him comfortable. If he gets too weak and in uncontrollable pain, you'll have to put him down."

"This is all hard for me to deal with. How long does he have to live?" I asked, the words sounding strange to my own ears.

"A few weeks to a few months. It's hard to predict."

"Doc, I thought we gave Bob all his shots. What went wrong?"

"Bob was a stray when you found him. He had probably already contracted the virus. There's no way of knowing."

The vet's words rattled in my head as I took Bob back to my apartment. I felt horrible. What's worse, there was no one I could talk to about how sad I felt. A creature that loved me and trusted that I would take care of him would soon die and nothing I could do about it. The feeling paralyzed me.

I didn't even have the luxury of staying with my sick kitty the rest of the day. I'd promised Bervard Dagobert I'd talk to his brother Perley. I had shirked that job too long already. After giving Bob a couple of full body strokes, I left him alone on the bed.

Perley's restaurant was on Poydras, so I started up Chartres in that direction. Clouds had moved north overnight, leaving behind a teal blue sky and a breeze so gentle it barely rocked the Boston ferns draping second-story balconies in the French Quarter. The atmosphere was electric, elevating my mood and energizing my steps as I hiked to Poydras. Perley's was the antithesis of Dagobert's. Instead of a stand-alone two-story building, the bistro was little more than a hole in the wall in a middle class, working neighborhood.

The customers didn't care, the place rocking when I arrived. Like Dagobert's, it had a long line of people waiting to get inside to eat. Perley had grown up in a family of restaurateurs and understood there was more to owning a restaurant than just cooking. Outside on the sidewalk, he smiled, pumping customer's hands as I walked up. He gave me no chance to go to the back of the line.

"Cowboy, you ain't got to stand out here. You family and you know that."

Perley grabbed my elbow and led me past the line of tourists, into his restaurant. When he opened the door, I found myself suddenly transported into bayou country. With Cajun music barely overcoming the clatter and chatter of thirty happy diners, the piquant aroma of gumbo and etouffee wafting from the kitchen quickly stoked my appetite.

"I guess you know why I'm here?" I said as he seated me at a little table in back.

"Yeah, Ber-vard tinks I tried to burn down Dagobert's," he said, his strong Cajun drawl further accentuated for the tourists. "Hell, you know that ain't like me to do none of that."

His response reinforced what I already believed. "Then it was just an accident? Like the insurance investigators said?"

Perley took a step away from the table, played briefly with his black mustache, and contorted his face into a distinct French grimace.

"I didn't say that."

Thinking I'd missed part of his answer amid the noisy restaurant din, I leaned closer.

"What?"

"Someone started that fire, all right, but it wasn't me."

"You're saying it wasn't an accident?"

"Tell you about it when I come back," he said. "I got to get a soufflé out of the oven before it burns."

He left me to ponder his words, not returning for ten long minutes. When he did, it was with a pitcher of lemonade. He placed the pitcher on the tablecloth's red checks, along with a cup of his soon-to-be-famous gumbo.

"Be right back," he said as I laced the already spicy gumbo with pepper sauce aptly named Cajun Fire.

Perley returned with another fantastic Cajun dish, seafood-stuffed bell pepper, and Mirliton dressing. Pulling up a chair, he turned it backwards, straddled it, and rested his elbows against its cane back.

"I didn't set that fire at Dagobert's. Delphine, Bervard's little squeeze did."

"Delphine is Berv's girlfriend's name?"

"Hell yes and everyone at Dagobert's knows she has Bervard in her sights."

"Why would she try to burn Dagobert's?"

"Cause she's nuts and got a temper like a banty rooster."

"That's no reason to set fire to the place. Where are you getting all this information from?"

"Kitchen talk. Delphine has hung around Dagobert's for almost a year now. Sammy LeCroix, the fry cook, says she and Bervard fight like an old married couple. When Delphine don't get her way, she punishes him."

"Why would he put up with that?"

"Cause she's young, kind of pretty, and most of the time she treats him like the King of Spain himself." When Perley grinned, his upper lip and oversized teeth flashed from beneath his mustache. "And hell, maybe he likes being whipped."

Ignoring his levity, I said, "What about the insurance policy you took out on the place?"

I could tell by his expression that my question had caught him by surprise. After twirling the chair around, he leaned back against the wall, letting me drift through a moment of silence as background music segued painlessly from Clifton Chenier to Louis Armstrong. Finally, he shook off his frown and began to explain.

"Wyatt, you know all about Mama and Daddy. Both of them drank like speckled trouts swimming upstream." I nodded but offered no opinion one way or the other. "Hell, Daddy didn't do nothing 'round Dagobert's 'cept lend his name to the place and pinch the waitresses' butts. He couldn't even cook. Mama had to keep the books and pay the bills. Only useful thing the old man ever did was hiring Sammy LeCroix to do the cooking for him."

Talk of two people once so close to me flooded my mind with old memories, some, not particularly pleasant. I resisted the point of Perley's story. Sensing my discomfort, he topped up my glass from the pitcher of lemonade.

"You all right?"

Nodding, I took a long sip from the sweating glass. Sirens blared outside as a fire truck raced along St. Charles Avenue. The front door opened briefly, and I became suddenly aware of the tourists still waiting in line. Perley continued his story.

"Mama always thought she'd die before Daddy because of her weight problem and bad heart. She loved Bervard but didn't trust him with money or business no more than she did Daddy. That's why she give me the money she'd saved for an emergency."

"Maybe you better explain," I said.

"Over the years, Mama managed to put back about fifty thousand dollars. After her last heart attack, she give it to me in case something happened to her. To help take care of the family with."

"But she got better."

Perley grinned again. "Hell, I'm surprised that tough ol' bird ain't still alive. She lost weight and give up smoking. The boozing finally got her, though not until ten years after it got Daddy."

"And what did you do with the money?"

"Had it in a savings account uptown. Last year, I finally

got around to doing what Mama wanted. The lawyer had me take out an insurance policy till he got the family trust in place."

"Then you have no designs on Dagobert's?"

Perley scoffed at my question, folded his arms, and leaned forward. "Hell, I saved my own money for years. Dagobert's is Dagobert's. I would never change anything about it. I just always planned to start my own restaurant. One I can control the way I want and cook what I want to cook."

I took the streetcar back to Canal. The rattling antiquity was so indigenous to the road it no longer even startled pigeons roosting on the General's statue when it rounded Lee Circle. Happy post-Katrina tourists, enjoying the weather and air cleansed by last night's rain, streamed in and out of the Quarter as we reached our stop. I hurried across the widest street in the world and bee-lined for Picou's bar. Bertram was alone behind the counter, polishing a glass.

"What's up, Cowboy?" he asked when he saw me. "Stomach bothering you?"

"My stomach's fine."

"Then why are your eyes bugging out like you got a caterpillar on your tongue?"

Bertram was full of it. A common Gallic trait, I'd noticed. He deemed himself a winner whenever he got a rise from someone. I had other things on my mind and refused to take the bait.

"Do you have any lemonade in this place?" I said, pulling up a stool at the bar.

"You break up with that little gal from Starkville?" he said, not answering my question.

"We aren't going together. Never were."

"Well, I just thought with you making them pitiful calf eyes and all. . ."

It was my turn not to answer. I turned instead on the stool and stared around the large, empty room.

"What you looking at?" he finally asked.

"All the people in here," I said.

"Ain't nobody in here but us."

When I grinned, Bertram knew I had him. "Exactamundo, Chief Run-at-the-Mouth," I said. "Maybe Pierre Bartender ran them off with his loud trap."

Bertram chalked up an imaginary point for me in the air and poured lemonade from the pitcher he kept beneath the counter. After a cool sip, I told him about the feuding Dagobert brothers.

"Sounds like Miss Delphine is the spark plug firing the whole deal," he said. "You gonna talk to Inez about it?"

"I don't know what to do. Inez already knows about Delphine, and I got the feeling the other night she might be plotting a little revenge."

"So?" Bertram asked.

"I think she has designs on me being part of her plan."

Chapter 34

Another hot day in New Orleans. Tony's eyes closed as he tried unsuccessfully to remember the events of the voodoo ceremony. Probably just as well, he thought. A female voice ruined by cigarettes interrupted his fantasy.

"Lieutenant Nicosia? You busy?"

Tony glanced up into the dark eyes of a smiling, middle-aged woman. Her front tooth was busted out, her graying hair curly with humidity.

"I'm a little busy"

"Your Chief said you could help me," she said, ignoring his attempted slight.

Tony shook off his headache and pointed to the metal chair in front of his desk. Without bothering to offer her a cup, he poured coffee for himself from a nearby pot.

"How can I help you, Mrs. . . . ?"

"Anna Moloni. I brought something that might interest you."

"What you got Mrs. Moloni?"

When she cleared her throat, a frowning teenager pushed through Tony's door carrying a computer beneath his arm. He placed it on the desk, and while fingering acne scars on his chin, waited for the detective's reaction. Tony switched his gaze to Mrs. Moloni for an explanation.

"Kevin bought it at a garage sale last Saturday. I thought it might interest you."

"I'm homicide, Mrs. Moloni, not burglary. If it's stolen property, you might want to talk with Detective Sullivan down the hall."

Anna Moloni stroked the side of her nose with a long finger. "You know what this is Lieutenant?"

"I think so."

Seeing sullen indifference glazing his eyes, Mrs. Moloni slowly scanned the room.

"Are we interrupting something, Lieutenant? Maybe I should ask your nice chief to find someone else to help me."

"No ma'am," he said, feeling chastised by her critical gaze. "What you got that's so important?"

Mrs. Moloni's broken-toothed smile returned and she removed a computer printout from her large, straw purse, handing it to Tony. He took the printout, doing a double take as he read it.

"This some kind of joke?"

"No joke, Lieutenant. Kevin found the file on the computer and printed it out. It looked like something that might interest the police."

"If this is real, Mrs. Moloni, it's just about the most interesting thing I've seen all year."

⚜

That afternoon, Tony leaned against the car seat of the unmarked Ford, shielding his eyes from harsh, summer sun glaring through the windshield. Between blinks, he glanced at the computer printout in his lap. Tommy was too busy negotiating traffic on St. Charles to notice. When they reached Terpsichore, Tommy turned south. Through the open windows, they heard the whistles of boats plying their trade on the river. Tommy wiped sweat from his forehead and tapped a nervous cadence on the steering wheel, shaking his head for the tenth time since they'd left the station.

"Maybe we should call for backup first."

"We just checking the place out," Tony said. "No need calling out the troops till we find out if the jerk at this house is our man. I already had one too many lectures from the Chief this week."

"You know I trust your judgment, Fat T, but. . ."

"Stop calling me Fat T."

"It's just that if the printout is truly the killer's journal, then. . ."

"Stop worrying. We're just scoping out the house."

199

Getting no response to his anxiety, Tommy shut his mouth and kept driving. They soon reached a neighborhood crowded with weeds, junk cars, and unpainted houses. Tony checked the address in his notebook as two black teenagers bouncing a basketball watched with interest.

"You passed it," Tony said. "Back up and pull in."

Tommy gave his partner an unhappy, sideways glance as he backed up and eased into the driveway. The teenagers followed the two detectives to the front door. Down by the river, a tugboat's lonesome whistle sounded.

"Detectives Nicosia and Blackburn, N.O.P.D.," Tony said, flashing his badge when a woman answered their knock. "We need to ask a few questions, ma'am."

The woman nodded. Instead of letting them in the door, she joined them on the stoop and closed the front door behind her. Except for her color, she could have passed as Anna Moloni's sister—an impression that would probably make neither woman happy, Tony thought.

"You live here, Mrs. . ."

"Kenner. Me and my son Andy," she said, pointing to the tallest boy staring at them from the driveway.

"What about your husband?"

Mrs. Kenner shrugged, her gray hair bouncing when she shook her head. "I ain't seen the man in ten years. He's probably doing hard time in Angola by now."

Tommy and Tony exchanged puzzled glances before turning their attention to the boy and assessing the likelihood of the skinny teenager being the serial killer stalking the city's backside. Tony somehow didn't think so.

Glancing at his notebook, he said, "You had a garage sale last Saturday?"

"Is the city sending out detectives now to collect sales taxes from poor black women?"

"Nothing like that," he said, removing his hat and swabbing his forehead with a handkerchief. "We heard you sold a computer, and we need to know where you got it."

"Black people own computers just like whites. You think we stole it or something?"

Mrs. Kenner's voice was indignant.

"I didn't say that either. How you got the computer doesn't bother me. Promise," he said, placing his right hand over his heart. "I only want to know where it came from."

Mrs. Keener cast a sidelong glance, perhaps a sign, to her son. The two boys, tossing the basketball back and forth, trotted off down the street. A green Chevy slowed, and Tommy's back stiffened when its engine backfired. Tony cleared his throat.

"Andy traded it from some kid uptown. Give him his old bike."

"You know the kid's name?" When Mrs. Kenner shook her head, Tony said, "Can we talk to Andy?"

"Not unless you got a reason to take him into custody."

"Like I said, we just want to talk."

"You leave him alone. We ain't got anything for you," she said, backing into the house and slamming the door behind her.

Seeing Mrs. Kenner watching through the curtain, Tommy jumped when the brakes of a city bus up on Magazine screeched.

"You think the kid stole the computer?" Tommy asked as they drove down the street.

"Sure he stole it," Tony said. "Hell, he's probably knocked over a dozen houses since last month. Probably wouldn't know where it came from even if he wanted to tell us."

"Should I have him picked up?"

"Not yet. He probably wouldn't be real helpful behind bars. Let me think about it before we do anything."

"You the boss,"

"Yeah, well just remember that next time you think about calling me Fat T," Tony said. "How are things going with you and Donna?"

"Not good. That girl has a wandering eye. Every time I think we're finished, she calls me on the cell phone."

"She's young, just like you. You both have plenty of time to get serious. Maybe you should just have some fun together and worry about permanent relationships later," Tony said.

"Yeah, how old were you and Lil when you got married?"

"Just out of high school. That's different. She was

pregnant."

"You never told me that."

"No, and don't go spreading it all over the precinct. It's just between you and me."

"Don't worry. Maybe Donna and I have no future. She'll hardly let me hold her hand anymore."

"Things have a way of working out. I hope our case does."

Before reaching Magazine Street, they passed a small park. Grass and weeds had grown up through cracks in broken concrete, and old paint flaked off a single park bench. Andy and his friend were shooting baskets through a hoop with no net. When Tony touched his elbow, Tommy slowed the car. After a glancing look, he motioned him with a nod of his head to keep driving.

Chapter 35

Lieutenant Tony Nicosia didn't spend his day off with his family. He drove instead down Terpsichore Street, stopping on a hunch at the little park he seen before. He found Andy shooting baskets alone.

"How you doing?" he asked, taking a seat on the park bench. "You like baseball? You're built like a baseball player."

Tony had a baseball glove on his hand, another on the bench beside him. Andy caught the second glove when he tossed it to him.

"Catch?" he asked, pitching him a baseball without waiting for an answer.

Andy needed no goading. They soon began firing grounders and high balls across the park at each other. They both quickly had enormous grins on their faces. An hour elapsed before they rested on the bench, relaxing as they caressed the soft glove leather.

"You got an arm, kid. You should give up that round ball malarkey and play a real sport."

"Ain't any diamonds around here," Andy said.

"Guess you're right about that," he said, draping his arm around the boy's shoulders.

"You on duty?"

"My day off."

"Why ain't you home with your family?"

"They're gone, mostly, doing this and that."

"You got kids?"

"Five," Tony said. "Two boys and three girls."

Andy's smile faded. "Ain't nobody but Mama and me. I never had no daddy."

"Maybe you're lucky. My old man came home drunk every night and hit my mother. When he finished with her, he came looking for Sis and me. Sis ran away when she was thirteen. Not long after that a truck ran over the old man when he stumbled out of a bar and fell on his face in the street."

"Damn!" Andy said.

"You damn right! Guess we all got our problems."

Andy patted Tony's shoulder. "I didn't mean to bring up bad memories for you."

"You hungry? Let's take a trip down St. Charles. I'll spring for a po'boy at Toukee's."

Andy piled into the passenger seat beside him and had a massive grin on his face all the way down the street. Although Toukee's was crowded, the waiter recognized Lieutenant Nicosia and found them an empty table in back. Tony ordered a Dixie for himself and a Coca Cola for Andy while they waited for their food. He watched in amazement as Andy devoured his first and then his second shrimp po'boy. By then, most of the lunch crowd had already departed. Waiters in white smocks ignored remaining diners as they cleared empty tables, clattering dishes, hurrying in and out of the dining area.

In the kitchen, the chef barked orders at his assistants. After seeing Andy lick the last morsel of French bread from his fingers, Tony motioned a harried waiter to bring them coffee and lemon pie. Andy ate his own, and then finished the last bite of Tony's. He wiped his mouth with the back of his hand, sighed, and leaned back in his chair. Tony leaned forward in his.

"You know why I visited your mother, don't you?" Andy lowered his chin, nodding without answering. "You're just like me at your age, in and out of trouble and never caught a break. I'm going to help you change all that, but you have to help me first."

"You putting me in jail?"

"Why hell no!" Tony said, reaching for Andy's hand. "We're friends now, and I'd never cross a friend. I got a serious question to ask you, and you're the only one that knows the answer. The computer your mother sold at the garage sale belonged to a bad person, a very bad person. You know who it is, right?"

"I only took it because he fired my Mama and we need the money right now. Mama is diabetic, and we don't have insurance."

"I'm sorry, Andy. In a year or so, when you're playing pro ball, it won't matter. You and your mom will have all the money either of you can ever spend."

"If I ever play pro ball, and if Mama lasts long enough to see it."

Tony motioned for two cups of coffee. "She will. Some other women won't be so lucky unless you tell me where you got that computer."

Andy stared at his new friend before speaking. "The street says never trust a white man or a cop. You don't seem that way to me."

"I'm not," Tony said. "You have my word of honor on that."

"I trust you," Andy said. "Mama worked for Senator LeBlanc over on Bourbon. When he fired her, and I went to help her get her things, I unlocked a window in his office. I came back when he was gone and took his computer."

"The computer belonged to Senator Gaylon LeBlanc?"

Andy nodded. "Are you going to arrest me now?"

"Arrest you, hell no! I might just give you a medal.

After extra pie and several more cups of coffee, Tony returned Andy to the little park. The boy waved as he pulled off in the car. As he did, he made a note to call the sports agent that had represented him when he played minor league ball.

Right now, things that were more important occupied his thoughts. All the loose ends were coming together, and he had just learned that Gaylon LeBlanc was the serial killer. That was the good news. The bad news was that Gaylon LeBlanc was the serial killer.

New Orleans is like no other city in the United States and probably the world. Family and hierarchy are necessary and in some instances more powerful than the law. Tony knew this. He also knew that former U.S. Senator Gaylon

LeBlanc came from one of the most prominent families in the city and was currently the president of the Crescent Club. Bringing the man to justice would be no easy task.

Mama's house wasn't far away, and he decided to drive by and see if the troops were on guard. They were. Mama was on the front porch picking flowers from a large pot. She waved and flashed a smile when she saw his car, motioning him to come into the house. Tony's emotions were a mixture of sheer panic and eager anticipation as he parked in the driveway and followed her inside. Mama greeted him with a kiss and a big hug.

"Tony, you look terrific. How much weight have you lost?"

"You noticed. No one else except Lil has. She thinks I have a younger girlfriend."

"Do you?" Mama asked.

"I may as well have. Our relationship has been frosty since I went home with my skin and hair darkened after staying out all night."

Mama laughed. "She didn't believe your explanation?"

"You mean that I was on a stakeout at a voodoo ceremony? Hell, it sounds so farfetched I hardly believe it myself. Where's Celeste?" he asked, changing the subject.

"With her father. He's keeping a short leash on her. Did you want to talk to her about something?"

"Just that she said the person that took her to the cemetery seemed strangely familiar. I wanted to ask her if the person she remembered could be Senator Gaylon LeBlanc."

"Come into the kitchen. I'll get you some coffee, and I think I need a shot of brandy to go with mine."

He followed her into the kitchen and sat at the table. "You saw the same man. Was it LeBlanc?"

Mama poured his coffee and a generous shot of brandy for herself. "How could I have been so stupid? Of course, it was. I have seen him a hundred times on television and even around town. It all makes sense now. Gaylon LeBlanc is the son of Sister Agnes, alias Mambo Aghnee. That explains the Vodoun connection. What now, Tony?"

"My ass, that's what," he said. "I may as well accuse the pope of these murders. Even if I get a conviction—and that's a big if—I'll be shoveling horse shit down at the police stables for the rest of my short, remaining career."

"Oh, Tony, it can't be that bad. Can it?"

"It can and it is. Maybe you better give me a shot of that brandy." Mama poured some in his coffee, and he felt slightly better after taking his first sip. When he finished his coffee, he said, "Gotta go now. Lil isn't speaking to me. If I get home after dark on my day off, she might strangle me in my sleep."

"Let me give you something to take with you." Grabbing a pencil, she scribbled a note on a scrap of paper. She handed it to him, along with a vial of powder as he paused in the doorway.

"What is it?" he asked.

"The same thing I gave you for your partner."

"I haven't given it to him yet."

Mama smiled and shook her head. "Then try it first. The note is the address of the florist I use. Take her a dozen, long-stemmed roses. In addition, Tony, make sure they are red roses. There is a cozy, little Italian restaurant a block from the university. Take her there and buy the most expensive bottle of Chianti they have. Discretely drop some of the powder into her wine."

"And then what?"

"Give her fifteen minutes, and then confess."

"Confess to what?"

"Whatever it is you feel guilty about. Tell her how much you love her and how you cannot go on without her. Make sure you've both had plenty of wine first. Whatever you do, do not hold back on the emotion. Wait," she said, rushing back into the kitchen and returning with her purse. "Take two of these before leaving the restaurant."

"What is it?"

"Yohimbe," she said. "You'll need it."

Chapter 36

Gaylon awoke at dawn in a bed he had not occupied in many months. He was alone, and his eyes slowly adjusted to the room's dimness as morning light began sifting through the ratty cotton curtains of the only window.

Mambo Aghnee sat at a dressing table with her back to him, combing her hair. She was naked. Gaylon slid from beneath the covers and began looking for his clothes. When Mambo Aghnee heard movement behind her, she turned to look, her face pinched into a horrible frown.

"You never explained why you killed Jason," she said.

Taken aback by the mambo's words, he said, "Yes I did. He almost got us caught when I killed the first woman for you. Staring at the body. Refusing to leave. I decided it was too risky to take him with me again."

"He was the reason I had you kill those two women. I did it for Jason. You knew I loved him. He wanted to be there."

"The potion you gave him wore off too quickly. He was a threat to me and to himself. He could have gotten us both caught."

You didn't have to kill him and defile his body," the mambo nearly spat. "What made you do that?"

"I had no choice. I would be dead now if I hadn't killed him first."

Mambo Aghnee strode across the floor toward the bed where he sat. From behind her back, she pulled a jeweled dagger and plunged it into his massive shoulder. He rolled away from her to avert a second attack. It never came.

Mambo Aghnee's anger was spent, and she stood, stark naked, sobbing and holding the bloody dagger. Her anger gone, she dropped the weapon, got a rag, and dressed his latest injury. When the bleeding stopped, she wrapped it tightly with a bandage.

"Gaylon, you are nothing more than my instrument. I am mostly to blame for Jason's death. He would still be alive today if I hadn't used my powers to free him from his hospital room. You just carried out my orders. I forgive you. Now I have new orders. Mama Mulate and her friend from Mississippi must die. They both will soon realize who you are even if they haven't already figured it out."

Gaylon grabbed his temple, grimacing in pain, and dropped to his knees.

"Oh, my God!"

Finally, the intense throbbing subsided, and he shook his head to clear the cobwebs.

"You understand, don't you?" she said. "When you do what I tell you, the pain will cease."

Gaylon stumbled to the chair where his clothes lay folded. With great effort, he dressed himself as Mambo Aghnee watched. She still wore not a single stitch of clothing. When he finished, he started for the door. Her words stopped him as he turned the knob.

"Tonight, after you take care of the meddling mambo and her friend, I want you to kill Sister Rose. It's time I take my rightful place in this mission and establish its true direction."

Chapter 37

Celeste and Mama sat at Mama's kitchen table, giggling as they smoked Ganja and drank shots of Cuervo.

"Hope the two cops across the street don't arrest us," Celeste said.

"They're the ones that need to be arrested. You'd think they'd never seen naked women before."

Mama's words sent Celeste into another giggling fit. "They got an eyeful on this stakeout," she said when her laughter abated. "Maybe we should give them another flash to keep them sharp."

An unexpected knock at the door interrupted their laughter. Dressed in little more than a revealing baby blue teddy purchased during a recent trip to Victoria's Secret, Mama answered the door. The person knocking was Tony, stunned at Mama's state of undress.

"I didn't wake you, did I?" he said.

His question sent Mama into yet another giggling fit. When Mama's laughter subsided, she gave him an overly friendly hug and motioned him into the house. She pointed to Celeste waiting at the kitchen table. Although the smell of Ganja was strong, he ignored it and sat between Mama and Celeste. Celeste had a teddy that matched Mama's teddy. Hers was pink and even more revealing than the one worn by Mama, if that were possible.

"How was your date with Lil?"

"Like a second wedding night. I'm just glad she is beyond her childbearing years. Am I disturbing something?" he asked.

"Do we look disturbed?" Mama said.

"I'm the one that should be disturbed. If Lil saw you two now, even after the other night, I'd be a bachelor by morning."

"Then maybe I'll call her," Mama said. "You're just about the sexiest man I've seen in a while."

Before he could answer, Celeste said, "Have you lost weight, Lieutenant?"

"Maybe a pound or two."

Mama grinned. "More like twenty pounds, I'd say. Guess my voodoo weight loss pills actually work."

"Yeah, well Lillian is worried I have a girlfriend because she hasn't seen me this skinny since we were dating."

"Do you?" Celeste asked.

"Do I what?" he said.

"Have a younger girlfriend."

Before Tony could answer Celeste's pointed question, Mama sat in his lap and hugged him.

"I'm flattered, Lieutenant," she said. "I didn't know you were attracted to little ol' me."

Celeste got into the act, hugging him and rubbing suggestively against his shoulders and back. Tony was too sober for comfort. He also feared the stakeout cops across the street had their binoculars trained on him.

"I love you ladies, but you're going to get me fired and possibly killed. Please, have mercy. I'm too weak to resist."

Cuervo, ganja, and Tony's words sent the two beautiful women into yet another round of laughter. Sensing his deep anxiety, they both returned to their chairs.

"We're sorry," Mama said.

"It's not your fault. Hell, if I had a couple of tokes from that pipe and a shot or two from that bottle I'd be the life of the party. I would also be single and unemployed by tomorrow. I was just checking to see if everything is okay. Now I think I better leave." He headed for the front door, trying to ignore Celeste and Mama. "You got my cell phone number if you need me. I won't be far away."

"Don't leave, Lieutenant," Mama said. "I need you now."

Celeste and Mama rolled with laughter as Tony exited through the front door, not looking back as he did. Tony was in a hurry and didn't see the police officers across the road were no longer watching the house. They were both dead.

Celeste was still laughing as she slugged another shot of Cuervo. Mama's mood changed abruptly as Tony's departure.

"Wait a minute, girlfriend. I'm sensing something evil in our midst."

"You think it's time to flash those two cute cops again?" Celeste asked.

Mama didn't answer. Instead, she went to the kitchen and started a pot of strong Creole coffee. Once the dark brown liquid began dripping from the grounds, she took her cell phone and dialed.

'Tony, I think you left too soon."

"Just in time if you ask me."

"You need to come back here."

"Mama, you know I can't. . ."

"Tony, we were all having fun before. Now I am serious. Baron Samedi is near. I feel his presence. Please, hurry."

Tony trusted Mama's instincts and did not hesitate. He did a one-eighty in the middle of the street and called for police backup as he roared toward her house, his siren blaring. He slid to a halt in front of the stakeout car and knew as soon as he opened the door that something was seriously wrong.

The car's door was ajar, the head of the person behind the wheel cocked at an impossible angle, his protruding tongue already turning blue. Tony didn't bother closing his bulging eyes. With his pistol drawn, he sprinted to the house and kicked in the front door.

Celeste was lying on the polished wood floor, either dead or unconscious. A man in black had Mama by the neck. He didn't let go until Tony put a bullet in his back. Before he could fire again, the man with pearl sunglasses released his grip on Mama's neck and knocked the gun out of his grip with a lightning backhand. As sirens of approaching police cars sounded outside, he flattened Tony to the floor and escaped with a frontal jump through Mama's picture window.

When backup arrived, Baron Samedi was gone. Tony was giving Celeste mouth-to-mouth resuscitation as a horrified Mama looked on. Tommy Blackburn was part of the body of arriving cops, every one of them with pistols drawn.

"Tony, we got two cops down outside."

Celeste coughed and gasped for breath as a paramedic quickly applied an oxygen mask to her face. She sat straight up, coughing but otherwise alive as Tony sprinted out the front door. He didn't stop until he reached the stakeout car.

"Blessed Mother of God!"

Ripping the gun out of Tommy's hand, he pointed it at his temple. Closing his eyes, he grabbed the trigger.

"Fat T, what, in hell's name, are you doing?" Without waiting for an answer, Tommy slapped the pistol out of his grasp. "Are you crazy? I swear to God I'll kick your ass unless you get your act together. I mean it." Tommy pinned him to the ground. "What in the hell do you think you're doing?

By now, the place was swarming with cops and paramedics. None seemed to notice the incident occurring between partners. Feeling he had no other choice, Tommy slapped his partner across the face. Then he did it again.

"Stop hitting me, asshole!" Tony said after the second hit. "Let me up."

"You grab that pistol again, and I'm going to take it away from you and jam it up your ass."

"I said I'm okay. Now get off me. You're breaking my back."

Tony's younger partner rose to his feet, keeping a watchful eye for any sign of odd behavior.

"You're scaring me, Fat T. You okay?"

"Hell no, I'm not okay. I feel like warmed over shit, and now I'm responsible for the death of two good men."

Tommy agreed with none of Tony's negativity. "You didn't do anything. If it weren't for you, those two women, along with the cops, would be dead. Now get a grip or I'm going to rub your face in the dirt again."

"I'm okay," he said. "But I swear to you now, by Mary Mother of Jesus, whatever it takes I'm going to kill that son of a bitch!"

Chapter 38

Lieutenant Anthony Nicosia and Sergeant Thomas Blackburn stood by the grave in dress uniforms, watching their second funeral in as many days. Chief Wexler gave the eulogy and then shoveled some dirt into the open hole. People were crying. Concerned relatives gathered around the bereaved widow, attempting, without success, to console her. Chief Wexler offered the woman and her family his personal condolences. Seeing Nicosia and Blackburn, he strolled over and joined them. Tony fussed with his uniform that was unexpectedly swallowing him in excess fabric. Wexler noticed without comment.

Instead, he said, "Lieutenant, Sergeant. I'm hoping you can tell me you have good news in the investigation."

Tony cast a sidelong glance at Tommy before answering. "Sir, we have a suspect."

"How strongly do you believe that he is our man?"

"Very strongly," Tony said.

"Is he in custody?"

"No sir."

"Why isn't he?"

"We have a few problems.

"Like what?"

Tony didn't stutter although he hesitated before answering.

"Sir, this isn't a good place to explain why we don't have the suspect in custody."

Wexler glanced behind him at the grieving widow. "I don't think you like attending police funerals any more than

I do. I'm going home to change clothes. Meet me at your office in two hours. I hope that gives you enough time to come up with an explanation why you don't have this strong suspect behind bars."

Tony and Tommy watched him leave the cemetery in a police limousine before offering their condolences to the slain officer's widow and his family. With the funeral party dispersing, they left in their car, changing out of their dress blues at Blackburn's bachelor pad. The place was a mess, empty pizza containers on the floor and beer cans on the coffee table.

"Is it my imagination or did another hurricane hit your apartment?" Tony asked.

Tommy knew what was coming. "What do you mean?"

"If a woman saw this mess she'd throw up. There clearly hasn't been a female over anytime in the recent past. Looks like things are not going so well with you and Donna."

"She's has a thing for that new young beat cop."

"You giving up?"

"I'm not getting much positive feedback. I asked Donna to the movies last Saturday, and she said no, not even bothering to make excuses."

"Maybe this will help," Tony said, handing him Mama's vial of powder.

"What's this?"

"Love potion."

Tommy snickered. "You kidding me, Fat T?"

Tony glared at his younger partner. "Do I look fat to you?"

Tommy gave him a quick once over. "Are you losing weight?"

"You have eyes don't you? I am at least ten pounds lighter than you so stop calling me Fat T. It's becoming a little annoying. Now, are you going to take this or am I going to have to stuff it up your redneck, Irish Channel ass?"

Tommy took the vial of white powder. "Fine, now what's it supposed to do?"

Tony frowned and shook his head. "You can lead a horse to water."

"What? Do I rub it on my pecker or something?"

"Might not be such a bad idea," Tony said. "First I think

you should tap a little bit into Donna's Dixie and see what happens."

Tommy glanced at the vial. "You sure this is legal?"

"Don't worry; it's not a date rape drug."

"What does it do?" Tommy asked.

"Hell, it's supposed to make Donna want you. I told you, it's a love potion." Tommy continued eyeing the vial. Try it, it can't hurt anything, and it might just work."

"I think you've been hanging around that voodoo woman too long," Tommy said as he followed him out the door.

They arrived at the precinct before Chief Wexler. When the boss finally walked through the door, he took an assessing look at Tony before sitting.

"Losing weight, Tony?" he asked.

"Yes sir, a little anyway."

"More like twenty pounds, I'd say. What diet are you on? I'm trying to lose a few pounds myself, and I'd like to know how you do it."

"I'm just watching my calories and such."

Wexler recognized a classic stall tactic when he heard one and honored Tony's privacy by not calling him on it. Instead, he asked, "Why isn't our suspect already in custody?"

"Extenuating circumstances, sir."

"Maybe you should explain what you mean."

"The suspect is a former U.S. Senator, current president of the Crescent Club, son of a former King of Rex, heir to one of the oldest fortunes in New Orleans. Would you like me to go on?"

Chief Wexler laughed. "You're saying the primary suspect is Gaylon LeBlanc?"

"Yes sir."

"You're kidding, aren't you?"

"No sir."

Wexler took the empty chair in front of Tony's desk and leaned his head backwards until he was staring at the ceiling.

"Why in the world did I ever leave Covington? We barely had any crime and rarely had a murder that couldn't be solved in ten minutes." After a moment of silence, he said,

"Better give me the details."

Tommy made a pot of coffee and poured three cups as Tony told his story. "The computer we recovered either belongs to the killer or a writer with E.S.P. The computer came from LeBlanc's house on Bourbon."

"How do you know that?" Wexler asked.

"Sir, I have my sources."

"Are they verifiable?"

Tony hesitated. "That may be a problem. The source is a minor, and he has a record of petty theft."

"But you trust him?"

"Yes sir," Tony said.

"Good. I trust your instincts. What else do you have?"

"LeBlanc's real mother is a voodoo mambo. LeBlanc kills his victims dressed as the voodoo deity Baron Samedi. All the killings, with the exception of the police officers, have voodoo ritual implications."

Wexler grinned and shook his head. "Lieutenant, Covington is looking better to me all the time. You want to accuse a former U.S. Senator of murder because he practices voodoo and it's making him strangle people and cut them up?"

"Now you understand why we haven't arrested him."

"You kidding? I can hear a Johnny Cochran want-a-be's defense right now. The mayor and D.A. are running for reelection, so they accuse a high profile, highly esteemed citizen of our community, of murder, stating the distinguished former U.S. Senator has strangled and butchered women because of his belief in voodoo. Does that sound like a case we can win, Lieutenant?"

"Since the D.A. is also LeBlanc's first cousin, I doubt it."

Wexler slammed the cup of coffee and refilled it from the pot without waiting for Tommy Blackburn. "We have a problem here, Lieutenant. Moreover, it seems like you have a problem." At the door, he said, "Have you even given this matter much thought?"

"Sir, it has occupied my every waking moment since I learned that Gaylon LeBlanc isn't only our primary suspect, he's our only suspect."

"All right," Wexler said as he started out the door. "I'll leave it in your capable hands." Having taken two steps down the hall he pivoted and stood in the doorway. "Just come up with an answer before next Monday. And Tony, no more dead cops."

Chapter 39

The attack on Celeste, Mama and the police officers assigned to protect them had resulted in a furious New Orleans police force and beefed-up surveillance of Mama's house. When I arrived to check on Mama and Celeste, I was frisked and questioned before allowed inside. Mama was drinking coffee at the kitchen table, Celeste on the couch with an ice bag on her head.

"I would have come as soon as I heard. Tony called and told me not to try before now. Is there anything I can do?"

"I'm okay," Mama said. "Celeste has a splitting headache. They checked her out at the hospital, and she'll be okay."

"I brought beignets from Café du Monde," I said, putting the bag on the kitchen table. "They always make me feel better when something traumatic happens."

"Sugar freak," Mama said with a grin.

Hearing my voice in the kitchen, Celeste dragged herself off the couch and joined us. She grabbed a beignet without waiting for a cup of coffee and ate until white powdered sugar glossed her nose and lips.

"You're right," she said. "These do make me feel better."

"Good. You'll be in heaven when you finish the whole sack."

"Those poor policemen," Mama said. "I feel so responsible."

"It's terrible that two men died. It isn't your fault. Tell me what happened."

"Mama saved my life," Celeste said. "Baron Samedi had me by the neck, and she threw a pot of coffee in his face. He released me and went after her. He would have killed us except Mama had a premonition before the attack and called Tony. He'd left here only minutes before. Baron Samedi was strangling Mama when Lieutenant Nicosia burst through the door and shot him. He dived through the window and got away."

"Now I feel like a prisoner in my own house," Mama said. "There is an army of police out there, and every one of them is as mad as hell."

"Good. He won't bother you here again."

"In case you've forgotten, I have a job. Granted it is only a short summer schedule. I still can't stay here until they catch the maniac."

"Celeste, you told me the person disguised as Baron Samedi looked strangely familiar to you. Did you get a better look at him last night?"

"Mama and I both know who he is. Tony told us."

"Then don't keep me in suspense," I said.

"Gaylon LeBlanc. Senator Gaylon LeBlanc," she added as if I needed further reference. Hopefully, he's in custody by now."

"Don't bet on it."

"What do you mean?" Celeste asked.

"If the killer is truly Gaylon LeBlanc, then the Lieutenant has a problem. I'm glad it's his and not mine."

I explained the situation to Celeste.

"Surely you must be joking," she said. "That man shouldn't be allowed to roam the streets."

"Tony will think of something," Mama said.

Before I replied, Maurice entered the front door without knocking. He and Celeste embraced, and he held her until all her pent up tears had subsided.

"I knew I should have taken you back to Starkville," he said.

"Oh Dad, he would have just followed us there. I'm all right now and well protected. Sit and drink some coffee.

Maurice, ever the clotheshorse, looked as though he'd just come from a GQ photo shoot. After watching him eat several beignets, I wondered how he kept his slim physique.

Good genes I guessed. At least his absentee parents had left him something.

"What are your plans, Mr. Duples?" I asked.

"Spend more time with the woman I now consider my mother. She had Arthur's body cremated. We are celebrating his life soon as she feels better. I'm not looking forward to seeing the old bastard's remains interred beside those of my real mother."

"You've gotten the closure you sought," Celeste said, her hands resting on his broad shoulders.

"Yes and I have Mr. Thomas to thank."

"Just doing my job," I said. "Now, I better leave and let these two get some rest."

"Will you join us at the cemetery when we bury Arthur? I think it would be appropriate."

"I'd be honored to accompany you," I said.

Before I left, Mama inspected my neck. "Where is the gris-gris I gave you?"

"In all the confusion this morning I forgot to put it on."

"Sure you did," she said. "It's okay because I made another for you. This one is the most powerful gris-gris I have ever created. I believe you're in more imminent danger than Celeste or I, and I don't know exactly why." She placed it carefully around my neck. "Now you must promise me you'll never take it off, not even for an instant until this evil has stopped. Do you promise?"

"Mama, I. . ."

"Do you promise me with all your heart and soul that you won't take it off?"

"I promise," I said, crossing my heart.

It was still early, and Bertram Picou's bar was empty except for someone sitting in my usual booth. Quite unexpectedly, it was Inez Dagobert, looking radiant, dark hair draping her shoulders and framing her pink blouse cut unusually low to display much of her ample bosom. Her smile when she saw me lit the room, and she gave me much more than a sisterly hug. Her sudden warmth left me little time to wonder what had happened to the normally shy and demure Inez.

"I wasn't expecting you," I said.

"No problem. Bert keeps bringing margaritas, and I'm totally tipsy. He said you'd be back soon, so I had him make a pitcher of lemonade."

As I watched, she poured lemonade into an icy glass and handed it to me. Handed is not the right word as she was practically sitting in my lap, close enough that her body heat generated stimulating waves of heat that surged through my extremities. Being a recovering alcoholic, I knew before the liquid touched my lips that a copious amount of vodka spiked it. I placed the glass on the table without taking a sip.

"Inez, what are you trying to do?"

"I'm so sorry. I should have known it would never work."

"What are you talking about?"

"I need your help. If you're a little loose, it'll be better. You remember, like old times?"

Inez's attempted deception stung me. "You know I have no tolerance for alcohol."

"I'm sorry," she said, hugging me and grinding her breasts against my shoulder. "Please forgive me."

Pressing her lips against mine, she thrust her tongue deep into my mouth, the kiss lasting long enough to get my attention.

"I think I better go," I said.

Inez pretended not to hear me. Bertram, by now, was watching our every move. Inez played to her audience by wrapping her arms even tighter around me.

"You look terrific. I always did think that you're the handsomest man in New Orleans."

"You aren't here to tell me how good looking I am."

"I want to talk about Bervard. Can we go upstairs to your room?"

As Inez stood, grabbed my hand, and pulled me toward her, I felt, suddenly and inexplicably, dizzy. I don't think that I answered her, my mind immediately reeling. The last thing I remember was the look on Bertram's face as Inez pulled me upstairs by the arm.

When I awoke several hours later, Inez was gone. The first thing that hit me was the odor of alcohol. I was naked, and my clothes on the floor reeked with the smell. I sensed that Bertram was waiting downstairs for an explanation. Worse, I found Bob locked out on the patio, his tail moving quickly when I let him in. Ignoring me, he nibbled at the morsels in his food bowl, concentrating on them instead of my unwanted strokes along his back.

"You got something to confess?" Bertram said when I finally went downstairs and took a stool at the bar.

"Why, are you a priest now?"

"I think you might need one."

"I didn't do anything. Inez slipped me something."

"And how did she do that? Spike your lemonade?"

"I didn't touch the lemonade. Do you think I'm crazy?"

"Then how else did she slip you something?"

I'd already thought about the answer to Bertram's question. "She must have had it in her mouth when she kissed me. She pushed it down my throat with her tongue."

Bertram laughed and shook his head. "Well, you smell like a brewery."

"I told you, I didn't drink any of Inez's spiked lemonade. She slipped me something that knocked me out."

"Are you sure about that? Inez left your room with a big smile on her face."

"I couldn't have done anything if I'd have wanted to."

"Maybe cause you were too drunk."

"I told you, not drunk, drugged. You think I'm stupid enough to fall for her spiked pitcher of lemonade trick?"

"She's a good-looking woman."

"She's a gorgeous woman, but I never laid a finger on her. Bervard is a close friend of mine."

Bertram poured himself a shot of Cuervo and tossed it back. "You told me you have a crush on her. You got to face it, Cowboy. If a woman wants a man, any man to make love to her bad enough, she is going to find a way to make him do it. I've known Inez all my life—hell, we are cousins—and I swear I didn't recognize her when she walked in the door. She had you in her sights. You were just as good as a dead duck."

"You're not giving me very much credit."

Bertram wasn't listening, his gaze suddenly locked on someone that had just entered the bar.

"Don't matter what I think. Berv just arrived, and he ain't smiling."

Chapter 40

I turned to see Bervard Dagobert charging across the room toward me. Unfortunately, I wasn't fast enough to prevent his roundhouse right hand from connecting solidly with my jaw. The blow knocked me off the barstool, onto the floor. Bervard didn't wait for me to get up, piling on top of me, his fists swinging wildly.

"You sorry asshole," he shouted. "Inez told me what you did."

I shielded my face from his raining blows. Bertram ended the fight abruptly with a tap to the base of Berv's skull with the weighted baseball bat handle he always kept behind the bar.

"You killed him," Inez yelled, entering the bar and catching the tail end of the fray. She rushed to Bervard's side, cradling his head in her lap. "I didn't know he was going to attack Wyatt, and you didn't need to kill him for it."

"He ain't dead, but he'll wish he was when he wakes up," Bertram said. "Better have a big bottle of aspirin ready 'cause he's going to need it."

As I held my own aching head, wondering what else could happen, little brother Perley bounded through the door followed closely by an attractive young woman. She was as slender as Inez was ample, her long hair black, olive skin flawless. She also had green eyes and could have passed as Inez's younger sister. I saw from the look in Inez's own green eyes that she was in no way related. The young woman was Delphine, the object of Bervard's affection and the cause of all the ensuing fuss.

225

"Why did you bring that slut?" Inez said, cradling Bervard's head even closer as if protecting him from the woman.

"I came soon as Berv called me," Perley said. "He told me he was going to kill Wyatt, and I'm here to stop him. Delphine and I were talking when he phoned."

My lip was bleeding, jaw beginning to swell and left eye turning black. A bump on my scalp had already risen to epic portions. The bump, along with my pill-induced headache, caused my temples to throb like a church organ out of control. Still, the story unfolding before me caused me to forget my aches, pains, and conscience. Inez continued caressing Berv's head, even as Bertram tossed ice water in his face. When Bervard opened his eyes, Inez's demeanor changed, and she slapped his face.

"You leave Wyatt alone," she said. "You're just as guilty as he is sleeping with that whore of yours."

"Now wait just a minute before calling anyone a whore," Perley said. "Delphy has feelings too, you know?"

Berv and Inez both stared at Perley. "Delphy is it now?" Inez said. "Since when did you two get so chummy?"

"We both single, last time I checked," Perley said.

Perley had a point. Inez and Bervard broke their stare and began looking at each other. Inez said, "Berv, I didn't think you loved me anymore. I didn't know you'd be so angry with Wyatt."

Bertram's club and Inez's slap had taken all the fight out of him, and he seemed to sink deeper into the comfort of his wife's soft arms. I noticed she had on the same sexy outfit, her long hair still draping her shoulders.

"I never stopped loving you. I still can't believe I've been betrayed by my best friend," he said.

"You're one to talk, carrying on with poor Delphy here," Perley said. "She's almost young enough to be your daughter. You never thought about nobody except yourself. Not Inez or poor Delphine here."

Perley had a grip on Delphine's hand, and she didn't seem to be resisting. Bertram raised the bat and shook it menacingly at Bervard.

"You screwed around on my cousin Inez long enough. I should have hit you harder. Maybe knock a little sense in

226

that hard Cajun head of yours."

"Don't turn this on me," Bervard said. "Wyatt's got some explaining to do."

"Yeah, and he'd have kicked your ass long ago if I had let him. A licking wouldn't do you no good. The only thing you understand is feeling the same way you've made Inez feel all these months. Inez turned the table on you and I think you got a taste of your own medicine from your loving wife and best friend. Now, I think it's you that's got some apologizing to do, and I think you better start with your Inez."

I opened my mouth to explain that I hadn't laid a finger on Inez. I never got the chance. Bervard started to cry and buried his face into Inez's awaiting and welcoming bosom.

"I'm sorry, Baby. I never meant to hurt you. Can you ever forgive me?"

Inez didn't need to answer. Her overprotective embrace answered for her, tears in her eyes conspicuous as she kissed Bervard's forehead.

"I forgive you, Baby. I'm just glad Susie and Berv Jr. didn't have to witness your craziness."

"Keep going, Bervard," Bertram said. "You ain't half done apologizing."

Berv extended his hand. "I'm sorry, Wyatt. I know you would never do anything sexual with Inez unless you were trying to send me a message I was too stupid and stubborn to get. Are we still friends?"

"You know you're still my friend," I said. I started to spill my guts, tell him I hadn't touched Inez, carnally or otherwise. A concerned glance from Inez kept me from confessing to him. "I talked with Perley. He didn't start the fire at Dagobert's. He's never done anything to hurt you or to destroy the restaurant. I think he has something to tell you."

Berv, Inez, and Bertram turned to Perley. "Mama left us enough money to make sure the doors to Dagobert's never closes. She didn't want to hurt your feelings that she entrusted it to me instead of you. You know you are just like Pop. You never been any good handling money. Next week, we're going to spend some of it to renovate and redecorate the place. Inez is going to manage the improvements. You know I love you, Big Brother, and I'd never do anything to hurt you."

"I love you too Little Brother. What about your place on Poydras, are you just abandoning Dagobert's?"

"I would never abandon my roots. I just have ambition beyond Dagobert's. If you're interested in what your little brother is doing, I'll sell you half of Perley's. Hell, I could use the help."

Perley got on his knees and embraced his brother and Inez. Before I could slip away, Bervard pulled me into the group hug fest.

"I've got the best family and best friend anyone could ask for," he said.

When the hugging and sloppy sobbing abated, Inez asked, "What about her?"

"Delphine and Bervard are done, I can promise you that," Perley said. "I called on her a while back to talk about the situation that's been going on for too long now. We found out we got lots in common. She likes modern Cajun cooking as much as I do. She's helping me out at Perley's, and we're seeing each other now."

Bertram and I watched as the foursome left the bar arm-in-arm, their differences apparently settled. When they were gone, I said, "First time I ever slept with a man's wife and had him hug me for doing it."

"I thought you said. . ."

"I was kidding. I didn't sleep with Inez, or anyone else's wife."

"Then why didn't you explain to Bervard what actually happened?

"Because he didn't need to know."

"You about a strange one," Bertram said, shaking his head.

Maybe Bertram was right. My encroaching headache and swollen jaw reminded me why I had quit drinking in the first place. Finding Bob on the bed did little to alleviate my pain. He didn't move away as I lay beside him on the bed, stroking his gaunt frame until I fell asleep.

Chapter 41

Gaylon left a trail of blood as he hurried away from Mama's house. It didn't matter because he had other things on his mind now. They included how he was going to stop the bleeding and get the bullet lodged between his spine and shoulder blade out without dying first.

The only person he even halfway trusted had stabbed him with a dagger less than twenty-four hours ago. He headed toward Sister Agnes with trepidation. There was little else for him to do and still stay out of the hands of the police.

Gaylon, knowing his mother Rose rarely visited, entered Sister Agnes' room without knocking. Agnes was not about, and he found a towel to cram in the wound that was still dripping blood. He couldn't quite reach it, so he wadded the towel against his back. Leaning against the wall, he staunched the flow of blood until Sister Agnes arrived. She seemed agitated when she opened the door and found him waiting for her.

"Are you crazy? Someone could have seen you come in here."

"No one saw me, and I had no choice," he said. "I've been shot."

Sister Agnes pulled his shoulder away from the wall and glanced at the towel, now sticky with blood and adhering to the wound.

"I should kill you myself. I heard the news. You spared the two I sent you to kill, taking two police officers instead. Are you totally unaware that you've probably led them directly to me?"

"No one saw me come here. Would you like it if I went to an emergency room instead?"

Despite her anger, Sister Agnes realized his argument. "What am I supposed to do? Even if I can stop the bleeding, I still can't take the bullet out."

"Do what you can or I won't survive until morning."

"I'm not through with you yet, and you'll do better than that. One of my minions is a medical doctor, though he probably hasn't seen a patient or been sober in a decade. I'll send a kanzo to get him."

"You trust him?"

"Does it matter now? The old drunk won't remember a thing in the morning. If he does, no one will believe him."

Sister Agnes changed out of her peasant-nun clothes and dressed in a manner appropriate for a Vodoun mambo. When she did, her character also changed to that of Mambo Aghnee. Gaylon was in a near death stupor because of loss of blood when the doctor arrived, a little rag doll of a man that hadn't bathed in years. Mambo Aghnee gave him something from a vial that seemed to sober him instantly. He acted almost professionally as he inspected Gaylon's injury.

"I'm Doctor Levant," the man said. "I need to remove the bullet from your back and stop the bleeders."

Mambo Aghnee's only medical instruments were forceps and a scalpel. She heated water, cleansed the wound, and acted as Doctor Levant's nurse, swabbing blood with gauze she tossed into a paper bag as he probed the wound. Mambo Aghnee had given Gaylon a potent painkiller, and his mind languished somewhere between dull reality and distant fantasy as the cutting blade did its work. The moan of a tugboat whistle on the river sounded like approaching ghosts and caused him to believe he was either dead or dying.

Despite being a longtime drunk, Doctor Levant had once been a competent E.R. doctor in downtown New Orleans and had dug many bullets out of gunshot victims in his lifetime. The procedure took less than fifteen minutes, including the time to stitch the wound with needle and thread.

"I took care of all the bleeders. He has lost lots of blood

though not enough to kill him. He's a strong man and should lead a long and productive life."

Mambo Aghnee already knew he would survive. Living a long and productive life was another matter altogether. In fact, she had plans to the contrary. She blew powder up Levant's nose and gave him a bottle of Ripple. Soon, the little man was back on the street without remembering he had saved a person's life by digging a bullet out of his back.

"You lost lots of blood," Mambo Aghnee said. "You'll be stronger in the morning. You will sleep on the floor tonight. You're still seeping blood, and I don't want you to stain my bedclothes."

Mambo Aghnee taped a towel to his injury, threw a blanket and pillow on the floor beside the bed, and gave him more painkillers before crawling under the covers and turning off the light. Gaylon moaned when the medication wore off, and his groans of extreme discomfort continued through the night. Mambo Aghnee ignored him. When she awoke the following morning, she found him sitting in her rocking chair, staring at the street below. She started a pot of coffee. She drank a cup without offering him any. As caffeine began working on her, she started in on him in an angry tirade.

"Even though you're a total incompetent there is still one job you must do for me. The most important job I'll ever ask of you."

He continued staring out the window at the rush hour traffic below. To reward his attention, Mambo Aghnee walked behind him and kicked him in the back. Gaylon groaned and sank to his knees.

"I'm listening," he said. "What is it you want?"

"You are a sorry excuse for a human being. I don't care now. You will do it, or I will cut out your heart myself and eat it raw. Hear me? You are nothing more than cow dung, and I wouldn't trust you to take out the trash. At least Baron Samedi knows how to kill someone."

Swollen red welts marked Gaylon's face where Mama had thrown scalding coffee on him. Seeing the marks, Mambo Aghnee slapped him hard across the cheek before performing an incantation and tracing a vever on his forehead. He took the abuse without whimpering, and a transformation began as Mambo Aghnee chanted over the vever.

"You summoned me, Mambo? For what purpose?" he said.

"Death," she said.

Baron Samedi smiled. "A subject I can warm up to. What is your wish?"

"Sister Rose must die. If it pleases you Baron Samedi, I beg that you kill the heretic and bring me her heart. I pray you do to her whatever else you see fit.

Mambo Aghnee had put a dark suit on her bed, along with a top hat and garish sunglasses. When Baron Samedi had changed into the clothes, she gave him a cigar. He grinned as he put it in his mouth. Without another word, he went out the door and down the hall to Sister Rose's apartment. There, he waited for almost an hour.

Sister Rose liked sharing breakfast with the people of her mission. Not that she had an enormous appetite. For her, attending a breakfast with her congregation was more symbolic than real. The woman weighed little more than one hundred twenty pounds even though she was almost six feet tall. The large hall was almost empty when she started upstairs to her apartment. The room was dark, and it took her a bit to see the person sitting in her worn Lazy Boy.

"Who are you?" she said, turning on the lights.

"Junior," he said. "Don't you know me, Mom?"

"Gaylon, why are you wearing that hat and those awful glasses? And get that nasty thing out of your mouth."

Gaylon grinned, showing his teeth without removing the cigar. "How you doing, Mom?"

"You're not my son. Who are you?"

"Gaylon is with me. You're absolutely right. I'm not Gaylon. You have sinned against your son, and I'm about to correct those sins."

Sister Rose approached Baron Samedi, still unsure he wasn't Gaylon. She touched his face. "Of what sins am I guilty?"

"You deserted Gaylon when he needed you most," Samedi/Gaylon said. "You betrayed your husband and your best friend."

"I did none of those things. Your father filed for divorce when I finally had the courage to confront him with his many indiscretions. My accusations earned me one of the worst beatings I'd ever endured. Still, I persevered. He fought me in court and got custody of you. He had all the money, the judges all his friends. All I had was my good name. Before he finished with me, he also took that. I wanted you badly. It didn't matter. I spent myself into bankruptcy. I yearned for you for years. I am so sorry, son.

"I am not your son. I told you that. Your son is here. I am not him."

"If you aren't my son then let him reveal himself. I beg you," she said.

"I have another purpose."

"What purpose could you have that's more important than dialogue between a mother and her son?"

"A powerful mambo has given me a job. I must carry it out."

"What powerful mambo? Are you a messenger from Sister Agnes?"

"You mean Mambo Aghnee?"

Sister Rose dropped to her knees. Outside a semi lumbered by on the street, agitating a dozen noisy pigeons perched on the windows.

"Gaylon, I love you and never wanted to hurt you. I must tell you something. Whitney was your real father. Even though I'm your mother I'm not your biological mother."

Baron Samedi's facial features changed slightly, and he placed the cigar in a glass sitting on a table. "Go on," he said.

"Your real mother is Sister Agnes. As you know, she was your father's assistant. They lived together in Washington. She was more of his wife than I ever was."

Sister Rose's words were powerful. They started a physical transformation, gradual at first that she could see on his face. She continued talking and her words began changing Baron Samedi back to Gaylon LeBlanc.

Gaylon removed the sunglasses and put them on the table. "Why didn't you tell me this before now?"

"I wanted to, believe me. Whitney told me if I ever talked to you about it, he would never let me see you again."

Baron Samedi's smile had washed away from the face

of the man staring at Sister Rose. His hat was on the floor, no longer covering his blondish hair. Baron Samedi's dark eyes were also gone, replaced by Gaylon's and his real mother's unique blues.

"If you knew about Agnes and my father, why did you wait so long to leave him. and why did you allow her to join you here at the Mission?"

"Agnes is my best friend. We loved the same man. I have more in common with her than any person alive. Your father was a righteous man in many ways even if he had a dark side that most people never saw. He could be cruel and unforgiving. I'm sure you know what I mean. The object Agnes and I share most is you."

Baron Samedi was now totally gone, and Gaylon's mind now aching as much as his body. An hour had passed when he hugged Sister Rose, kissed her goodbye, and promised he would come again soon. He didn't leave the mission immediately, returning first to Sister Agnes' quarters. She was staring out the window, an ugly frown on her face, her arms tightly locked, and her dagger clasped firmly in her hands.

When Gaylon entered the room without knocking, she said, "Did you bring me something?" He didn't answer, and Mambo Aghnee turned to face the visitor. She immediately saw it was not Baron Samedi. "You," she said with a sneer. "Where is Baron Samedi?"

"Sister Rose sent him away."

"And just what do you mean?"

"You sent me to kill my mother. For that task, I don't need Baron Samedi's help."

Chapter 42

Lieutenant Anthony Nicosia had seen many bloody crime scenes during his career, though never one quite as horrible as the one he and his partner Tommy Blackburn now witnessed. They stood inside Sister Agnes' room at the Camp Street Mission. The nun/voodoo mambo laid dead on the floor, her eyes open and mouth agape, frozen in a silent scream never uttered. She was naked, her body battered, bruised and bloody. Vevers incised in her flesh stretched from her ankles to her forehead, and an ugly red welt encircled her pale neck. Only a gaping hole in her chest remained where her heart had been.

"Good God almighty," Tommy said. "No one deserves to die like that."

Tony nodded. The room crawled with forensic experts, photographers, and detectives. They were dismantling the area for any smattering of information to connect the killer with his deed. He knew this time there'd be more evidence than they'd ever need.

"Let's talk to Sister Rose," Tony said.

Tommy followed him downstairs to a table in the great hall. Sister Rose was waiting, her head bowed. "Is she really dead?" she asked when they sat down beside her.

"Yes," Tony said. "And please don't try and cover up for your son. We already know who committed the murder."

Years of service had given Sister Rose the ability to distinguish lies from reality with exceptional ability. She already knew the Lieutenant was telling the truth and wept as she made her confession.

"Gaylon came to my room, intent on killing me. I told him I was not his real mother. I explained about my ex-husband's many indiscretions and his longtime relationship with Agnes. I didn't realize he would react so violently. What will become of him?"

"Your son is a sick man. He needs help. Will you testify against him?"

"I cannot do that," Sister Rose said.

"You have to. You can't help him by attempting a whitewash. If you talk, I'll see to it he gets the help he needs."

"Lieutenant, I know you mean well."

"Your son has committed some horrible murders. If you love him, it's your responsibility to help us stop him and put an end to his killing spree."

Sister Rose cradled her face in her hand. "Please don't make me give you an answer."

Tony squeezed Sister Rose's shoulder, and then nodded for Tommy to follow. The criminal investigation would continue for several hours, their job already completed. When they exited the mission, he took a deep breath and shook his head.

"I need whiskey. Are you up for a drink at Carlucci's?"

"There won't be anyone there. Every one's here at the crime scene."

"You saying I ain't good enough company for you?"

"You know that ain't what I said, Fat T."

Tony ignored the nickname. It no longer held water as he'd lost almost thirty pounds. His clothes barely fit any more. Lillian had already started taking in his pants and buying him new shirts. Nearly three decades of marriage doesn't end easily. Thanks to Mama, theirs had become stronger than ever.

"I'm going to Carlucci's. You can come if you want or go home and watch N.Y.P.D. Blue. Meantime, I got real cop work to do."

Tommy Blackburn would have followed his partner to hell The last thing he wanted right now was to drink with him at Carlucci's Bar. It didn't matter because he didn't think he had a choice.

There were only a half dozen patrons in the bar when they arrived and none of the usual crowd. Tommy ordered a cold pitcher of Dixie and a double shot of Scotch, neat. Tony downed the shot and then ordered another. Tommy poured him a cold glass of Dixie Beer while he waited for his next shot to arrive.

"You okay?" he asked.

"Hell no, I'm not okay. Don't you ever get tired of investigating murder scenes? I've seen lots of terrible things in my twenty-five odd years as a cop. It got crazy during the corrupt years and again after Katrina. It was never as miserable as this summer. We know who the murderer is, and we can't bring him in."

"Something will work out. The Chief won't let this drag on forever."

"Chief is a decent, hard working man. Gaylon LeBlanc is an ex-senator. The president of the Crescent Club, for God's sake. Not to mention he comes from one of the most powerful families in the city. The Chief doesn't stand a chance. If we arrest him, we'll never make the charges stick."

Tommy went to the bar to get Tony's third Dixie and Scotch shooter. When he returned, he said, "Then we'll find another way to bring down the son of a bitch."

Several hours had passed, Tony quite drunk when Donna, Paul, and Doc Warner entered the bar. They ordered several pitchers of Dixie on their way back to the table to join Tommy and Tony. Seeing Tommy, Donna sat in his lap, put her arms around his neck, and squeezed, kissing him passionately without letting him go.

"Thanks for waiting for me," she said. "I can't believe how much I missed you."

The young foot cop that Donna had been seeing walked slowly past the table, hoping to catch her eye. With her attention focused on Tommy Blackburn, she didn't notice.

Tony's head lay buried in his arms, on the table, oblivious to the new arrivals to the bar. When Doc Warner asked him to play a game of darts, he poked his head up long enough to say no.

"Bring me the same thing he's having," said Doc Warner when Jimmy arrived with their pitchers of Dixie.

237

"You having a bad night, Doc?"

"The worst," Doc Warner said.

"I thought so," Jimmy said. "I've never seen Tony this drunk."

"Stay tuned," Doc Warner said. "I'm about to join him."

Carlucci's quickly filled with cops returning from the crime scene and others getting off duty. Ernie, Jon, and Sergeant Carnahan soon arrived. Still reasonably sober, Doc Warner engaged Carnahan in several games of darts. Tony was almost asleep on the table when Mama and Celeste entered the front door and searched the smoky room until they located him. Mama rubbed his back until he responded.

"You okay, Tony?"

"I been better," he said.

"This will help," she said, lifting his head and blowing white powder up his nose.

Within minutes, he shook his head and drank a large swallow of Dixie. When Jimmy brought another shot of Scotch, the detective brushed it aside with the back of his hand. Mama downed it, not wanting good spirits to go to waste.

"Tell Mama what's the matter."

"We just came from the murder of Sister Agnes. I think we both know her better as Mambo Aghnee. The man that killed her is virtually immune from prosecution. Gaylon LeBlanc, the same person that killed the two police officers and tried to kill you and Celeste. He whacked his own mother, and what he did to her shouldn't have happened to a dead rat."

Mama glanced furtively at Celeste. "You don't look so good, Tony."

"I haven't had a knot in my stomach like this since I was in basic training. I was hoping I'd never have this feeling again."

"Why don't you come home with us? Everyone seems preoccupied, especially Tommy. I don't think anyone will miss you."

"Story of my life," Tony said as he followed them out the door without an argument.

Chapter 43

Celeste, her father and I were once again at the St. Louis No. 1 Cemetery, this time to bury Arthur Duplesses. Celeste, Maurice, and Megan Duplesses, now out of the hospital stood together, watching as a Catholic priest said words and someone pushed the urn containing Arthur's ashes into the ornate vault that also bore the remains of Maurice's maternal mother. Maurice had adopted a new mother, and he had his long arm around Megan's shoulder. The old woman didn't seem to mind.

Arthur had occupied a prominent spot in the hierarchy of New Orleans royalty. He had even served as King of Rex; some might say the highest summit a Big Easy resident could hope to achieve. Amazingly, in his will, he'd left everything to his only son, Maurice Duples, showing life's pathways often take extraordinary and unexpected turns. I watched as a cemetery worker closed the tomb.

Maurice had hired a band that consisted of trumpet, sax, and bass drum musicians. They played Amazing Grace and several other funeral staples. After the ceremony, a stretch limousine took us all to Rue Bourbon. The band followed us, marching up the center of the street. The procession continued to Bourbon Street where we got out of the limo and joined the band. In deference to Megan, we stopped after walking a block.

"We have dinner reservations at Antoine's," Maurice said. "We can remember Arthur's life and maybe say a few words."

Antoine's, one of the oldest and most exclusive

restaurants in New Orleans, is located near the intersection of Bourbon and St. Louis. The restaurant has fifteen dining rooms, "each with its own personality," the advertisement said. It also had many private dining areas to accommodate parties such as ours. Luxury like Antoine's wasn't cheap, but Maurice could afford it.

Everything at Antoine's is Ala carte. We started with oysters Rockefeller, escargot basted in a red wine sauce and shrimp remoulade. We proceeded to gumbo Creole and crawfish bisque. We then had trout, shrimp, crab, and chicken prepared in a variety of ways. Along with the entrees came spinach in a light cream sauce, buttered carrots, broccoli in a special hollandaise sauce and asparagus to die for. We also had an Antoine's salad, a house specialty. After finishing with cherries jubilee, flamed at our table. Maurice said a few words to commemorate Arthur's death.

Fine dining is neither inexpensive nor fast. Three hours had passed, and it was dark outside when we spooned cherries jubilee into our mouths and finished our last cup of coffee. Maurice and Celeste ordered brandy ice to finish off the night. When they had finished their first, they each ordered a second. Megan and I were the only ones sober at the table as Maurice and Celeste had also consumed several bottles of expensive wine, both red and white. We left the private dining room happy and sated, and Arthur well remembered. The limousine was waiting at the curb. Before entering, Maurice shook my hand.

"I'm taking Celeste to Starkville tomorrow. If the police want to argue, I'll have them deal with my lawyer. I appreciate all you've done for us."

Celeste kissed her father's cheek, not following him into the limo. "You take Grandma home. Wyatt and I have a few things to talk about yet."

"It isn't a brilliant idea to wander off alone. The murderer is still out there, you know?"

"There are more policemen watching us than everyone else on Bourbon Street. We'll be okay."

"Are you sure?"

Celeste gave him a hug and nudged him into the back seat of the limo. We watched as the elegant black car rounded the corner at Dauphine. As they disappeared into the night, Celeste kissed me.

"Your father seemed more relaxed than I've ever seen him," I said.

Celeste nodded. "Finding Arthur and Megan is the best thing that ever happened to him. He now has a mother he can cherish. He's already forgotten what a sorry asshole his father was. He asked me to give you this."

She handed me a sealed envelope. I opened it with my finger and stared at a check for ten-thousand dollars.

"This is more than he owes me."

"Dad has money he'll never spend, and you earned every penny. Don't insult him by trying to give the rest of it back. Now let's go to Pat O'Brien's and have a Hurricane. I'm not through drinking tonight."

Pat O'Brien's, the courtyard bar on St. Peters just off Bourbon is a New Orleans landmark. I followed Celeste as she flirted with every male tourist and college student along the way. It was Friday night, the place rocking. Dueling pianos in the main bar were playing ragtime, jazz and pop hits—as interpreted by the two female song stylists that had been there long as I could remember. Often, a man with a banjo accompanied them.

As a waiter seated us, they launched into the fight song of the University of Alabama. The performance drew raucous applause, and I sensed our eastern neighbors heavily weighted the audience. Celeste reached across the table and squeezed my hand.

"Since I'm returning to Starkville tomorrow, I want you to know how much I appreciate everything you've done for us. I wish I could have met you before you and Mama hooked up."

I hardly knew what to say. "Mama is a close friend, but we aren't intimate, and she isn't my girlfriend. I'm sorry you have that wrong impression."

Celeste had already become happy from the bottles of wine and various diverse and specialty drinks she and her father had consumed. Both her hands wrapped around a chilled glass of rum and fruit juice that alone could intoxicate a moose. She took a long sip through the straws before answering.

"You don't have to say that just to spare my feelings."

"I wouldn't lie to you."

Celeste seemed amazingly sober for someone that had drunk as much alcohol as she had, and I wondered if Mama had given her something.

"I want to return to the graveyard and do something before leaving town. Will you take me?"

The banjo player and the two singers took a break, and much of the crowd in the main room went out to the courtyard. Celeste stared at me, waiting for my answer.

"The cops keeping tabs on us will freak," I said.

"I'll go to the bathroom now. Follow me in a minute. There's a crowd of people outside waiting to get in here. We can lose the cops watching us. At least it'll be fun to try."

"Not a good idea. The cemetery is an even worse place to visit at night with that homicidal maniac stalking you."

"Please, Wyatt. You'll understand when we get there. I'm going with you or without you. Please?"

I didn't know if she meant it or not. I did know how stubborn and forceful she could be.

"I'll go with you although I think it's an absolutely insane idea."

Celeste leaned across the table and kissed me. Her plan to evade the police worked to perfection. I met her on St. Peters and we headed south to the darkness of Rue Royal. I felt powerless to resist as she led me up St. Louis to the St. Louis No. 1 Cemetery although I followed her with much apprehension. Once inside the cemetery gates, we followed the path of broken shell. Celeste held my hand tightly and demanded a tour, even though darkness and shadows masked all but the vaguest outlines of crypts and ornate statuary.

"New Orleans cemeteries are called Cities of the Dead. Being here now, I can see why. Some of the crypts are large as houses. The place is home to marble gargoyles, angels, and spirits too numerous to count. The inscriptions on the graves detail the history of every man, woman and child that lived and suffered in New Orleans."

"It's both morbid and marvelous," she said. "Would you please take me to my grandmother's grave?"

We weren't far from where we had just laid Arthur Duplesses to rest. When we reached it, Celeste went to

Marie Laveau's grave instead. From her purse, she removed lipstick, which she used to create three large red crosses on the side of the crypt. She closed her eyes and made a wish.

"The last time I made a wish here, it came true. I couldn't leave without making another. This one is far more serious." Her task completed successfully, she turned to me with a smile. "Since you and Mama aren't an item, then maybe there's a chance for you and me after all. I'd concocted all sorts of complicated fantasies about how I would make love to you. My favorite occurred here, by Marie's grave. Will you fulfill my dream tonight?"

Celeste's question took me by surprise, and she never gave me a chance to answer. Just as well, as it would have caught in my throat.

Chapter 44

The night after Celeste's departure, I sat alone at my usual booth in Bertram Picou's bar. I'd left a message for Mama, and she had yet to return it. Inexplicably, it caused me to feel abandoned and dejected. The bar was crowded and Bertram too busy to stop by for a visit. As I sat there, feeling sorry for myself, Tony and Tommy came winding through the crowd.

"I thought we'd find you here. Mind if we join you?"

"I'm kind of busy right now," I said with a grin.

"Yeah, I can see," he said. "You remember Tommy?"

"How are you doing, Tommy?" I motioned Bertram to bring them each a cold Dixie. Shirley brought two beers and a glass of lemonade as I tried to guess the reason for their unexpected visit.

"Did you lose some weight?" I asked.

"Thanks for noticing. We didn't come here to talk about my schoolgirl figure. I need another favor."

"I didn't really think you were here for a social visit."

"You know me too well, Cowboy," Tony said. "Got a minute?"

"Spare time is my biggest asset. How can I help?"

He spread a computer printout on the table. The print quality was inferior, nine pin dot matrix. Dull ink from an ancient ribbon further impaired my ability to interpret the text. Despite its poor print quality, the document took less than a paragraph of reading to comprehend its significance.

"I heard LeBlanc was your prime suspect. Is this for real?"

Tony nodded. "A kid heisted a computer from a townhouse down on Bourbon. The information you're eyeballing came off the hard drive."

"This is either overwhelming evidence or else the delusion of a mentally disturbed diarist."

"It's evidence all right. I have a problem, and it's a powerful one. Gaylon LeBlanc owns the townhouse—ex U.S. Senator Gaylon LeBlanc. And like you said, this document pegs him as our voodoo strangler."

I already understood his predicament. Gaylon LeBlanc, millionaire industrialist, supporter of local arts and former state senator, had power which was something worth far more in south Louisiana than money. He regularly rubbed elbows with judges, bankers, politicians, and others of wealth and establishment. Accusing the senator of any crime, much less murder, could prove a career-ending mistake.

"What about the kid that stole LeBlanc's computer?"

"Show the printout to Chief Wexler. Let his testimony do the rest. I'm not a lawyer anymore, but it doesn't take a fool to see this is overwhelming evidence."

"I did that already. Wexler asked me how I knew the computer came from LeBlanc's house. Maybe the kid got his heists mixed up."

"Maybe he did," I said.

Tony's frown warned me he didn't appreciate my analysis, even in jest.

"The kid's mother was LeBlanc's housekeeper. He fired her unexpectedly a few weeks back. When her son arrived to help her with her cleaning supplies, he conveniently left a window unlocked. He went back that night and relieved LeBlanc of a few items. LeBlanc never reported the robbery because he apparently didn't want police nosing around his house."

"Don't matter anyway," Tommy said. "We got about an armadillo's chance on I-10 of securing a search warrant. Even if we tried, me and Fat Tony would end up riding bicycle patrol over in the Iberville Project. Besides, Tony won't arrest the kid."

"Shut up, Tommy. He's off limits. Get that through your thick, Irish Channel skull."

"Off limits, hell! Tony got him a tryout with the Mets."

"The kid's decent enough to play in the majors. End of story."

Tommy shut his mouth and drummed the table with his fingers, moving his massive head in a barely perceptible shake. Flagging down Shirley, I ordered him another Dixie.

"Since this isn't a social visit, what do you want from me?"

"I'm sure you've heard the killer takes souvenirs from his victims—hands, nipples and who knows what else. We think he keeps the trophies somewhere in his house. If we had evidence on LeBlanc that grisly, even his allies would dump him."

"I'm sure you heard about the murder at the Camp Street Mission," Tommy said. "The heartless bastard killed and butchered his own mother."

I had heard. I'd already visited Sister Rose to offer my condolences. I'd left the mission a thousand dollars lighter, although I somehow felt the better for it. Bertram was leading a group of Texans in a rousing, albeit out-of-key rendition of My Calenda across the crowded bar. Neither Tommy nor Tony noticed. Both had grown animated as they discussed the relationship between LeBlanc and the voodoo strangler. I kept quiet and listened, waiting for the inevitable second shoe to drop. It soon did.

"We know LeBlanc's schedule pretty well," Tony said. He usually eats late before taking a walk, a long walk."

Bumped on her way through the crowded bar, Shirley dropped a tray of hurricanes. Tommy flinched, his eyes closing during the resultant explosion of flying shards. In tears, she crawled between customer's legs on her hands and knees, picking up the shattered glass.

It took Bertram only a moment to respond. After vaulting the counter, he rushed to his beleaguered girlfriend's side, yelling for customers to move out of his way. Tony's attention, veins protruding from his neck, was riveted on me. He was bug-eyed as he stared unnerving bullet holes through my head.

"We need a ruse, a reason to enter LeBlanc's townhouse without a warrant. Something like a small house fire," he finally said.

"You want me to break into LeBlanc's townhouse and start a fire? Why don't you just give me your pistol and let me shoot the bastard?"

Tommy glanced at his partner as if assessing the slim chance my suggestion might be something other than sarcasm. After Shirley's accident, he had drained his Dixie in a single pull. Now his nerves seemed less jangled as he leaned across the table on his elbows.

"Fat T says you can get in and out of a house slicker than a cat burglar."

Tommy was right. During my college days, I'd earned extra money working for H.U.D., repossessing houses. Doing so usually entailed waiting until the current owner left the house, and then breaking in and changing the locks before the police arrived.

Most homeowners have no idea how vulnerable their property is. There are many ways to enter a home without a key. Long ago, I'd become an expert in every one of them. I wondered what else Tony had told Tommy about me.

"I don't know if that's a compliment, especially coming from the police."

"You're an insider in this deal," Tony said. "You know what to expect and how to take care of what we need to do."

"Which is?"

"Just start a small fire in the trash can. We'll keep a fire truck waiting around the corner. When the smoke hits, we'll be there with firefighters and police. We'll take care of everything else. With pictures and compelling evidence, even LeBlanc's powerful friends will dump him. I need someone I can trust that isn't on the force to pull it off. Will you do it for me?"

I had my doubts about Tony's assessment of LeBlanc's friends. It didn't matter. I already knew the two detectives weren't going to let me reject their proposal. The visit from Lieutenant Nicosia and Sergeant Blackburn did little to lift my spirits, and I decided to go upstairs, hit the bed early, and try to forget my problems. When I opened the door, I realized they were just beginning.

I'd left the patio door ajar so Bob could go out on the balcony if he wanted to. A gust of summer breeze had blown the door open. I saw Bob, hung between the wrought iron rails surrounding the patio. He wasn't moving as I sprinted for the open door.

Bob was dead. He had tried to crawl through the rails as he had so many times before, to get to the fire escape leading to the alley below. The rails were slightly wider at the top than the bottom. He had gotten stuck and too weak to free himself. There had been no one there to rescue him. My wretched day had suddenly grown darker as I freed his body from the rails.

I buried him in the large, palm tree pot, the place he loved to lie in and watch the world go by. I said a few words before closing my eyes, feeling empty inside—the same way I'd felt when my parents had died.

Chapter 45

Summer darkness comes late to the Big Easy. Nine-thirty, even ten. Long past dark I leaned against crumbling mortar, somewhere on the far end of Rue Bourbon, my eyes dimming from staring much too long at the front door of a Creole-style shotgun house. Gaylon LeBlanc finally appeared. Out the front door he waltzed, dressed in black with a cape that draped the ground. He moved slowly. After locking the deadbolt with care, he gazed around, listening to night sounds radiating from up on Canal Street. He didn't seem to notice me standing in the adjacent alleyway.

Something had eaten away at my gut ever since I'd agreed to break into his house. Some nagging doubt I couldn't quite identify. Shoving the thought to the back of my mind I quickly surveyed the area, finding everything dark and deserted—at least almost deserted, except for an old black wino stumbling like a misplaced apparition down the sidewalk. The old woman had wandered a long way from her usual haunts on the other side of Canal. Her unexplained presence disturbed me profoundly.

After adding the anomaly to my growing list of paranoia, I returned to the job at hand, retracing LeBlanc's steps to the house where the door lock took less than ten seconds to open. A stray dog howled over by the Iberville Project, and the old house gasped when I entered. Breathing deeply of sticky, August air, I slipped into the darkness.

LeBlanc lived in a shotgun house, thirty feet wide and maybe twice as long. Such houses were, quite simply, nothing more than small rectangles probably worth a million dollars because of their location on prime real estate. Streetlights, reflecting through stained glass over the front door, cast dancing shadows and multicolored reflections off dull walls. The house was otherwise dark. When a cat knocked over a trashcan in the alleyway outside, his screech pulled a knot in my throat, backing me against a wall until my heart reset.

LeBlanc had raised the temperature of the air conditioning, and the place had already begun to steam. Outside, early rain had left cobblestone streets damp with humidity. Inside the narrow hallway reeked of must and antiquity. Shaking off my nerves, I proceeded through the first door in search of what I had come for.

My light cut a precise swath through the darkness. I found LeBlanc's office, a small room dominated by a giant, mahogany desk. Side chairs, computer, and some three-drawer file cabinets completed the decor. After jimmying the desk drawer and rifling through it, I turned my attention to the nearest trashcan.

LeBlanc's trash consisted mostly of wadded paper, and the contents of the can made my next job easier. With a disposable lighter borrowed from Bertram, I lit the edge of a crumpled newspaper. What followed took less than a second. Like Shirley's hurricanes, dry paper ignited like kindling wood, exploded with a loud pop and lighted the room. For a moment, I stood there, hypnotized, staring at billowing smoke and growing flame until something behind me freed my gaze from the fire.

The sound sent my blood pressure racing toward the roof. In a moment of recognition induced by adrenaline rushing to my brain, I recalled specific answers to the questions still eating away at my gut. The sound came from the shuffling gait of a person with a limp scrapping across hardwood flooring. LeBlanc had a gimpy foot, and leg. It was a fact I should have remembered. Tony had watched his every movement since learning he was the killer.

Like everyone alive, LeBlanc had his routines. He probably went up the street for a latte every night and was away from the house for ten minutes or so. Tony had suckered me, and I had an idea why. I had little time to reflect on my faulty memory, or Tony's duplicity as gloved hands caressed my neck, quickly slipping a garrote around it and tightening. I could smell LeBlanc's breath when he spoke.

"Looking for something?"

I grabbed his strong hands, struggling to breathe as life quickly began to flow from my body. Billowing flames had already jumped from the trash, lighting papers on the massive, mahogany desk. LeBlanc needed to kill me quickly and put out the fire. But he had a problem. Sirens of approaching fire trucks screamed outside the window and someone was already in the process of kicking down the front door. With his hands still tight around my throat, he wheeled me around to face the noise of splintering wood. When two street cops burst through the door, pistols drawn, LeBlanc and I realized they weren't there to admonish us for playing with matches.

Both cops dropped to their knees, raised their pistols, and began unloading them at us. Ten seconds of chaos that felt like an eternity followed. Pandemonium mingled with gunfire, muzzle flash and the stench of burning gunpowder and loosened bowels.

I opened my eyes long before my ears stopped ringing, cordite, and blazing paper joining with the pungent odor of blood as I struggled to pull myself off the floor. Gaylon LeBlanc was dead beside me, his body riddled with bullets. I touched the gris-gris around my neck when I realized I hadn't even been nicked.

⋐⊂⟨⟩⊃ᕽ

Fire trucks were arriving outside, blocking the streets. Firefighters quickly extinguished the flames while police cordoned the house and began dispersing the growing crowd. Anesthetized by a fresh bottle of cheap vodka, the old black wino stumbled through the broken front door followed by one of the cops that had shot LeBlanc. The old woman was a plant, brought from across town to provide the police a story. Now the pieces were coming together, and tomorrow the Picayune would sing a decidedly different tune from what had happened at LeBlanc's townhouse.

It'd probably sound something like this: Seeing flames pouring from former U.S. Senator Gaylon LeBlanc's house in the French Quarter, two police officers called the fire department then knocked to alert the Senator. Screams from inside the house indicated someone was in need of assistance. It had prompted them to break down the door. They unexpectedly encountered a wild LeBlanc in the process of slicing up an old wino—forced to use deadly force when he attacked them with the knife. A computer printout found on LeBlanc's desk linked him to the murders committed by the now infamous Voodoo Strangler.

The story would appear almost plausible.

Tommy Blackburn materialized from the confusion, leading me out the back door to an unmarked police car. I joined Lieutenant Tony Nicosia in the back seat as Tommy took the wheel.

"You all right, Cowboy?"

"You set me up!"

Tony offered no apology. Instead, he said, "LeBlanc didn't deserve to live through twelve years of appeals, even if we could have made the charge of murder one stick. And that's a big if. The only way to handle a killer like that is to shoot him down like a mad dog."

"At least you could have told me what was going down."

"Would you still have done it?"

I didn't have an answer to his question.

Tommy turned at Governor Nichols, stopping the car on Decatur. "You a real hero," he said as I opened the door.

I didn't respond to his comment, and Tony said, "Forget about it, Wyatt. It's the Big Easy."

As their taillights faded in the distance, I reflected on his deceit and my own complicity. I didn't feel like a hero. Much like the city itself, I felt more like an old whore.

I walked toward the French Market where early morning sun was still hours from rising. It mattered little because the brick streets were already awash in activity—stall keepers sorting produce and stevedores unloading trucks filled with melons and plump, red tomatoes.

Dew, coating waxy magnolia blossoms, created a potent fragrance that wafted through the square, mingling with the ripe bouquet of fresh fruits, flowers, and pepper sauce. I stopped and took a deep breath.

Damp, night air began to revive me, and I thought

about seagulls and seashores, trying desperately to store the night's incident in that black repository hidden deep in all our souls. I headed for Café du Monde, hoping like hell a sugary beignet and cup of black, Creole coffee, might kick start my heart and help bastion my fleeting sanity. At least until the sun came up.

Chapter 46

Tommy Blackburn and Lieutenant Tony Nicosia stood inside the bedroom door of LeBlanc's camp on Lake Pontchartrain, observing as a forensic team uncovered a growing collection of gruesome human souvenirs.

"I was wrong about the murder by Lee Circle being the strangler's first," Tony said. "He killed at least two in Washington. From the looks of his collection, it doesn't end there. I just wish we could have stopped him before he turned my summer into a living hell."

"No one could have caught him any faster, Fat T," Tommy said.

Tony didn't even flinch at his nickname. It didn't matter anymore. He was bumping one-seventy-five, and felt better than he had in years.

"Tell that to the widows and children of the two dead cops."

"Let it go, Tony. It wasn't your fault."

Though Tony wanted to believe what his partner said, he couldn't quite get it out of his mind. Perhaps it was time to have Mama blow some more magic powder up his nose to elevate his mood a little.

"Maybe you're right," he said. "Lil and I are taking advantage of the month break the Chief is giving me. We're going to Italy and the Greek Isles. Hell, we might never come back."

"You have to. Donna and I are thick now. She's cleaned up my apartment and is talking seriously about moving in with me. I may need a best man."

Tommy followed him out the door. When they reached the car, Tony said, "Just don't let your supply of love potion run out. Mama's making me another batch before Lil and I leave for Italy.

Chapter 47

I remained in bed for twenty-four hours—until Bertram pounded on the door and would no longer take "Go away," for an answer.

"Cowboy, you got a visitor,"

"Tell whoever it is I'll see them tomorrow."

Bertram's keys rattled in the lock, and he entered without an invitation. Mama was with him. "Let me talk to him alone," she said.

Bertram backed out of the door, shutting it without commenting. Mama sat on the bed, bent over, and cradled my head in her arms. I think she may have even deftly drawn something on my forehead although I couldn't be sure. After kissing my cheek, she blew something up my nose. Strangely, within seconds, my demeanor lightened. Sensing my mental change, she opened the dark curtain blocking sunlight from the patio

"Whatever you did to me just now, you're free to keep doing it," I said. "My head's not pounding for the first time in days."

"Stress can do that to you. Are you okay?"

"I should be dead. I was standing right in front of Gaylon LeBlanc when two cops unloaded their pistols at us and riddled him with bullets. I wasn't even grazed."

Mama touched the bag still around my neck. The gris-gris protected you."

Having no better explanation, I didn't argue. "Nicosia used me to take down LeBlanc. He knew he had little chance to convict him, so he devised another way to solve his problem. I still have enough lawyer in me to worry about it. He didn't care if an innocent person died along with the killer."

"You're being far too hard on Tony. He couldn't have known LeBlanc would attack you so quickly and use you as a shield. Once the plan was initiated, there was no turning back."

Something in Mama's voice caused me to say, "You didn't know anything about Tony's plan beforehand did you?"

"How could you even think that? At least everything turned out all right in the end."

Mama's response wasn't exactly a denial. It was the best answer I was going to get, and I decided not to force it. She was wrong about how things turned out. You don't face almost certain death and experience gut wrenching fear without deep scars remaining etched permanently on your soul. In the end, logic is no balm for nerve endings frayed by an overdose of terror or the Grim Reaper's unexpected touch of your shoulder. Mama could see something else was on my mind, and pressed me for an answer. I told her about Bob.

"Your kitty died? Oh Wyatt, I am so sorry. I don't know what I'll do when I lose Bushy and Cliffy. Is there any way I can help?"

"I buried him in the palm tree's pot, outside on the patio. Maybe since you're a priestess and all, you could say a few words."

"I'd be honored," she said.

I followed her out to the balcony. It was a beautiful day in the Quarter, sun shining brightly, the temperature neither too hot nor too cold. Mama fished in her purse and removed a small plastic crucifix, which she placed on the spot where I had buried Bob. She closed her eyes and chanted something in a language, probably some African dialect, I didn't recognize.

"Wyatt, I want you to know Bob's spirit has passed, and his soul is in peace."

I didn't know if cats had souls or Mama was one of the world's greatest bullshitters. At that moment, I didn't care. Her words gave me comfort and helped ease my nagging guilt. I went inside and sat on the bed.

"Thanks, Mama. You don't know how much better that made me feel."

"I think I have a pretty good idea," she said. "Why don't you take a shower and change clothes? I am starving, and I have not had breakfast at Brennan's in forever. I'll buy."

Mama's offer to treat anyone to anything came as a shock. "I don't know that I feel that much better."

"Trust me," she said. "If you don't just yet, you soon will."

Taking her advice, I showered and walked with her to Brennan's, famous all over the world for its eggs Benedict. The waiter who probably hadn't seen Mama for months smiled and called her by name—as if she ate at that particular restaurant every day. After breakfast, we conversed over strong, perfectly brewed coffee.

"Are you going to get a new kitty?" she asked.

"I don't think so. I wasn't exactly the world's best pet owner when it came to Bob."

"Cats are independent creatures. They need their own space and Wyatt, you weren't responsible for Bob's disease. You gave him all the attention you were capable of giving. Most of all you gave him love. In the end, that's the most any of us can ever hope for."

"Maybe," I said. "At least Bertram is glad he's gone."

"You're not being fair to poor Bertram. He treats his collie better than he treats himself."

Maybe that was part of what was bugging me. Why couldn't I be at least as decent a person as Bertram? Did I have an inherent character flaw or defective gene? Mama gave me little time to consider an answer because she had a question of her own for me.

"You haven't called with any new business in a while. Have clients stopped calling?"

"My answering machine is full. I just haven't felt like doing anything."

Mama reached across the table and grabbed my hand. "Wyatt, you mean we're partners?"

"Are you kidding? This is the most lucrative thing I've ever done, including my stint as a trial lawyer. Most of all I love it, and it'd be empty without you."

258

Mama patted my hand. "I'm happy for you and Celeste. Actually, I am jealous. I always felt as if we have lots in common."

"You have the wrong idea about Celeste and me. She has her own life, and I'll probably never see her again."

Mama was still holding my hand and staring at me with her brown eyes. "Wyatt," she said. "Are you really going to be okay?"

I smiled and said, "I've never been okay a single day in my life. It doesn't matter because I think I can make it the rest of the way."

Chapter 48

A week had passed when I glanced over the pet adoption section in the Times Picayune. There was a picture of a cat. The caption read Ninja, a friendly, shorthaired, black cat. The article described Ninja as an eight-month-old that had been at the shelter since he'd been a kitten. It went on to say he had a loud, happy purr when you pet him.

After Bob's death, I was reluctant to take on the responsibility of a new pet, and I was still smarting from his loss. Reality finally caught up with me. I couldn't deny I missed waking every morning to a raspy tongue licking my face. I missed the leg rubs and the purring for attention. Most of all, I was tired of being alone. I set out for the shelter with my cat carrier and returned with Ninja. When Bertram saw me, he called me over.

"Hey Cowboy," he said. "You been a little pe-kid lately, so I got you something to cheer you up." From behind the bar, he lifted a squirming yellow kitten that was the spitting image of Bob, including the stump for a tail. "I tried to find an exact replacement for that mangy tomcat of yours, but all I could find was this little female. Her name is Kisses. I hope you like her."

END

Biography

A native of Louisiana, Eric Wilder loves gumbo and southern mysteries. Thanks for reading *Big Easy*. You might also like *City of Spirits*, *Primal Creatures*, and *Black Magic Woman*, the second, third and fourth novels in the French Quarter mystery series. Please check out his Facebook fanpage at Facebook.com/louisianamysterywriter.